Vampire Slayer

One Foot in Darkness

By
Dani A. Camden

PublishAmerica
Baltimore

© 2006 by Dani A. Camden.
All rights reserved. No part of this book may be reproduced, stored in a retrieval system or transmitted in any form or by any means without the prior written permission of the publishers, except by a reviewer who may quote brief passages in a review to be printed in a newspaper, magazine or journal.

First printing

All characters appearing in this work are fictitious. Any resemblance to real persons, living or dead, is purely coincidental.

ISBN: 1-4241-0436-X
PUBLISHED BY PUBLISHAMERICA, LLLP
www.publishamerica.com
Baltimore

Printed in the United States of America

*For my children,
Ashton, Kessler and Emma*

You are my love…

Special Thanks To:

My amazing husband Chandler: Thank you for your unfaltering support, your unconditional love and your limitless patience. You are my rock!

To my mother: Thank you for teaching me the beauty of imagination and the glory of the written word!

To my father: Thank you for teaching me that I COULD write this stuff! Now, if only I can switch from Am to D!

And to my mother who didn't have to be, Linda: I was lucky to have found a friend in you! Thank you for all of our late nights!

Chapter One

Sweet Dreams

She stamped her foot and up it flew. Naturally, his curiosity forced him to look down to see where it had come from. He was just in time to catch the outer side of her right leg snap back into place. His mind tried to wrap its way around what had just happened. He quickly jerked his eyes back up just in time to see she had it in her hand and was sprinting for him. He wiped the blood from his nose and readied himself. Just before she could stick him with the accursed thing, he jumped over and landed behind her. But before he could grab her shoulders she lifted her right arm and nailed him with a powerful back fist. He fell backward into a puddle. She seemed to tower over him, even though she was barely over five feet tall. He tried to move, but he felt a crushing weight on his chest forcing him back down. He tried to grab at it and his hand was swatted away. His vision was blurred but he could still make out that it was her foot standing on his chest.

"Didn't your mother ever tell you not to wander down dark allies all by yourself?"

"How?! Who are you?" He gargled.

"That…is a good question," she stated matter of factly. She lunged down sharply and plunged the wood deep into his left breast. He grasped it quickly as he looked at her in agony before he erupted into a cloud of dust. She stood up to dust herself off and began to sigh. But instead of her witty retort, she began to gag and cough. "Damn! *Cough.* When will I learn…*Gag*…not to breathe in after they do that! I'm going to be tasting that for a week!" No sooner had the words exited her lips, than the heavens opened up and rained down heavily. She threw her arms up and said, "Of course! As if an evil undead guy in my mouth wasn't enough, let's add water to his ashy remains, which are all over my clothes, thereby staining them permanently! Great! This is just what I need now!" And then she stormed off down the alley, into the rain, into the dark of the night.

~~~~~

Her head hit the pillow. Soft, cool, comforting. She didn't even bother undoing the few braids she put in her long brown hair. All she had accomplished in preparing for bed was removing her soaking clothes and boots and putting on an oversized t-shirt that was laying on the floor.

She pulled the fluffy comforter up and over her chest and cuddled it close. Her eyes closed and her mind drifted. Her head rocked as she felt her thick hair soaking her pillow.

She knew the dreams would come again, as they had for the last two years when all this started. She felt the darkness come and slowly carry her into listlessness.

"Emma." It always started with that woman calling out to her. As if she were being told that the lesson was about to begin, so she better be listening. In the darkness a light appeared. As it got closer, it became clear that it wasn't a light at all. It was a person. A woman, to be exact. A woman, with long white hair in a long white dress. She stretched out her hand and bid her to follow. She tried to keep up with the woman, but she always seemed to be just out of reach. Finally, the woman stopped and opened double doors. A blinding light exploded from the doorway, and Emma was engulfed in it.

Yelling and pushing everywhere. Panic was so thick in the air you could taste it. It was dark and the air was harsh from being filled with dust. Her body ached and her limbs felt heavy, yet she knew she must fight. There was no one else left but her. She had been trained all her life and this very well could be the end of it. She was surrounded by them. One swung at her and the breeze from the swift, moving arm made the cut on her left cheek sting all the more. They snarled and roared at her. She sensed that the redhead to her right was about to make his move. She jumped as he lunged for her, and was able to leap frog over his shoulders, turn around and shove her stake through his heart from his back. He fell to dust before her. The other six tightened and growled, gnashed their teeth. This only scrunched their faces all the more. Their yellow eyes gleamed through the dusty air; their lips curled up showing more of their gnarled fangs. And then there was the smell of death all around, dank and metallic. By now the remaining people had fled the village. The beasts closed in on her, grinning and creeping. She stood firm, feeling out the moment. They encircled her and began to creep around, ripping at her skirts and pulling at her hair. She closed her eyes, trying to push the fear into her stomach so she could use it. Out of the darkness came a new figure. He was tall and handsome. His long dark hair blew gently across his face and revealed his menacing grin. He spoke in French.

"Mes amis, I believe she has been tenderized enough. I can handle her from here." He breathed in deep. "Your aroma is intoxicating, ma chere! I can hear your heart pounding from here. The fear of a slayer! It makes my skin tingle. Tu sont magnifique!"

This was it, she knew it in her blood. She grunted through her teeth, "You are a devil of the worst kind! Je crèche a vous!"

"Oh ma chere, we are not so different, tu et moi. Nomads of a sort. Hunters. Death is our obsession, our passion. It is a part of us."

"I don't think so. You're a monster. You feed off of innocence. It is my duty to protect it." She gripped her stake sternly as if the stake itself gave her more power and strength.

"I'm bored with this banter. I think I would like to get straight to the screaming now!" And with that they ran toward each other. Her skirts billowed in her wake, as did his black velvet jacket. She leapt forward with the stake in her right hand stretched out in front of her. He deflected her attack and swept her to the side. When he did, the stake tore the sleeve of his gentlemen's coat. "Do you have any idea how hard it is to find a good tailor when you are on my schedule?! I think I will hurt just a little bit extra for that." She wasn't fast enough and he picked her up by her delicate throat. His dark, handsome face distorted into its demon form. "Don't worry, ma cheri, I'll make sure you feel everything! And don't worry, I am not like most men, I can go all night!" He erupted into laughter as he threw her to the ground and tore her skirts from her body. He beat her head into the road until she was barely conscious. She couldn't move, but she could feel. And for hours she did feel everything until he had his fill and became bored with pleasuring himself, feeding and dismantling her. "Really, you were magnificent! Merci bebe!" And he tore her head from what was left of her torso.

Emma sat straight up in bed, screaming. Her face glistened with sweat. "Damn it!" She rubbed her face roughly, thinking it would rub the images out of her mind. All it did was bring some of her own memories to the surface. Flashes of her own foot being ripped from her right leg as she tried to scramble out into the daylight from a couple of vamps who had spent the night torturing and feeding on her family. She glanced down at the fiberglass limb that rested next to her bed. "It's not fair," she mumbled. "Why couldn't this, this super boost happen earlier?" With that she picked up her plastic leg and threw it across the room; subsequently it went through the wall and into the living room. "Well, good thing I already went to the bathroom." With that she reached for a bottle on her night table, tossed a few pills down her throat and lay down and waited for the sweet, light dizziness to take over and force her to pass out into blackness. "Sweet oxicodone, take me away."

A stream of sunlight made its way through the dark drapes of her bedroom. Emma's eyes shot open. She groaned as she rolled away from the light. *I really should line the windows with foil*, she thought to herself. Reluctantly, she pulled herself up and rubbed her face. She was still a little numb from the muscle relaxers. She felt her bladder tingle and leaned over the side of the bed in search of her leg, when out of her peripheral vision she caught the large hole in the wall and suddenly remembered the fit she had had in the middle of the night. "Damn! Jimmy's gonna kill me. AGAIN!" That was not the first time

Emma had lost her temper in this manner. On three of her bedroom walls was evidence of patch work. "Plaster and drywall tape, Martha. That's what I call the décor of this room!" she mocked. Standing up from the bed she grabbed her silicone liner, and crossed her arms across her chest, holding her breasts steady. Using her left leg she hopped out of the bedroom, down the hall and into the living room to retrieve her leg. As she plopped down onto the couch and began to roll her liner on over her right leg, the front door opened.

"Goddamn, Emma! How many times do I have to keep patching these walls?" Jimmy had come back. He was tall and handsome with wavy brown hair. He had Emma's high cheek bones and intense hazel eyes. He walked over to where Emma was sitting and picked up her maltreated limb. The spring-loaded hatch on the outer side was stuck open and would not stay shut. "Emma! Holy Shit! Do you have any idea how long this is going to take to fix?! Is there any way you could, oh, I dunno, hit a pillow?! Take deep breaths, count to ten?"

"Shut up, smartass. I'm sorry, I'll try better next time. I'll go back to throwing lamps."

"Why don't you try not throwing anything?! Maybe we could give that a shot!"

"Look, just be glad that all you got was the height and weren't cursed with this awful temper and tragically striking good looks!" Emma batted her eyes and smiled coyly.

"Alright, lemme go get your beater and I'll start on this one after I eat, ok?! It was the one in France wasn't it?"

"Yeah. That one always wakes me up."

"Have you tried the notebook thing yet? It helps me." Emma rolled her eyes.

"Why? If you write them down why do I have to? Do you think we need two copies? Besides, I have someone to talk to about it. How many other people do you know share dreams with another person?!"

"Well from what I've read, MANY twins do that!"

"And in how many of those cases was one of the twins a slayer?"

"Emma, I don't think a slayer has EVER had a twin. I think we are an enigma." Jimmy padded down the hall to retrieve her "beater" leg from her closet. "Lucky for you I'm a genius."

Emma smirked. "He's never going to let go of that." Jimmy returned to the room with her leg.

"Why would I? It's only fair. You got the cool super strength, I got the super smarts!"

That night Emma watched Jimmy work in the basement on her leg. What once was considered the "family room," complete with an air hockey table, big screen TV, mini kitchen, and card table, was now called "the shop." Jimmy had this place equipped and armed to the teeth. The back corner was reserved for the work Jimmy did on all of Emma's prosthetic legs. This included regular maintenance, weapon installations, adjustments, and whatever cosmetic demands Emma could conjure up. At first glance, it would seem like a dungeon with all of the feet, tools and weapons hanging from the ceiling. A large stainless steel work counter was against the wall with a peg board above it, and an old butcher block table was across from that. Everything looked well used. Across from Jimmy's shop was Emma's training area. A red punching bag hung from chains in the corner and wrist wraps lay discarded underneath. Various weapons hung on the wall. Axes, swords, chains, bo staffs, daggers, and an old canvas laundry bag full of stakes. Lining the walls around the little gym were dumbbells, medicine balls and a couple of yoga mats. To the front of the basement was the kitchenette with an old yellow couch and TV. Emma sat there now half twisted around so she could see Jimmy. The TV played the news but was muted.

"How much longer?" Emma prodded.

"About half as long as it would take if you keep asking me questions," he responded from underneath his welding mask. Sparks flew up above his head. Jimmy flipped up the mask and closed the hatch on the leg. It snapped perfectly into place. He stood it up on the table and pushed down hard on the heel. The trigger tripped and the hatch popped open.

"Voila!" he proclaimed. "Stake launcher is a go! I have some new upgrades I want to add, too. I might get a chance to install them if I wasn't so tied up fixing what you break every night!"

Emma turned around and made mocking faces and moved her hand as if it were a puppet. She jerked back around sharply and asked, "Hey, what about that 'Barbie' foot you promised? I hate the high heeled foot I have now, it looks like shit! The colors don't match and the toes are too narrow!"

"Oh, I didn't tell you?" Jimmy announced as he removed his mask. "I couldn't find enough material in the Western hemisphere to make a foot that big!" Emma grabbed her shoe and hurled it in his direction. Jimmy ducked just in time. "Oooo, not as quick as you think you are eh? Maybe you should practice more. And didn't we discuss this no more throwing shit?"

"Just because you are a minute and a half older doesn't make you my father!" As soon as she had said it she regretted it. For the last two years they both had made it a point to avoid any references to parental figures. They both looked solemnly at each other for a short moment and then down at the floor. Emma stared down. She studied the old dirty rug under her feet, trying to memorize the fibers and see if she could see beyond what her eyes allowed. She tried to superimpose the image of how it looked when her parents were alive to how it looked now. All she could see was the dirt and the fraying. She breathed deep, searching for the familiar smell of popcorn and root beer that used to be synonymous with this room. But now all she smelled was burnt copper, old sweat and old dirty basement. The tears threatened to breech the wall she had fought so hard to build. She breathed in hard to force herself to stop this self-pitying and come back from out of the past.

"I know," Jimmy said suddenly. "But pushing it out of our minds doesn't do any good either." He wanted so much for his sister to let go of her guilt. There was nothing she could have done. Fate plays cruel tricks on us all. He knew all too well. He could never tell her that as much as he loved his twin sister, he resented her and was jealous of her abilities. He had tried to take solace in the fact that he was much smarter than she was, shared some of her slayer reflexes, and the fact that they shared a slight telepathic connection to each other, which included the slayer dreams. But he could never get over that fact that SISTER got to be the bad ass! *But then again*, he said to himself, *I do have a penis, and that inherently makes me better.*

"You know, when you talk to yourself like that and I am nearby, I can hear you. And the fact is it's not really a penis unless you get to use it!" Emma quipped as she bounded up the stairs.

"I use it!" he yelled back. Emma popped her head under the dropped ceiling at the top of the stairs.

"Going to the bathroom and jerking off to the underwear section in the latest K-mart ad doesn't count!"

As the sky began to turn black, Emma prepared for her patrol. She packed her backpack with stakes, bottled water and her discman. Jimmy handed her her leg fixed up and ready to go. He had already loaded it with a new slim stake. She pulled on her high black boots, laced them up and slid a dagger into each one. She doublechecked to make sure that the boot on her right side could still accommodate for her tricked out leg. The spring action hatch on the side still opened and shut no problem and there were a few new updates as well. She clicked her heels and a wooden blade came jutting out of the toe. She stepped down on the ball of her foot and twisted, and a series of spikes stuck out from her shin. "Cool." She threw on her black jacket and bag, and walked down the hallway.

Jimmy met her at the front door in the living room. This evening's reminder that his masculinity needed affirmation, made him decide he was going to patrol with her tonight. He had put on a long khaki raincoat and slung a single-strap backpack across his broad shoulders.

"Where do you think you're going?" Emma questioned. "Don't you have to open the store tomorrow morning?"

"If I am a couple hours late and some guy, who's a bigger loser than me, can't get his first edition copy of *Klingon for the Galactic Traveler*, I think I'll get over it. Besides, the only people who actually come in to buy books don't come in until after one p.m."

"Alright, I guess I could use the company. But don't talk too much. Wait a minute, don't you have that book?"

"What self-respecting scientist doesn't? But don't tell anyone." He grinned. She smiled back at him and walked out the door.

They walked together down Fairbanks Road. It was shortly past ten o'clock, and most people were at home by now. Or, they were in a better part of town.

"For the last time, I am not going to learn *Mok'Bara*! It's not real! It's make-believe!" Emma fired.

"There are classes where you can learn it! They have exhibitions at conventions!"

"Yes! *Star Trek* conventions! I am not learning some made-up Klingon martial art!"

"But don't you see, no one would expect it!"

Emma stopped for a second and stared off in thought. Her eyebrows furrowed and she shook her head vigorously. "NO! This is stupid! Like the time you tried to make me wear the Klingon battle armor you built!" Jimmy nodded his head and smiled to himself.

"That was really cool, too! I did an awesome job! Mom would have been proud!"

"Jimmy. Please."

"And why can't we talk about them! About it! It's been two years!"

"Because! I'm ashamed! I hid! I hid like a baby! I could have done something!" Emma cried.

"And how do you think I feel!" Jimmy yelled back. "I wasn't there! Last thing I said to Dad was he could kiss my ass! That I wasn't running his stupid little book shop that no one cared about anymore! Emma, I told them that I was better than them! I have to live with that for the rest of my life, that I wasn't there to help them! To help you."

Emma sniffled and righted herself. She didn't like feeling like this. Guilty for pushing her issues off onto him. She felt bad. She turned and hugged him tight. "I'm sorry, big brother. I keep forgetting that you saved my life."

Two Years Ago

The front door slammed and Jimmy jumped into his blue Dodge pickup truck. John Hogan ran out after him. It was too late, though. Jimmy had already pealed out of the driveway and sped off. John hung his head. This wasn't the first time they had come to this place. And always one of them walked away. He wanted so much to be close to his son again. Jimmy was a good kid, a parent's dream really. But he could be so full of himself. John wished he could find a way to make him see that his attitude would only make him miserable.

"John! Honey, come back inside. Let's do our best to enjoy the rest of the evening. Emma leaves for school tomorrow and she has cheerleading camp next week. Jimmy will cool off and come back later. Let's all just go back downstairs and watch the movie!" Katherine called from the door.

John smiled reluctantly at her. She was always a breath of fresh air. Her long, wavy, dark hair never lost its luster in these past twenty-five years. She batted her large brown eyes pleadingly at her husband. It always broke her heart to see him like this. All she wanted was an evening with her family. Even though she would complain about not ever having enough time alone with John, she missed having all the children there with them.

John shuffled back up the walk to where his lovely wife was standing in the front doorway. He put his arms around her tiny frame, and kissed her gently on the top of her head. "Let's go, shorty. What movie is it tonight?"

"*The Wrath of Kahn.*"

"Great. I haven't seen that one in a whole week!" They stepped in together and shut the door.

Emma looked up and saw her parents walking down the basement stairs. "Don't worry, Dad, he'll be back in the morning. He feels bad, too."

"I hope you're right, sweetie. Hey, who's got the popcorn?"

"I do!" a small voice spoke up from behind him. She was tall and slender and only fifteen years old. Emma will never forget that image of her. Standing there in her pink "angel girl" pajamas with her light brown hair pulled up into a ponytail and holding a huge bowl of buttered popcorn with a smile on her face. She was sweet and graceful and never cared about "diets." John turned around and shoved his large hand into the bowl, pulled out a pile of popcorn and stuffed it into his mouth. "Daddy! Save some for the rest of us will ya!?"

Then the doorbell rang. They all looked at each other, confused. It was nine o'clock at night and they weren't expecting anyone. John volunteered to get the door, commenting on how if it's one of the neighbors that Mom would end up standing there talking all night and they would never get to the movie. John proceeded up the stairs and back to the front door. The women all huddled together on the couch in front of the TV, eating as much of the buttery popcorn on top as they could.

Upstairs John answered the door. There stood two clean-cut men in nice polo shirts and khaki pants.

"Excuse me, sir," said the one on the left with the blond hair, "but our car broke down and we were wondering if we could use your phone real quick." John was a kind man and honestly wanted to accommodate anyone who asked for his help, and so he was more than happy to invite them in and offer his phone.

"Sure, boys, come on in! The phone is over there on the table next to the couch. Would you like something to drink? The family and I are downstairs watching *The Wrath of Kahn*, you're welcome to join us as you wait for your ride."

The second man shut the front door and turned around. John looked up at him and was horrified. The young man's face had been changed into a disturbing form. His eyes were now yellow and his teeth had grown sharp and long. "We aren't that big on *Star Trek*, sir, but I think we will take you up on that drink. I believe we are a bit thirsty!"

They both grabbed John and threw him into the wall by the fireplace. He managed to get the poker and swung at the intruders. They both laughed at the man struggling to save himself and his family.

Down in the basement, the three women sat huddled on the couch, staring up at the ceiling. Scared and confused, they remained frozen. Finally, Katherine could wait no longer and she stood up from the couch and slowly walked to the stairs. The girls begged her silently to return to them and she shushed them. Very carefully she began her ascent. She slowly took one step at a time to ensure that her socked feet made no noise whatsoever. When she had reached the top, she carefully pushed the door open and peered down the hall into the living room. Her eyes widened with terror. She saw her husband being beaten over and over again with the fireplace poker. With each devastating blow, blood flew into the air and into the faces of the attackers. Each time this happened, they pointed and laughed at each other. John was still conscious. He tried to roll and when he did he groaned in pain. He tilted his head and locked eyes with Katherine. She felt the tears stream down her cheeks, hot and wet, pooling on her chin. The attackers started again. It was as if they were drunk from the violence. John kept looking at Katherine. He mouthed to her, "Run." At first Katherine couldn't fathom the idea of leaving her husband to these demonic butchers. But in her heart she knew it was too late for him and that she needed to get her daughters out of there quick. She realized suddenly that she had forgotten to breathe. She blinked, looking at her husband, and mouthed, "I love you." His eyes glazed over and she knew he wasn't there anymore.

The bastards were like dogs now, lapping the blood up off of John and slurping at the pool of it on the floor. She went to make her retreat. Slowly she began to back away. But the step creaked and the monsters jerked around. They saw her and they snarled as they grinned. Before they could fall upon her, Katherine turned around and yelled for her daughters to run.

Emma immediately jumped up and ran for the far wall with the high rectangular windows. She tried climbing the shelf but in her urgency she kept slipping. Her socks seemed to be working against her. She went to ask Shea to give her a boost; it was then that she realized Shea wasn't there with her. She was still standing in front of the couch, frozen.

"Shea!" she whispered loudly. But she didn't move. She wanted to grab her and pull her toward her, but she was scared, too. Frantic, she spun around looking for a place to hide. And then Emma remembered when they were children. When she and Jimmy wanted to hide from their parents or from their bothersome little sister, they would hide under the stairs. What once was a closet was now covered by paneling and had been forgotten about. She and Jimmy had found it by accident when they were six. They were play wrestling when Emma got thrown into that paneling. Jimmy had noticed that crack perfectly straight on one of the seams and he was able to bend it back from the wall. When he did that, they saw that there was a small door there and pushed it open. Once inside they could pull the paneling back in place and shut the door. No one ever knew about their secret "clubhouse." They would even bring flashlights in there and no one could see the light from inside.

The only problem now was getting there from where she was, all the way to the front of the basement and not get caught. She gathered up all of her courage and ran for the clubhouse. She reached for Shea's arm to pull along with her, but as her fingers touched her arm, they saw their mother's feet dangle from below the dropped ceiling. Shea screamed. Emma thought she would die of fright right then and there. She tried to pull Shea along with her but she was running for the stairs, all the while screaming, "Mommy!" Tears poured down Emma's face. She wanted to yell out for her sister, but she didn't want to give herself away like Shea had done.

Now they know you are down here! she kept screaming in her head. As much as she wanted to help her baby sister, her fight or flight mechanism had just made up her mind for her. She kept going for the hidden door. She slid behind the air hockey table that was there now and pushed her fingers into the crack. All she could hear was her heart pounding as she pulled the paneling back. She shoved the little door open and threw herself in. As quickly and quietly as she could she pulled the paneling back into place and shut the door. She squished herself as far back as she could to the back of the little closet, as far back as the stairs would allow her to go. She heard Shea run up the stairs to get to her mother. And when she got close one of the intruders grabbed her as well.

"Well! Looks like we have a young one!" He sniffed her neck and then licked it. "She's fresh, too! Nice and ripe and never been picked!" the dark-headed one sang. "We are gonna have fun tonight, baby girl, and Mommy is gonna get to watch! Too bad Daddy was in too big of a hurry to get dead, he coulda watched, too! I bet you taste like peaches!" He bit into her neck so hard that Emma could hear the crunch of his teeth penetrating her skin. He pulled back harshly. "I better save some for later. I want you awake so you can scream for me!"

Emma sat in her hole and rocked. She was ashamed of the things she felt now. She was glad that it wasn't her! She just kept praying that they wouldn't find her. She scolded herself for being so selfish. But what could she do? She heard them drag her mother and sister up the rest of the stairs and down the hall. She assumed they had taken them into her sister's room. That's where it sounded like they were. A few moments later she heard the basement door open and footsteps come down the stairs. Emma froze, afraid that any movement would give her away. Her breath was halted and her eyes were wide and searching. It was as if she could feel his movements. She heard him walk the perimeter of the basement and then force open the door to the closet where Daddy kept all of his best and rarest books. Then the book closet door shut and he was silent for a long moment. It felt like forever to her. Was he searching for her? Had Shea and Mom told him there was another one in the house? Emma gathered herself up into as small of a ball she could get herself into. Then, just like that, she heard him bound up the stairs whistling something happy. Emma's tears fell in relief. He hadn't known she was there!

All that night, she could hear them laugh and holler with delight. She could hear the screams of her sister and mother. She never moved from that spot far in the back, under the stairs.

It had been quiet for a long time. She guessed that two hours had passed since she had heard any sounds or felt any movement. Slowly she began to crawl and feel around on the floor, hoping that just by the grace of God something had been left behind from her and Jimmy's clubhouse days. She was in luck! There in one of the far corners was a candle and a lighter! Slowly and carefully she attempted to light the lighter. Finally it lit and she was able to light the candle! She rejoiced in her mind that Jimmy was such a bookworm. The candle set on a piece of broken glass stuck in the corner on a ledge. It was stubby and white and obviously hadn't been used in a while. Below it was a small stack of books. She picked them up and sifted threw them. *Encyclopedia Brown* and *Adventures of a Fourth Grade Nothing* were right on top. "Judy Blume? Hmmm." Underneath that were a couple of dinosaur books and one on *The Ferengi Rules of Acquisition*. But when she had picked up this final book, a soft green glow caught her attention. She looked back down at the floor and saw a digital clock. *Thank God Jimmy was always so anal about punctuality!* By this clock the time was seven a.m. *Had it really been that long?* she thought to herself. *If these things really were vampires, then isn't it safe to assume that they have to sleep during the day and that they can't go out in the daylight?* This was her chance. She needed to act quickly. Suddenly, her limbs began to tingle. She brushed it off as fear and lack of sleep. She got this strange sensation of confidence. She looked at the digital clock and thanked Jimmy under her breath for leaving this stuff in there. She thought of him for a moment, how he was lucky not to have been there, but how she wished he was there. *Jimmy. Where are you, big brother? I need you so badly right now!*

Three miles away Jimmy awoke with a start and jumped up off of Brian Kelly's apartment floor. He wasn't quite sure how or why, but he knew Emma was in trouble and he needed to get home as soon as possible. He kicked the empty beer cans out of his way and grabbed his keys off of the makeshift milk crate coffee table and ran out the door. "I'm coming, sissy. I'm coming."

Emma removed her socks, blaming them for her failed escape last night. She took a deep breath and pulled the little door open. "Ok, now to open the paneling, you can do this! You can!" Shaking, she stuck her right hand out in front of her and gently pushed the paneling. It gave, and slowly it opened. She closed her eyes and breathed in deep again and prepared for her next move. Emma slowly peeked her head from around the bent paneling and looked around. She saw no one, so she slipped out. She crawled under the air hockey table and slowly stood up. Checking out the stairs, she saw blood spatter in the wall near the basement door; it was cracked. She covered her mouth and tried not to vomit. Reminding herself that she had to get the hell outta there, she turned and headed for the metal shelf under the window. But as she inched closer she heard them stirring upstairs in the kitchen.

"Hey, do you smell that?" the blond one asked.

"Yeah, it smells like, *sniff,* a candle?" answered the dark-headed one. "Is it coming from the basement? I thought you said no one was down there!"

"There wasn't. I checked, I swear! There wasn't anywhere anyone could have been!"

"Do I have to do everything for you?" He started walking to the basement door.

Emma panicked and started to run. Just then the door flew open and the dark-headed one saw her! "Hey! Where did you come from!?" he yelled. "And where do you think you're going!?"

Emma didn't stop; she raced for the shelf and started climbing. The vamp caught her legs and tried pulling her down. Instinctively, she kicked back and he was knocked back a bit. Both of them were shocked. The vamp looked down and back up again, but before she could question where it had come from she reached up and pulled the little curtain off of the rectangular window. The vamp was blinded and ducked out of the sunlight. Emma yanked open the window and started to tear her way out. Suddenly, she felt his hand around her right ankle. She was slipping back! "NO!" she screamed. The pain was unbearable! She couldn't shake his grip when, out of nowhere, she felt this overwhelming sensation of the tingling in her limbs again. This time, it was intensified and all over her body like an electric shock, and she was the electricity! It was like someone had flipped a switch and suddenly she was on for the first time in her life! She knew she had the power to get herself out of there! Emma reached forward and grabbed onto the clothesline pole that was stuck in the yard. She pulled with all of her might, but that damned vampire wouldn't let loose of her foot. His grip was as solid as hers. She wedged her shoulder up and was able to get her left arm through the window and now pulled with both arms to free herself. She bit down and gritted her teeth, using everything she had to pull. A sharp pain shot up her leg as she felt the bastard sink his nails into her heel cord to get a tighter lock on her. She pulled herself up far enough to get her left knee up to the windowsill and was able to use it as leverage. She pulled hard one last time and was free!

She was out of the basement and lying in the grass under the sun. She breathed in deep and allowed the early sunlight to warm her face. But then something didn't feel right. She looked down and saw that her right foot was gone! Her mouth dropped open as she looked back into the window and saw the vamp there in the shadows holding her foot and waving.

"Not bad, but at least I got a souvenir!" He then started laughing manically. Emma crawled backward using her hands and her remaining left foot. When she got to the middle of the yard, the sun was directly over her and she was sure they couldn't get to her there. She fell back and felt the throbbing pain of her mutilated limb. As she slipped off into subconsciousness, she called out to Jimmy one last time.

A minute later Jimmy pulled up into the driveway and found his twin sister bleeding to death in the front yard.

"EMMA!" he screamed as he shook her. He took off his shirt and tore it to make a tourniquet. He looked around, and got up to go inside to call 911. Her hand reached up slowly and touched his leg.

"No," she whispered. "Don't go in there! They're still inside! All gone. They got them, all gone."

"What do you mean? Who's in there? Who's all gone? Where's Mom and Dad?"

Emma closed her eyes and relived the events in her mind. Jimmy jumped back in horror.

"No. I don't believe it! What the hell is going on?! I'm taking you to the hospital!"

He put her into the truck and tore off for the emergency room. The police never found the ones who did it. It ran on the news for two weeks as "a great tragedy." John had been bludgeoned to death with a fireplace poker and drained of his blood. Katherine and Shea Hogan had been repeatedly raped, sodemized, tortured with curling irons and knives, and drained of their blood. Emma recovered quicker than anyone could have imagined and the twins inherited their family's house and book shop. They both dropped out of college and, for reasons even they were not sure of, they both stayed in the house.

One evening Jimmy was going through the books in the closet when he found one of the oldest books he had ever seen. He described the Legacy of the Slayer. It seemed to explain what had happened to Emma. With that book and the helpful use of the World Wide Web, Jimmy and Emma were able to learn about what a slayer was and what she needed to do. From that day on, it had been their personal vendetta to rid the world of those who had rid them of their family. This was their life now.

CHAPTER TWO

Walnut Grove and Layla Fellows

Present Day
They let go of each other and took a step back.
"I'm sorry, too. You were there and heard everything!"
"Yeah, good thing you were being a bitch that night! You may not have been there in the morning to help me." They both scoffed. They turned and continued to walk down the street, past the liquor store and the thrift shops and down by the building that used to be the beauty school. Now it was just an empty building. Jimmy and Emma stood there for a moment and looked up at it. It was just a flat one-story brick building with boards on the broken windows. They had to start doing that to places now. Teenagers, who have nothing else to do in this town, get drunk and walk around looking for windows to smash so they have a place to party. Just then a couple of kids came running and bumped into them on their way.

"Hey!" Jimmy yelled. "I hope I never have kids!"

"I hope you never have kids either! You're enough for the world! Like this place needs any more reasons to suck."

"Like I need a lecture on coolness from the girl who once dressed up as Wilson the volleyball from *Castaway* for Halloween!"

"Oh come on! That was awesome! No one else thought of that!"

"Yes I know. And there is a reason for that!"

Emma pierced her lips together and looked down. She mumbled under her breath, "Trekkie."

"TrekkER! TrekkER! For the last time, it's trekker! Trekkies actually believe they are IN *Star Trek*! I am just a fan! Therefore, TREKKER!" Jimmy instructed.

"Whatever, it's all GEEK to me."

They both smirked and looked in one of the broken away boards to see if they could make anything out.

"Well, this is where the news said those kids were last seen. You ready?"

"What else am I gonna do on a Friday night in Walnut Grove, Missouri?"

"When you say it you make it sound so boring, so..." Jimmy searched for the word that best described their hometown in Middle Missouri.

"So 'Retirement Community'?"

"Yes! That's it! Like a big old folks home!"

"And we must be in the basement." Emma frowned. She looked around to make sure no one was around. Jimmy reached forward and tried the door.

"Locked from the inside."

"Well, I guess we'll have to knock!" Emma took a step back, raised her right leg and kicked the door open. The twins stepped into the old salon. Jimmy kicked aside the bits of broken plywood and broken metal from the lock.

"Maybe we should have rung the doorbell?" He snickered.

"Nah, I wanted to be discreet." Emma shuffled around in the large room. There were still mirrors hung consecutively on the opposing walls. Still a counter here and there. There was even a derelict hair drying chair off in one of the corners. It was dark and smelled like rat feces and mildew.

"Maybe they're not back yet; maybe they left and moved on," Jimmy suggested.

"No. They're here. They're hiding." Emma slowly laid her bag down and walked casually across the floor. Her ears perked. She looked over in the back right corner at a metal door that was shut. The handle turned. She and Jimmy looked at each and she grabbed the dagger from her left boot. Jimmy dropped his bag and produced a stake from the inside of his coat. They stalked closer to the door, preparing for the worst. The door slung open. There stood a young vamp of medium build in bagging, ripped up jeans, a Warrant t-shirt, and holding a beer. He was laughing as he turned back into the doorway to say:

"Uh huh, yeah, that's what she said!" He turned back around and froze. "Uh, did Rudy send you?"

Emma turned and looked at Jimmy and they both shrugged in agreement to go with it. Emma responded:

"Yeah, I was supposed to ask for...Oh darn! I forgot your name again!"

"Huhuh, Crusher!"

"Yeah! That's it! Crusher! You know, I would have taken you for a Steve."

"You know I get that a lot. So, dude, are you like, her manager or pimp or something, because we told Rudy that we only wanted chicks, man."

Jimmy and Emma look at each other again and tried not to laugh.

"Um, I'm her bodyguard. You know, in case people get too friendly, ya know?" Jimmy quickly stammered.

"Wait a minute!" The vamp halted. "Where's your stereo? We told Rudy that you had to bring one!"

Emma felt around her chest. "Oops! I must have left it in my other bra!" She threw her dagger across the room so that it stuck into the vamp's neck and pinned him to the wall behind him. She sashayed across the floor until she reached the vamp bleeding on the wall and tried to pull out the dagger. Emma stood in front of him and danced a little sultry and then turned around, bent over and slapped her behind.

"Hey, where's my tip?" she demanded. "That's ok, I'll give you one. Warrant? Wasn't cool then, definitely not cool now. And I guarantee you NO ONE is buying the name *Crusher*!" And with that she pulled a stake out of her sleeve and dusted him. Jimmy came up from behind her, yanked the dagger out of the wall and wiped it clean for her.

"Seriously, I REALLY didn't need to see that. That was just wrong. I thought the slayer dreams were bad, I am really gonna have nightmares tonight!" Jimmy complained.

"Oh please! I have real talent. Admit it! I could have a brilliant future as a featured stripper!"

"Oh yeah!" Jimmy agreed. "I can hear your stage name now! 'And now, get your big bills out for PEGGY THE PIRATE!'" He then erupted into laughter. Emma slapped his chest and shushed him. There was a noise of scooting chairs coming from the room behind the metal door.

"Way to go stupid! Peggy the Pirate? You've put some thought into that one haven't you?"

Jimmy hung his head in shame. "Yeah, I've been waiting for the setup."

"How long?"

"A couple of months now."

"Ahh, not bad, really. Clever."

The door opened and another stood there looking confused and wearing a Linkin Park shirt.

"Oh my God! Your taste in music is actually worse than that guy's!" Emma proclaimed as she referenced the pile o' dust on the floor to her left.

"Hey!" the gruff-looking vamp interjected.

"I mean c'mon now! Has the music industry really produced anything half way decent since 1992?"

The pissed-off vamp punched Emma in the face.

"Hey! No need to resort to physical violence now! I'm sure we can resolve our musical differences with adult conversation. But wearing Linkin Park? Really? It's like you WANT people to know that you have no taste!" The vamp swung at her again and she blocked his punch and gripped his fist tight.

"Geez, even your fighting skills aren't original! Let me make it simple for you. You can't keep doing the same thing over and over again. Like this!" Emma twisted his arm behind him and kicked him in his rear and he slid across the room into the wall. Then she ran over and picked him up by his hair and slammed his face into the concrete floor. "See what I did there. I did two different things consecutively. That means in a row." She took a step back to allow him to get up. He stood and cleared the blood from his eyes.

"You talk too much, little girl." He grunted.

"Ya see, I keep telling her that but she never listens to me. I guess it's because she talks too much," Jimmy remarked as he stood back, watching.

"Just like a woman. Too much talk." The bloody-faced vamp scoffed along with Jimmy.

"Really? 'Cause I was thinking that you haven't been around many women in your, *ahem*, 'lifetime'!" Emma teased as she thrust her hips, making a sexual reference. This really ticked him off. He took off running for her and she stuck her arm out and yelled, "Olay!" as he missed her and ran past. He yelled and ran at her again and this time he tackled her.

"Oh yeah? I'll show you how much practice I get!" Emma clicked her right heel and the wooden dagger came jutting out and she shoved it into the vamp's groin. He howled in agony and Emma flipped him off of her.

"Oh, I'm sorry! I didn't think that would hurt! Didn't know anything was there!"

"You BITCH!" the vamp managed to sputter out. Emma pulled out her stake, flipped it in the air and stabbed it into his chest. He burst into dust.

"You have issues. Serious ones," Jimmy scolded. "You play around too much."

"Oh c'mon, Jim! Why can't I work out some aggression while I am working? The women at the DMV get to!"

They walked to the back room and looked around to make sure they had gotten all they had come for, and they had. A typical vampire nest. Filthy and smelly. An old broken TV, a cooler with warm beer, and a couple ratty mattresses on the floor. Jimmy knocked over some boxes and glanced half-heartedly. Emma lifted one of the filthy mattresses disgustedly with her thumb and forefinger and quickly dropped it. Jimmy darted around to her direction.

"You find something?"

"Yeah. The reason why the invention of the flushable toilet was so important." Emma gagged. They stopped and looked at each other. A soft sound came from the closet in the back corner. They nodded at each other in agreement that they both heard it. Then another sound came from the closet. This time it was more of a whimper. They turned and walked softly over to the closet. Jimmy almost tripped over a wadded-up blanket when Emma grabbed his sleeve. She pointed to the hand sticking out from underneath it. She squatted down and lifted a corner of the tattered, green army looking blanket.

"Oh my God." She gasped as she stared down at the mutilated corpse of a young man. His eyes were open, dried and had lost their color. He didn't even look like a real person anymore.

"He looks like wax," Jimmy blurted. The young man was covered in bites and his face was severely beaten. A closer inspection of his hands showed that they were both broken and so were all of his fingers. They were all twisted and bent out of shape.

"Looks like we were at least a day or two late," Emma said as she became choked up. Then there was the whimper again and Jimmy and Emma were snapped back into the world, remembering the reason why they were headed in this direction in the first place. They slowly stood up and stepped over to the door. Emma placed an ear to the door and waited patiently for another sound. When the soft sob and thud came again, Jimmy stood against the wall as Emma cautiously opened the door. There in the dark, a young woman shuffled back against the wall and covered her eyes with her arm.

"Please," she pleaded softly. "Please, don't hurt me anymore. Please let me go. I won't tell anyone. I swear! Where's Bobby? Please. Please." Her face and arms were bruised and cut. Her blonde hair was stringy and greasy. She huddled there trembling in nothing but her bra and panties. Emma kneeled down and reached her hand out for the girl's arm.

"Hey. It's ok, they're gone. I got rid of them, you can come out." She slowly dropped her arm and looked up. She smiled quickly and then began to cry.

"They were horrible. I, I, I think the one was gay."

"What makes you say that?" Emma questioned.

"Well, he was wearing a *Warrant* t-shirt." Jimmy removed his coat and wrapped it around the girl. But when he moved, it gave the young girl a clear view of the boy on the floor in the blanket. Her eyes grew wide with horror.

"Bobby!" she screamed. Jimmy quickly jumped around and recovered the body.

"Come on. Let's get you to a hospital." Emma lifted her up and ushered her out of the building.

That night, after they returned from dropping the girl off at the hospital, they stayed up, cracked open a twelve pack, and reminisced over some old family albums that they had kept in a closet for the past two years. It felt good to talk about happy memories again. With the photo album open and empty beer cans on the floor, Emma passed out on Jimmy's shoulder. Jimmy didn't have the heart to move her. For once she looked peaceful, and he could sacrifice a couple hours of comfort for that. He stared at a picture of him and his father standing in front of the book store, arms around each other and smiling big. He touched the image of his father and the tears welled up.

"I'm sorry, Pop. You were a better man than I could ever hope to be." He bowed his head and closed his eyes tight. He didn't want to allow himself to cry. He was surprised when he felt a firm hand grip his right shoulder. He stopped, looked up and there stood his father, smiling down brightly at him.

"It's ok, son. Are you going to get that?" With that Jimmy awoke with a start. He sat straight up on the couch and looked around, bewildered. Emma sat up from the other side of the couch with bloodshot eyes, looking confused.

"Hey, did we sleep down here all night?"

Jimmy looked out the window that Emma had escaped out of two years ago and realized that it was daylight.

"It was a dream?" he questioned himself out loud.

"What?" Emma asked. Just then the doorbell rang. They both looked at each other.

"You saw Dad!" Emma proclaimed. As if shot by electricity they both jumped up and ran upstairs for the door. Emma looked out of the peephole of the front door and saw that a girl was standing there impatiently. She was short and looked as if she was of eastern Indian descent. Her hair was long and she wore it loose down her back. Emma thought to herself that she looked kinda like a hippie with her long red gauze skirt and off white cotton peasant shirt. The girl impatiently tapped her black mesh slippered foot and drummed her fingers on her hips in anticipation. She stopped suddenly and looked up at the peephole and snapped in a British accent.

"Are you going to stare at me all day or are you going to let me in?"

Emma jumped back and looked at Jimmy, shocked.

"Who is it?"

Emma shook her head from side to side to answer.

"Well come on. It's bloody freezing out here! If you let me in I can tell you who I am. But first you have to turn the handle and pull the door toward you. This will create an opening where I am able to pass across the threshhold into your home. I have not yet mastered the art of walking through walls," the girl demanded. Emma stepped back and opened the door. The girl stepped inside and looked up at Jimmy. "Well you're a tall one aren't you? You going to get those bags or do I have to drag them in here myself?" The twins looked behind her and saw two large dufflebags and a trunk on their front porch. Then they looked back at each other, utterly bewildered.

"Uh, you did say that you would tell us who you were," Emma stammered.

"Layla. Layla Fellows. Now, you, slayer, you think you could use some of that super strength to carry those bad boys in here?"

The twins were dumbstruck! How the hell did she know that?! Jimmy couldn't help replaying the song *Layla* in his head.

"Yes, yes, very original. No one has ever made that connection before," Layla blurted sarcastically. "Father was a Clapton fan. Go figure." She moved past them and plopped down on the couch and sneezed. "Sorry, I'm allergic to tacky."

"Hey!" Emma defended.

"How did you do that?" Jimmy asked as he stepped in front of the beautiful yet sharp-tongued intruder. "And what makes you think you are staying here?" Layla sat upright and looked back and forth at the two, a little confused.

"You mean you didn't know I was coming? He didn't tell you?" The twins yet again looked at each other in confusion.

"Who?" prodded Emma. Layla huffed and rolled her eyes.

"Lord. Your father! I told him to tell you I was coming! I told him to make sure you were home. I swear."

Jimmy and Emma's mouths dropped open.

"How could you have possibly spoken to him? Our FATHER has been dead for two years!" Emma shouted.

"Yes! I know! I'm not stupid! In fact it was right over there." Layla pointed to the fireplace. "And I did speak to him just last night, that's what I do. I'm a medium, or a witch or whatever you like." She smiled and then whispered, "I see dead people!" She erupted into laughter. "It kills me every time! I love it! Good movie, too."

"You're a lunatic!" Emma blurted. Jimmy stood there aghast. He almost couldn't believe what was happening. He recalled the "dream" he had had that night. His father standing there holding his shoulder, asking him, "Are you going to get that?"

"Emma. No. She's not crazy. Remember when we woke up. You knew that I had seen Pop. I thought it was real, then I thought it was a dream. Now, I know he was really there. He may have been in my dream, but he was really there! He told me that it was ok and to get the door." Emma stared at him with a questioning look on her face.

"You've got to be joking."

"How many times do we have crazy dreams?! The slayer dreams even! Suddenly I have one where I see Pop and I'm crazy!"

"You do realize that this is a complete stranger that we are just airing all of our laundry out in front of? Let's just put an ad in the paper! 'Vampire' problem? Then call The Hogans! We'll bust n' dust those pests for a low, low rate!'"

"Emma! She read my mind! That thing about Clapton? I had that song stuck in my head! And she talked to Dad!"

"I will not!" Layla suddenly objected. The twins stopped arguing and looked at her.

"Excuse me?" Emma asked. Layla was looking off into the kitchen. Jimmy and Emma looked in that direction also, but saw nothing.

"You're daft if you think I'm doing that!" Layla continued. She looked back at the twins and rolled her eyes. "This bloke here," as she pointed to the kitchen, "wants me to go tell his girlfriend that he will never leave her and never stop loving her!" She then turned and faced the kitchen. "You're DEAD! Do you not get that? She's alive and you're not! Then if you're never going to leave her what in the bloody hell are you doing here following these two around?"

"Uh, Layla," Emma interjected, "there's no one there."

"Are you completely mental? Or do you not remember that not five minutes ago I told you I see dead people? I wasn't just reciting a popular line from a hit movie you know. And for the record your mother cannot believe how much you have torn up the walls in your room, missy! Very, very upset and she says you need to lay off the muscle relaxers." Jimmy chuckled. "And you, sir, she says she knows what you have been doing in the book shop when no one's around!" She looked over to her left and grinned. "Duran Duran? Really?" Jimmy stood up straighter and cleared his throat.

"Why exactly do you think you are going to be staying with us?" he asked.

"Well, I don't think, I know. And I'm moving in not just staying here. Your sister said I could have her old room. She's very sweet really."

"What?!" Emma yelled. "I don't know you! I don't know why you are here! Why would I just let you move in, and especially to my baby sister's old room!"

"Because. I am here to help you. I have some answers you have been looking for. And if you don't stop whining, your sister has authorized me to tell Jimmy about you and Brian Kelley!" Layla stood up, brushed herself off, and folded her arms across her chest.

Emma's face turned red and she quickly ran out the front door and collected Layla's things, lugging them back into Shea's old room.

"What?!" Jimmy yelled in amazement.

"It's a good thing I came when I did, too! The dark forces are definitely at work in this hole in the ground you call a town."

"Really?! Have you seen something? Some message?"

"No, love, it's more like what I haven't seen! Do you know that this place doesn't have one Krispy Kreme? And there's a Tractor Supply next door to a Fashion Bug! What in the bloody hell is a Fashion Bug?! Does it look like a lady bug? How can you live here?!" Layla stood up and wandered around the living room looking at nick nacks and blowing dust off of pictures. Every once in a while she would mutter to herself. Emma returned to the room and announced to Layla that her things were placed in Shea's room and that it was down the hall, second on the right.

"I know where it is. You think the girl would give me her room without telling me about it?" She walked down the hall and disappeared.

Emma quickly jogged over to Jimmy and stood close to him.

"What in the hell is going on here? And why are we just letting her stay here?"

"Emma, she knows all that stuff! She says that she's here to help. That she has some answers for us! And besides, she's way hot!"

"Oh there we go! There is a chance that Jimmy might get laid so let's make her at home as quickly as possible!"

"By the way, Saint Emma, what about Brian Kelley???" Emma's face promptly turned red again.

"Nothing," she said. "Tell her you like her shoes, chicks love that." Emma turned and walked to her room.

Jimmy scoffed and went downstairs to clean up the mess from earlier.

The shower felt rejuvenating. The hot water beating down on her face and shoulders and running down her back was a welcome pleasure. She could taste the steam as it rose from the tub and her body. Her senses started to come awake from the drunken stupor she put herself into last night. The fog was beginning to lift from her mind and she remembered looking at the pictures with Jimmy. How they laughed as they looked at pictures from Halloween. How they cried when they spoke about how much they missed those things. And then blackness.

"Guess I passed out," Emma said to herself. She opened her shampoo and began to lather her hair. It smelled of roses.

"Roses," she pondered. "I remember something about roses last night." She closed her eyes in an attempt to better focus the memory. Then she saw it, The White Woman again.

"Another dream, I had another dream. A new one?"

As she relaxed into the image more pieces came together. The white woman was very close to her. She held her index finger to her lips and shushed her. She turned and this time curled her finger to tell her to follow. They stood in a desert. Barren, completely. She stretched out her right arm and pointed off in the distance; they saw a rose spring from the sand. It was the most beautiful rose she had ever seen! And it smelled so sweet; she could smell from all the way over where she was! Emma wanted to walk over to it, to touch it, but the woman stopped her. She told her that it wasn't her time. They continued to stand there, and as they did the rose wilted. Emma felt so sad; she wanted to touch it so badly. But as soon as that rose wilted another shot up in its place! This happened several times. A rose would wilt, another would spring up. After a while, Emma noticed that each time a new rose sprang up from the scorching sand, she would be that much closer to it. The White Woman clasped Emma's hand.

"Look!" she prodded. Emma looked and saw that as one rose wilted another came up, but the other rose had not disappeared! It remained and, in fact, became radiant again. Emma smiled in awe of the two roses sharing the plot of sand.

The horizon became darker. The darkness came closer and closer, but the roses were as radiant as ever. The darkness kept coming. Emma was afraid. She looked toward the White Woman, begging her to help.

But she simply held her finger up to her lips, shushed and smiled. Emma turned back to the roses and blinked. There was a flash of light and then the desert was filled with roses! The smell was overwhelming. They were beautiful! And with that the darkness receded. The White Woman took her hand again and this time led her through the field. She stopped after a while and stooped down. She pulled Emma with her and put her hand on one of the roses. She felt the petals; they were so soft and delicate. She reached down to pull it up and the thorns stuck her fingers. She yanked her hand back and nursed her bleeding fingers. The White Woman reached forward and wrapped Emma's hand in her skirts.

"It hurts, I know. It is a difficult task. Best we leave it here and not uproot it; let it continue to bloom. After all, it is not alone anymore."

Emma came back to her senses. Doing so, she lost her balance on her left leg and fell into the tub. Soap ran into her eyes and stung.

"What does that mean?" she asked out loud. She remembered what Jimmy had said about Layla earlier. "She is here to help us. She has some answers." Would she know about this? Emma finished rinsing her hair and decided to find out for herself.

Emma put on a t-shirt and jeans and wrapped her hair up in a towel. She looked for Layla in—now her—room. She wasn't there. She walked downstairs and discovered her and Jimmy going through some of the books Dad had in that closet.

"Did you know that Layla's parents were members of some ancient Sumerian brotherhood?" Jimmy asked excitedly.

"Of course I don't! I don't anything about her remember?" Emma replied. Jimmy rolled his eyes and gave her an exhausted look.

"My parents were of the Brotherhood of the Abgal Da. They died in an attack on the British Motherhouse. Not many survived. In fact, fearing another attack, they tore down the Motherhouse and relocated it."

"What are you talking about? Who's Abigail and why was her mother's house attacked?" Emma asked, frustrated.

"No, Abgal Da. It means 'Warrior Priests.' The Brotherhood of the Abgal Da was formed thousands of years ago in ancient Sumeria by a sect that worshiped a Goddess called the Ba Musal."

"What does that have to do with Emma?" Jimmy interrupted. Layla stopped and rolled her eyes toward Jimmy to scold him.

"Ok, don't do that, I need to stay focused!" Layla whipped around and pointed to the air. "And you shut up, too! I don't care about your rubber ducky!" They watched as she yelled into thin air like she had missed a few doses of her meds. They both scooted a little farther away from her.

"As I was saying before I was so rudely interrupted, she was not only their patron Goddess, she was a warrior and their protector against the parasitic forces of darkness called the Uradda, which came to be known millennia later as Vampires. For thousands of years, she was their Goddess and Savior. But she had already been ancient when The Brotherhood came into existence and so her time was coming to an end. Fearing the vulnerability they would suffer losing their warrior Goddess, The Brotherhood concocted a spell that would allow their Goddess to pass her spirit on to a suitable vessel. And since each woman, carriying within her the warrior spirit, was mortal, a new Ba Musal was born every generation to ensure the safety of their people."

"How did they do that?" Emma asked.

"Yeah, I mean it's just one spirit, how did they make it into…" Jimmy trailed off.

Layla rolled her eyes in aggravation. "Ok, kiddies; let's not forget you have about fifty freaking dead people in here also asking me a jillion questions. You are going to make my cute little head explode. I have no idea how they did it, they just did. Just like in everything thing else there are loopholes. Magic is full of them. Or full of it. Probably both; anyway, don't interrupt me again.

"As time went on the numbers of the Uradda grew to staggering amounts. And The Brotherhood became aware that a single warrior against the thousands of Uradda that were springing up was not enough. They came to the conclusion that to fight an army you needed an army. And so The Brotherhood decided that they would have to find a way to awaken the spirit of the Ba Musal in ALL the dormant vessels!

"They traveled the world searching for the magics powerful enough to create such a spell. And during their exploits they ended up recruiting more and more followers. This created a network that spanned all four corners of the globe! Eventually, due to the changing of the times, they were forced to keep their society a secret and hid behind the guise of scholars and socialites. As each generation passed, the Ba Musal, now, thanks to the likes of Bram Stoker, called the Vampire Slayer, was still awoken. And so, to make sure they were able to be near when the next was awakened, The Brotherhood set up Motherhouses in places they considered to be of 'mystical interest' throughout the world.

"Being that my parents were members I was raised on the Legacy of the Slayer, and demons and evil, blah, blah, blah. I have always had the power I have now. Luckily, my parents were who they were and knew how to help me cultivate my abilities. I had been in Indiana assisting at that Motherhouse in setting up a new mystical research facility when I got a message to come here and see you."

"A message?" Emma questioned. "From whom?" Layla smiled.

"You know who," she cooed. "The Sentinel, or as you two call her, The White Woman." Emma and Jimmy were stunned, but they were beginning to expect it from Layla.

"The Sentinel?" Jimmy asked. "The Sentinel of what?"

"Of whom, you mean," Layla corrected. "She is the Sentinel of the Legacy; the embodiment of the spirit of the Ba Musal!" They looked at each other, perplexed. "Have a seat, darlings, I have something I need to show you." Layla jaunted up the stairs and the twins sat on the couch.

"Do you think this chick is for real?" Jimmy asked Emma.

"Oh now you're the one asking me this! And yes, I believe she is. I had a dream last night. A new one. I was with the White Woman, or Sentinel, or whatever, and we were standing in…"

"A desert," Layla interjected. "It is very common for a slayer to meet with her in the desert. Symbolizes the harshness of this world and of the task at hand."

"Yes, it was a desert," Emma replied. She went on to describe the dream to them. Jimmy looked at her, sort of hurt.

"Why didn't you tell me? I didn't have that dream!"

"It wasn't for you to have, big boy. You are only meant to see what you are meant to see," Layla schooled.

"Do you know what it means?" Emma asked Layla.

"Yes I do, and I think you know, too, you just haven't let yourself know it yet."

"Do you get off in speaking, like, super mysterious? I thought you were so blunt that you said whatever crossed your lips," Jimmy teased.

"Shut up, you git, or I will make sure you forget how to speak, and you will spend the rest of your life trapped in your own mind." He took it that Layla was not exaggerating.

Emma now looked at him exhaustedly. She looked back at Layla and said: "I think it means that the rose represents the slayer, but I thought there could be only one in every generation. Why was there two, then many, and what does it mean that it's not alone anymore?"

Layla half smiled. "Remember I told you that Brotherhood had been searching for powerful magics? Well, finally a few years ago, The Brotherhood was able to accomplish the task they had set out to do millennia ago. The Army of the Ba Musal was born. Unfortunately, they didn't realize the magnitude of vessels that were out there and now search the world, sort of 'collecting' them for training and preparations in general."

"Well, how come this is the first I have heard of this? I mean if it happened two years ago shouldn't someone have contacted me?" Emma asked.

"Well, ya see, the states got a bit missed. The Brotherhood's members are all over the globe looking for and training new slayers. I guess they kinda forgot about back here."

Layla took a deep breath and a drink of her soda. "Good Lord, don't you people have anything other than diet? This isn't even real soda!"

The twins sat there blinking, trying to take everything in.

"I'm confused," Jimmy remarked.

"Good, then I have said it all correctly!" Layla proudly stated.

"You said you had something to show me?" Emma questioned.

"Right." Layla flopped a folder in front of her. "This folder contains information on what I have just explained to you. And even some info on some of the Ba Musal that came before you. When you get an opportunity it's yours."

"So what you were saying earlier, is that there are thousands of slayers in the world now?" Jimmy posed.

"Actually hundreds, but since the spell is having a bit of a trickle down effect, it may grow to thousands. And I guess the fact that each girl is born with it, new Ba Musal are literally being born all the time. Makes for some interesting nappie changes I bet!" Layla chuckled to herself.

Jimmy stood up, stretched and scratched his head. "And on that note, I have to go over the books for the store. You ladies play nice now!" Jimmy kissed the top of his sister's head and hurried up the stairs.

Emma ran her hand over the folder briefly. It hadn't all quite set in yet. Hundreds of slayers? It was a relief to know that she was not the only one going through this. But then something started to eat at her. Why couldn't she have had this great epiphany a day earlier? A year earlier? Her family would still be alive! She could probably still have her right foot!

"Oh bloody hell! You are the most depressing person I have ever been around! You are the freaking James Bond of slayers! And Jimmy's your Q! Don't you see that? You are the only one with this limb! The only one who has all of these kick ass gadgets! Why doesn't that make you happy? I mean come on! You get half price off for pedicures! That would be enough for me right there!" Layla preached. "I'm going to take a bubble bath. Those right bastard spooks will probably follow me in there, so please, if I start yelling and cursing it's not at you or your brother. Unless I catch him peeping, then you may have to pump him full of those muscle relaxers you like so much."

Layla walked off, leaving Emma alone in the basement. She looked down at the file. She was curious, but for some reason she couldn't bring herself to read through. Too much like nosing through someone else's life. She took the towel off of her head and lay back on the couch.

"An army of Slayers!" she mused. "Bond, Jane Bond!" Emma laughed. She kind of liked this gig after all.

~~~~~

That afternoon Layla insisted on getting to know her new surroundings better. And apparently, to her this meant scouting for perspective merchants of inexpensive footwear.

~~~~~

The newly-formed trio wandered slowly down the sidewalk of the L-shaped outdoor mall.

"I know you said that this place was small, but this is quite possibly the most pathetic mall I have ever seen," Layla said, sipping a soda from "Sammy's Subs."

They passed the town's one and only brand name department store and then the local discount chic clothing shop. They stopped and looked in at the large picture windows to see the many clothing racks, circular and linear, full of a prism of bright colors. Jimmy looked in as well and spied a pretty sales clerk with pretty blonde hair falling around her shoulders in large ringlets. In her tight pink blouse and denim skirt she adjusted the window display right in front of him. He smoothed his hand through his hair and straightened his jacket. She felt someone staring so she looked up at him. Jimmy jerked and mustered his most suave smile and winked. The girl rolled her eyes, laughed and turned away from the window.

"I'm never getting laid again." He sighed and jogged to catch up to the girls who had continued on without him.

"I mean how do you stay sane in a place like this? You don't even have a club here do you?" Layla complained.

"What do you expect; it's the retirement capitol of Missouri. You want a good time you have to drive an hour and a half north to St. Louis," Jimmy answered.

"We may not have a club but there's a pool hall and a..." Emma trailed off. She noticed in front of the record store a group of middle-school-aged kids hung out. There were three boys in baggy pants and dark t-shirts and a couple of girls with black make-up and fishnet fingerless gloves. The boy with the shaven head played around on a skateboard, bumping into people with the one with the Mohawk, and the other boy with long, greasy hair smoked cigarettes and laughed. The girl with short bottle-blonde hair pointed out Emma to the dark-headed girl and they stared intently. They caught the attention of the boys and they all studied her. Mohawk and shaved head looked at each other and shared a laugh while they pointed and continued to stare.

Emma looked down and remembered she was wearing a dark denim skirt and flip flops, revealing her shiny fiberglass prosthetic. She could hear them comment how the plastic-looking leg portion's coloring didn't match up with the rubber foot, which, over time, had become stained with black marks and slowly began to yellow from wear. Emma became agitated with the attention her not-so-fabulous accessory was drawing. She looked down again at the limb and more and more imperfections began to catch her eye. Several red and black scuff marks around the bulbous ankle, a tiny chip no more than a fraction of an inch in size and a few scrapes and scratches up the front on the shin. Jimmy, Emma and Layla got closer to the group and she could hear the boys make pirate jokes and the girls scold her choice in wearing a skirt with such a disadvantage. The tops of Emma's ears burned. She could feel her blood boiling and her face turning red. She hated these kids. She wished she could just go over there, pull their pants down and spank them all in front of the world. Maybe a little humiliation would teach them a lesson. But since she couldn't do that she would just tell them what she thought.

"WHAT?! You never saw a girl with a fake leg before? How about I just take a picture so you can show it to all of your friends and that way you wouldn't have to watch TV anymore! You could just come up with more and more funny little comments to make!" she yelled as she got closer to the one with the shaven head and pointed a finger in his face.

"Careful, Ted, she might take her leg off and beat you with it!" the one with the Mohawk said. Ted then turned and they all laughed and celebrated his comment.

Emma fumed and rolled her eyes. She then snapped back sarcastically. "Oh, Ha ha ha! Like I haven't heard that one before! Get some class!"

"Grow a leg!" the blonde girl yelled.

"Grow a personality!" Emma spat back. Jimmy grabbed her arm and started to drag her away. The kids pointed and laughed as Jimmy and Layla pulled her into the Chinese restaurant.

"Let go of me!" She grabbed his hand and forced it backward.

"Hey! Remember we set ground rules about that after you broke my hand last year! Why are you arguing with a bunch of kids?" Jimmy asked, rubbing his hand.

"They started it! They shouldn't have been staring like that!" Emma yelled. The older couple seated in the back of the restaurant looked up and began to say "excuse me" when Layla cut them off.

"Oh go back to your Kung pao, you old codgers; we'll be done in a minute!"

"Maybe they haven't ever seen a fake limb before; they handled it badly, yes, that just means they have shitty parents! You're the adult, Emma, it's your responsibility to act like one! Maybe what they really wanted was to know more about it!"

"Oh yeah, Jim, that's it! Why? So I can tell them my sob story and they can pity me? Tell me what a brave little trooper I am?" She could feel the tears welling up in her green eyes, intensifying their color. She wanted to reach up and wipe them but that would just be admitting that the tears were there.

Layla grew weary with Emma's display. "No, dear, I don't think there's any more room left in your pity party, it's already full of you," she said flatly with her hands on her hips.

"That's real easy for you to say, Ms. No-Assembly-Required!" With that, Emma flung open the door and stormed off down the sidewalk.

Maybe a little shopping would take her mind off the previous encounter, she thought. Ironically shoe shopping always seemed to make her feel better. She walked into the Shoe Emporium and began searching through the rows and rows, hunting for the perfect pair like she hunted down vampires. She inspected each one from the toe to the stitching. Finally, she found the perfect pair of black leather boots with a slender heel and pointed toe. Her excitement mounted as she kicked off her flip flops and sat on the stool to try on the boots. However, when she sat and looked down to start pulling on the boots, she realized what she had forgotten and her heart sank deep in her chest, making her lose her breath momentarily. She had her flat foot on today. Her high heeled one had been torn up and Jimmy hadn't finished fixing the one he had been working on yet. Her frustration grew again. She gripped the boot by the foot and squeezed harder and harder until its arch snapped. Realizing what she had done she threw it to the floor, grabbed her flip flops and stormed out of the store. She stood out on the sidewalk barefoot with the world swirling around her faster and faster. People walking by happily with bags full of their purchases continued on. How nice for them that they didn't have to worry about these things that filled her mind. Too many thoughts whirled around her head, making her feel unsteady on her feet. Wasn't her family's sufferings and death enough? Why did she have to be a freak on top of that? Not just the missing foot with its unattractive plastic replacement, but what man wants a woman who's ten times stronger than him? Even her brother felt castrated by her abilities.

    She slapped her forehead, punishing her weakness for crying and took off in a sprint for the gas station across the street. She flew in and went straight to the back and locked herself in the bathroom. There she allowed herself to cry and feel the pain that the kids' words and stares had caused. She let her thoughts linger on their comments and her wallowing depression turned into rage. She spun around with her fists clenched so tight that she began to draw blood. Without thought she flung both of her arms over her head and brought them back down again and again on the condom and tampon dispenser mounted on the wall. It crumpled like foil, making a pathetic metallic groan. She stared at what she had done and rushed out of the bathroom. She continued out of the gas station and walked with her head down all the way home.

    Luckily, Walnut Grove being the town it was, it didn't take long to get to and from anywhere. Emma walked into the house and went straight to her room. It would be dark soon and she was definitely in the mood for some violence.

Chapter Three

The Lessons We Learn

Jimmy walked casually in the front door. He had just come home from closing the book store. It had been an interesting day for the Hogan twins. A hot Indian girl showed up at the front door proclaiming she had the answers and that Emma was not the only slayer in the world! And now, she was living with them! He dropped his corduroy bag by the door and walked across the living room toward the kitchen. He grabbed a cup out of the cabinet and turned to open the fridge. He stopped in his tracks when he realized the door was open. Since Emma was still out patrolling, it had to be Layla.

"Oh, hey, how was your evening?" he asked. As he did so, the door shut and there she stood. Layla. In only a blue tank top undershirt and matching panties. She pulled a spoon out of her mouth and laid an armful of junk food onto the table. Jimmy didn't even glance at the assortment of chocolate pudding, cheese sticks, snack cakes, and potato chips on the table. He was struck dumb by the appearance of her. She stood up straight and licked the remainder of the pudding from the spoon and set it on the table. She smoothed the stray hairs back from her face toward her ponytail. Her entire being seemed to glow ethereally and every move she made was deliberate and graceful. She smiled at him and reached down for a chip and slowly eased it into her mouth.

"And by the way, the loo has been clogged for two hours and shit is threatening to spill all over the damn floor. HELLO?! Are you listening to me?" Jimmy had suddenly become aware that most of what he perceived in his mind of the last couple of minutes was not fully reality. He dropped his cup and stammered as he went to recover from this embarrassment. She stared at him impatiently. "Well? What's wrong with you? I ask a question and you answer, that's how this thing called conversation works."

"I, uh, sorry." He picked up his cup and placed it on the table, but he was so nerve wrecked by being in front of such a beautiful woman who was only wearing her slightly translucent underwear, that it toppled and fell again. "Sorry!" he exclaimed and bent down to retrieve it. Layla herself became aware of what had befallen Jimmy and began giggling.

"Have you not seen a girl in her underroos before?"

"Well, not normally in my kitchen late at night and usually I have known the person for more than twelve hours!" Jimmy answered.

"Oh Christ! You and your American modesty! Get over it! It's just a body. You people are so hypocritical. Brittany Spears can wear pasties and a thong on national television, but God forbid I walk around in my knickers!" Layla preached as she waved her arms around and spooned pudding into her mouth.

"Does she do that a lot? That little scene today at the mall?" Layla asked with her mouth full.

Jimmy cocked his head to the side and shrugged. "Unfortunately, yes. She's tough as nails, believe me, but she doesn't handle things like that very well. Like putting salt in a wound. She's been through a lot. People point and stare and some, like today, have even said things to her face. One time right before we dropped out of college, well she was a cheerleader and after she got her first leg she tried to get back into it. But there was this girl, Christine I think. She was always jealous of

Emma. Anyway, she forced Emma back off of the squad by making comments like 'She shouldn't be allowed to get the spot because her leg might fall off in the middle of the routine and ruin everything.'"

"Oh that's mature!" Layla said, rolling her eyes in disgust of the despicable comment.

"Yeah, well, cheerleaders are vicious. First she thought it was kinda sweet and up lifting to hear people say things like 'good for you' and 'you can't even tell when you wear pants!' But after a while it just started sounding like they were just being nice and trying to make themselves feel better."

Layla nodded and offered Jimmy one of her snacks and he declined. "Suit yourself!" she said. "But she acts so at ease with it, like she's come to terms with it."

"To a point it's true! I don't know everything that goes on in her head but what I do know is that she doesn't want that leg to be her trademark. She doesn't want to be known as the girl with the fake leg. But unfortunately not many people around here have seen anyone with a prosthetic leg, let alone a pretty young woman with one. God, she'd kill me if she knew I was telling you this!" He rubbed his face roughly, trying to keep himself from looking at her chest through her sheer top.

"Slayers," Layla scoffed, shaking her head. "Worse than men with that crap. No offense."

"Don't worry; I had my 'masculine' removed a couple years ago!" They both smiled and laughed quietly.

Jimmy took a deep breath and did his best to look her in the eye instead of the thin tank top Layla wore in the apparently very cold kitchen.

"So you were saying that the toilet is overflowing?" he stammered as he blinked.

"Ah, naw, that was just a piss-take. Seriously, I'm easy. No worries."

"I am so lost right now." Jimmy turned and pulled the juice out of the fridge and began to fill his abused yellow plastic cup. Layla sat and began to load up on sugars and other carbohydrates. Jimmy sat next to her and sipped his orange juice. He watched in amazement as the slender spitfire stuffed cheese sticks dipped in marinara into her mouth.

"How are you eating that right now?" he asked slightly in awe. "It's after ten, aren't girls, you know, worried about their weight and stuff?" Without missing a beat, Layla answered him smugly.

"What? Are trying to say I'm fat?" It seemed that she had caught him again. He looked up, flustered. He searched quickly for a way to redeem himself.

"Oh geez, I'm only joking! Do you not possess a sense of humor?" Jimmy stared at her blankly and blinked.

"I will never get women. You people make no sense. You're either really happy or really pissed or really depressed. All women must be bi-polar. I swear. That fat question is like the unanswerable question. No man can ever get out of that one alive!" Jimmy hung his head, staring down into his cup of orange juice. Layla just smiled and giggled at him.

"You know you could relax a bit more. I'm not going to hurt you. Unless, that is, if you ask me too!" She grinned widely as she crunched down on another cheese stick.

"Aren't you British women supposed to be all ladylike?" Jimmy asked.

"Bollocks!" Layla hurled back. "If I want to say something why not say it? I prefer to be honest about my feelings and opinions instead of covering them up with smiles and curtsies and very well I thank yous!"

"Well, you could be a little nicer, though," he presented.

"PONCE!" Layla suddenly yelled seemingly in Jimmy's face.

"What the hell?!"

"Not you, lamb! The poof behind you!" Jimmy whipped around to see who was there and not to his surprise there wasn't anyone.

"How rude are you? Did you not notice I was having a conversation here? No! I am busy and you are an arse!"

"What exactly are they saying to you when you do that?" Jimmy asked. She furrowed her eyebrows and bit her lip as she thought.

"They think that since I can see and hear them, that somehow they aren't really dead, that there is still some chance that they can enter into this world again. But the thing that they don't quite grasp is that their bodies are long gone, and there is nothing I can do. They can't accept the fact that their time has passed. They believe I am here to help them fulfill their last requests and ambitions. If I fulfilled every spirit's ambitions, I would never, ever, ever be able to fulfill my ambitions while I am alive! And if I do it for one, then I must do it for all. I think the main thing that they do not know is, the things that they want me to pass on to their family members and such; those people already know! They already know that they loved them and so on. If you truly cared for someone during your life, they will know! It's not my job to finish their lives for them!" Jimmy looked at her thoughtfully.

"Well, what does this guy want?" he asked her eagerly. "I mean he went through the trouble of interrupting, might as well do something for him."

"You want to know what I can do for him? Like I said, if I fulfill his wishes, I have to do it for all of them! They watch me help him and then they become relentless in nagging me! Let me show you how I handle this, if I can't ignore them anymore." She pushed back from the table and stood up from her chair. Layla walked confidently around the table and behind Jimmy, close to the doorway to the living room. She squared her shoulders and looked up sternly.

"Look here! Whether you like it or not, you are dead! Ok, as in no longer in this dimension! There is nothing more for you here! Yes, yes. YES! You ARE DEAD! Do you see that big, bright purple light above your head? Yes that one exactly. Yes, you twit! If you just let go, everything will be as it should be! Trust me, she knows! Now, please, you are really cramping my style and I would like to get back to my grub! I'm not sure, but I hear that they have a Disneyworld in sweater heaven. OK, then off you go!" And she wiggled her fingers in a sort of wave, dusted her hands and walked back to her chair.

Jimmy looked at her, perplexed. "What did you just do?"

"I told him to GOOO TOWAAARRDSS THE LIIIIGHT!" Layla mocked.

"The purple light?!" he questioned.

"Yes, the light is purple," Layla responded. Jimmy nodded.

"Thought it was a white light."

"No, purple."

"Is it a dark purple, you know like a blue-violet, or more periwinkle?"

"Kind of a shiny periwinkle actually." She nodded and sipped her soda.

"Do you see them all the time? The spirits? Or, only at certain times of the day and what not?"

"I see them all the time, well, what I mean is, I see them when there are any 'them' to see. Normally, at any other place, maybe one, maybe two. But here! Do you realize how many lost souls you have in this house? Following you two around! I am astounded! I might go crazy here! It's a slayer thing, I'm sure of it. It's like they're attracted to your aura. They sense the power, the strength."

"What do you mean 'your'? Emma is a slayer. Not me. I am her trusty sidekick and leg gadget guy!"

"Oh no, love! You and your twin share that aura! Now, don't get me wrong, you are NOT a slayer. But you do share the spirit of the slayer! Which is why you can know when the other is in need, and why you have the abilities to sense each other's thoughts! You are twins in spirit as well as in flesh!"

"When you put it that way it just makes it sound creepy!" Jimmy finished his juice and tossed his cup into the sink. "Well, I think I am gonna turn in for the night. If you need anything, let me know. Night." And he turned and walked away.

Layla stood up abruptly and the sound of the scooting wooden chair against the laminate floor forced him to turn around.

"Thank you," she said in a nervous way as she rubbed the palms of her hands on her hips.

"For what?" Jimmy asked.

"For believing me and letting me stay," she cooed. "Anyone else would have called me a looney and told me to bugger off. But you didn't and I appreciate that."

Jimmy didn't know what to say. He just stood there trying not to look at her breasts. "Well, if you try your best not to call me a ninny, a git, daft, and all those other crazy words you make up anymore, then we will call it even! Oh, and helping with the bills, always a plus!" And then he turned and walked away. Layla stood there and watched him walk down the hall and listened as he closed the door to his bedroom. She smiled to herself.

"He is quite adorable, isn't he?" she said out loud.

"I told you," said a mysterious voice from behind her. A tall, languid woman stepped forward and Layla turned to greet her. She was slender with a long, silken, dark blue, sleeveless gown. The color of her eyes matched it and were almost too bright and striking to look at. She had long black hair that was soft and shiny and fell down her back to her buttocks. She reached forward with her milky white arm and rested a hand on Layla's left shoulder.

"How much longer?" Layla asked without turning around. She continued to smile.

"Not much," the woman answered gently. "Timing is everything, my child. And patience is a virtue you tend to lack."

Layla turned and looked at her with a raised eyebrow. "I just don't like beating around the bush!"

"Are you questioning me?"

"No, Lady Aslyn. I just feel deceitful," Layla said as she showed the first glimmer of humility since she arrived at the Hogan home.

"You have told them no lies. You have no reason to feel deceitful."

"But my reasons for coming here!"

"Did you not tell them that you were here to help? That you have answeres? That is your reason and purpose for being here!"

"Forgive me, my Goddess," Layla said as she bowed her head. "I will continue to do as you ask. It is time when you proclaim it."

Aslyn reached down and lifted Layla's chin with her delicate right hand.

"The time at hand is trying, I know. But you have survived one of the most difficult tragedies a human can go through. The sudden death of your parents. You are something very special. Only you can show the slayer and her brother the path they must walk. All things work together for the good. Remember that." She stepped back and faded into nothing.

Suddenly, Layla heard the front door open and close and there was Emma standing in the kitchen doorway.

"What the hell is all of this? Do you not ever stop eating? Since you say you will be living here now, that means you have to clean up after yourself. And that also means you replace what you eat. Oh my God, did you eat all of that? In the same sitting? Do you have a tapeworm?" Emma set her bag on the chair that Jimmy had been sitting in and walked to the sink. She poured herself a glass of water and gulped it down quickly.

"What are you doing back so quickly? I didn't expect you until right before dawn," Layla submitted.

"Small town remember. Besides, I think the activity will be kinda low since I hit one of their hot spots and cleaned it out." Emma leaned on her left arm on the counter and looked at Layla. She then realized that she was only in her underwear. Emma blinked. "Uh, did you need something to sleep in, or some other form of bodily coverings?"

"You're telling me, that you are more comfortable staying strapped into those binding leather boots and coo-lots than you would be in an undershirt and panties?"

"I didn't say that."

"Then what is the big deal! I am comfortable!" Layla defended.

"And cold, too, as it would seem!" Emma said as she looked down and then up quickly, then smiled.

"Oh, do I threaten you? Are you jealous of my ample yet perky bosom?" Layla accused. Emma pierced her lips and briskly walked out of the kitchen, down the hall and into her bedroom. Two minutes later, she returned, wearing a matching tank and panty set. It was dark green and the tank had a golden shamrock on it and the panties had the words "Luck of the Irish" on their front.

"There, now, how's this for ample yet perky?!" Emma said as she turned round fully.

"See, now don't you feel better?" Layla asked.

"You know what, you're right! This is very relaxing! I guess I am too used to living with a guy."

"We're both girls here! Nothing we haven't seen before! And now that your brother sat here and talked for a while with me in my knickers, I don't think he will have a problem with it in the future!"

"You mean my brother saw you half naked? Well, that's just great! It was hard enough getting him to run the book shop alone! Now, he'll never leave the house!" Emma threw her arms up in the air and told Layla she was going to bed.

Layla looked around the kitchen and began to clean up from her little bedtime snack. When she had finished, she stretched her arms and yawned deeply.

"Shit! I'm quite knackered myself!" She yawned again. As she walked down the hall toward what was now her bedroom, the multitude of souls that "haunted" the twins continued to try and reach out to her. In this state, it looked as if they were standing in water. They were out of focus and quivering. Their voices sounded as whispers, distant and hollow. But when she focused on one, or one was determined and strong enough to bring themselves into focus, she could see and hear them as clear as she could anyone else. She reached for the door knob, but when she did one such soul came into clarity and stood right beside her. So close, that Layla thought she could feel his breath. But that would have been impossible. He was nothing more than a spirit. She stood there in the dark with the spirit as he loomed over her menacingly. His eyes glowed white and cast forbidding shadows on the rest of his face. His brow was furrowed and his lips were thin. His nostrils flared as he "breathed" heavily.

"And what in the great googily moogilies can I do for you?" Layla demanded. He continued to stare down at her and his eyes continued to gleam eerily. "OK, here we go." She rolled her eyes and huffed. She then began to recite in monotone voice her well rehearsed speech. "You are dead, get over it. Do you not see the purplely light…" She trailed off, because as she looked up, she noticed there was no light. "Wait, you're not…"

"I am not one of your pathetic spooks, little girl!" he bellowed in a powerful and deep voice. "I am beyond what you can control with your simple castings and powers over the dead!"

"What are you then?" she questioned with a bit of nervousness in her voice. He stepped closer to her and looked down directly into her eyes. She could see that his irises were not black but, in fact, the darkest, deepest red she had ever seen. She inspected his face further and discovered that the color of his skin was grey. His jaw was wide and square and his forehead was low.

"What I am is not of consequence. What I can do to you is—" He reached forward and clasped his hand around Layla's neck. He lifted her up three feet from the ground and pulled her close to his face. Layla was shocked! No spirit had ever been able to touch her! They would have to have enough strength to punch their way into this dimension and momentarily recorporialize. This thing, whatever it was, was very much in this and the next dimension! How was this possible! He was telling the truth, he was in no way a spirit. She tried to struggle. But every time she tried to cry out for help he would only tighten his cold, steely grip. That's what his massive hand felt like; cold steel.

"Why do you try to fight? I am something that not even your 'Aslyn the Azure' can defeat! You meddle in things you do not yet comprehend! The scales have been tipped and the opportunity has presented itself! There is nothing you can do to stop it!"

Layla pulled frantically at his fingers. She looked at him coldly and gritted her teeth.

"If there is nothing I can do," she gargled, "then why are you here threatening and trying to kill me!?" He squeezed her neck tighter and she began to feel a cracking as the muscles around her windpipe began to weaken. Her head felt like it was going to explode as she was deprived of precious oxygen. Her instincts took over and she began to kick viciously. He just tightened his lips and flared his nostrils. She kicked more and was able to reach the wall. She kicked again and again. After the third kick Emma came jutting out of her room. She leaped forward and kicked him as hard as she could in his lower back. This made the large creature drop Layla and turn around.

"Sorry!" she professed to Layla. "It took me a sec to get my leg on! I couldn't find the liner!" Layla just grabbed her throat, gagging as she tried to breathe, and waved and nodded her head in acknowledgment as Emma prepared to engage the beast. He squared his shoulders and cracked his neck. Emma stood with her fists clenched and arms ready.

"You think you have power? What you consider power, is what I use to blink an eye! There is nothing you can do to affect me!" He started forward and began to swing his arm around to give Emma one hell of a right jab. Just at that moment Jimmy emerged from his door and sleepily looked around, wiping his eyes.

"What's going on out here? WHOA!!" he exclaimed as he saw the fist coming straight for Emma who was standing right in front of him! He knew that as soon as she dodged that, it would have followed through straight to him! He jumped back and slammed the door. Just as he did Emma ducked and the massive gray man's fist went right through Jimmy's door. Jimmy gasped and fell back.

When Emma ducked, she punched the man right in his crotch. He just looked down and smiled.

Emma looked up and grimaced. "Now how did I know that was going to happen?" She scurried backward and stood up. Jimmy came out of his room and shot at the intruder with a crossbow. It stuck in his chest. Jimmy clenched his fist and celebrated by exclaiming "yes!" but it was premature. The man simply reached up, pulled out the arrow and threw it into the wall next to Jimmy's head.

"Oh shit!" Jimmy gulped.

"Way to go, dumb ass! I think you just pissed him off more!" Emma grumbled. She ran at him and jumped to reach his jaw with her left fist. When she made contact, it wasn't even enough to make his head turn. She stood back and shook her hand, mouthing, "Ow." She stepped backward, trying to come up with her next move. The only things she had really ever come up against were vampires. She had no clue what this thing was in her hallway! She twisted the ball of her foot to reveal the spikes that Jimmy had installed in her shin.

"What else do you have in your bag of tricks?" He grinned. And with that a bright yellow light began to grow from behind him. He stopped and turned. Everyone looked in the direction of where it was coming. There stood Layla at the mouth of the hallway. Her eyes were completely white and her hands were down by her hips, shoulder width apart, fingers spread apart with palms facing each other. Energy was building up between her hands and was so powerful that it was blowing back her hair. She was chanting loudly and it seemed to resonate through the entire house.

"Nefiim, Elohim, Annunaki Dingir. Ninhursag Nibiru, Enki Nin-ti Nibiru!" Over and over again she repeated this. And as she did the light grew larger and brighter and began to ripple. It became so bright, that they had to shield their eyes with their arms and hands. The man just stood there glaring at Layla. The ripple grew bigger and began to tear. A great force blew out from the tear and then began to suck inward. At first, it didn't faze the massive creature, but then Jimmy and Emma noticed that his feet were starting to slip and scoot forward. He forced his hands downward in an attempt to hold himself in place. But it was to no avail. He growled in frustration as he was continually pulled toward the rift. The twins began to feel the power of the suction that was pulling in the giant gray monster that had invaded their home. The man clenched his fists more and a black fog started to emerge from his feet. His momentum slowed and he began to yell back at Layla.

"Your curse cannot take me, witch!" Layla just chanted louder and stronger.

"Nefiim, Elohim, Annunaki Dingir. Ninhursag Nibiru, Enki Nin-ti Nibiru!" The force from the rift increased so much that the twins had to hold on the door jam to keep from being taken up in it. The thing lost his grip; his feet slid out from under him and was sucked into the rift. As soon as he was gone the rift closed and Layla dropped to the floor, unconscious. The twins' feet touched the floor again and they let go of the door jams. They ran over to Layla and checked to see if she was still breathing. Jimmy ran into the bathroom and brought back a cold wash rag. He handed it to Emma and she slowly dabbed her face with it. Layla blinked her eyes and gradually came around.

"He's gone right?" she whispered. She brought her hand up to her throat and stroked it gently.

"What the hell was that?" Emma asked.

"I opened up a portal to the Nibiru dimension." Layla stood up with help from Jimmy and was escorted to the couch.

"Dimension? How did you do that? And what is Nibiru?" Emma prodded.

"I told you before; I am what you would call a witch, or medium. I possess some abilities. Some have to do with the spirits of the departed; others have to do with nature. What you saw was me casting an ancient Sumerian spell to open up a particular dimension. I am not sure how long it will keep him, though. I don't know what he is. At first I thought he was another one of those annoying spooks that insist I help them complete their unfinished business."

"When did you realize that he wasn't?" Jimmy asked.

"Oh, I don't know, maybe when he grabbed me by my throat and almost killed me!" She leaned back and rubbed her throat. It was red and raw and beginning to swell. Emma went and got her a glass of water.

"Take small, slow sips. Swallowing is gonna be rough at first so take your time," Emma said as she handed her the glass.

"What happened, I mean was he waiting there for you? Or was he one of the souls that are following you?" Jimmy persisted. Layla seemed to gag on the water and coughed.

"Look, first of all, all these 'bodily challenged' individuals are following you, too! They are attracted to the slayer aura. I have said this before. And when I see them, at first, it's like looking up through water. Nothing is focused or clear. But if one was strong enough, or if I focus on one of them, then they COME into focus and I can see and hear them as well as I see and hear you! They just have that purplely light above them, and they shine brighter."

"Because of their auras?" Emma asked.

"Because they are nothing BUT auras!" Layla corrected. "This one, though, it was like all of the sudden he was there! I knew something was off. There was no light above him and I couldn't see his aura! I don't know what he was."

"But you know what he was doing here, don't you?" Emma accused.

"If you think that I have brought trouble into your lives then you must have missed your flight to reality! Trouble was already here and trouble is all over. And now TROUBLE has threatened to make its move!" Layla instructed. She looked at the twins sternly without blinking. They looked at each other and seemed to be in a sort of conference. Jimmy looked up and Layla knew that he knew she was keeping something from them.

"What is going on here? Why are you really here?" Jimmy asked. Layla rocked her head back against the couch cushion and muttered something they couldn't make out. And then she said:

"I think it is time now."

The twins looked at each other.

"What do you mean? Time for what?" Emma asked.

"I believe you are right." The voice came from behind the twins. Layla looked up and smiled.

"Emma, Jimmy, meet Aslyn the Azure." The twins could not believe what was happening. There stood this tall and lovely woman with striking blue eyes. She looked back at them calmly and smiled gently. Aslyn bowed her head slightly in a sign of respect and graciousness.

"Is she a witch, or a demon?" Emma stammered.

"Not exactly." Layla coughed. "She is a Goddess."

CHAPTER FOUR

Pearls of Wisdom and the Voices of Self Degradation

"A Goddess?!" they both exclaimed in disbelief.

"How is that possible?" Emma asked.

"Well, when a mommy Goddess and a daddy God love each other very much, they share a special hug," Layla reported sarcastically.

"Layla, as much as I adore your penchant for biting wit, I do not believe that now is the correct time," Aslyn exacted. Layla immediately quieted and resigned to be accommodating. Emma decided to get her answers straight from the horse's mouth.

"Aslyn, first of all, what are you doing in my house, secondly why should I allow you in my house and lastly how is it that you are considered a God?? I mean, I thought there was only one God. Now there's a Goddess?" Aslyn smiled slightly and looked at Emma.

"I understand your concern. I am a being that can control interdimensional travel. I simply choose to be where I wish, and it presents itself to me. Doors and walls are as meaningless to me as the wind to you. I assure you that my intentions are not at all malicious. I need your help. So does the world, or more accurately, your reality. And you are correct in your belief of the one Almighty God. She is there; I am nothing in comparison. She is the womb from which all life was sprung. I am more of a captain, or an overseer if you will. And there are many of us. We existed before the birth of man, and before the age of demons. Each of us had our own area of authority. This is where most of mythology is based in. Some of us were benevolent, others were very wicked. But then the age of the God Kings passed and demons cursed the Earth. Then man came, and he found a way in which to cleanse the world of the foul ones. The age of man was born, and soon they found that there was no more need of us. Man forgot and wrote us off as myth. But this did not mean we left. Oh some of us laid themselves down into the Earth and slept, but some, like myself, remained and kept watch. Until two years ago. That is when the balance of power was tipped."

"You mean when they turned the Slayer into an army?" Emma interjected.

"That's correct. While helpful in the battle against the foul ones, it has also allowed for an unbalance in the nature of the universe. Old Evil has been awoken and is taking its opportunity to seize this world for its own devices."

"How does that make an opportunity? If there is essentially now more powerful soldiers of good, then how does that make a way for evil to arise?" Jimmy asked anxiously. Layla rolled her eyes and began to explain, when Aslyn gave her a stern eye to make her ease off. Aslyn lifted her left hand with her palm facing the ceiling and looked at it. An old-fashioned brass scale appeared.

"Imagine this scale represents the balance in reality between dark and light." She then waved her hand slightly, behind the scale. A piece of rice paper unrolled behind the scale. "Now, imagine that this delicate rice paper attached to the scale, represents the fabric of reality. Like the paper, reality is fragile. Any slight movement of the scale in either direction…" As she said this both trays of the scale filled. The left with white pearls, the right with black pearls. But then the white pearls began to fill higher than the black pearls. "…and the scale will tear the paper." With that, the left side of the scale tipped down and the paper tore in the middle and there was a flash of blue light, then the whole image disappeared. Aslyn turn back to the three and raised any eyebrow.

"You're saying," Emma spoke up, "that there always has to be a balance between good and evil, basically."

"That is exactly what she is saying," Layla wheezed, in her typical sharp manner.

"But that means that there must ALWAYS be a slayer to fight a battle that can never be won!" Emma challenged.

"I understand how you must feel. But it is not a fruitless life. You, and all slayers for that matter, are VERY important. It isn't a battle that can never be won. It is one you can win every day! Every day that the rest of the world can go on living in relative oblivion to the existence of preternatural forces attacking their existence is proof of a job well done. But now, the balance has been tipped." She held her hand up and the scale appeared again with the left side of overflowing white pearls tipped down and the brilliant light still streaming from the tear in the rice paper. "This creates a rift in reality, and that rift is a door to another dimension! The more it tears, the more it rips, and a bigger tear means more open doorways to places you don't want to be!"

"So, what do you want from me? I didn't do this! We didn't even know it had been done! Until yesterday, I thought I was the only one in the world! Sorry, I was left outta the super hero loop," Emma forced.

"A balance must be reestablished. There are things being let into this dimension that will shred this world. Things this world has not faced in eons." Aslyn stopped and looked down.

"What do you mean? Are you saying that dinosaurs are coming back, because that would be awesome!" Jimmy blurted. Everyone looked at him sternly. "What? Don't tell me that you never imagined seeing a real live dinosaur? I mean come on! Never mind," he defended and conceded the floor back to the Goddess.

"No, Jimmy, not dinosaurs. But some far more ferocious. Demon Kings who rule over legions of demon warrior spirits who live for domination, the stench of terror and the thrill of death."

"Demon Kings, wow, do they get a crown?" Jimmy asked.

"This is not a joke, boy! This is very real! You had one in your house tonight! Naberius! Demon King and ruler of sixty-six legions! His whole purpose is to cause discord! Trouble! Madness! Dread is an aphrodisiac for him! He wants your world drenched in blood and clouded with ash! He wants to rule this dimension as he rules nine others!"

"Now why couldn't you just give me a little heads up on that one? That would have been helpful! Might have literally saved my delicate neck," Layla announced. Aslyn shot another stern look in her direction and Layla once again slunk down into the couch.

"I had no reason to believe he would attack you let alone know where you are. The rift must be growing for him to be able to punch through like that! Also, that means he must see you as a threat!" There was a moment of silence and then Aslyn took a step back.

"He won't attack again for now. Naberius possesses the most dangerous trait there is."

"What's that?" Jimmy asked.

"Patience," Emma responded. She stood there with her arms folded, looking off toward Aslyn without blinking, looking very pensive. The other two looked at each other in surprise. Aslyn looked concerned. She tapped her lip with her finger.

"There must be balance," she muttered. "There is no way to reverse the change in the line of slayers. Even I cannot do that. The only hope now is to find a way to close the rift before too many enter and the scale tips again! Before too much of the madness takes over."

"You mean it's started already?" Emma posed.

"Well of course! It started two years ago when the army of slayers was created! Haven't you seen the signs?" Jimmy and Emma looked at each questioningly and then back at Aslyn and shook their heads, murmuring no. "Well they were there! I don't see how you could have missed them! Increase in war throughout the world, the SARS virus, gas prices, Justin Timberlake going solo, THE RED SOX winning the WORLD SERIES!"

"Yeah, that was pretty messed up." Jimmy nodded along with Emma. "How were we supposed to know that they were signs that reality was out of wack, I mean other than the Red Sox beating the Cardinals."

"How could you not?! Don't you remember about the change in the WB's line up?"

"Oooo, yeah!" Emma exclaimed. "Remember they got rid of that show last year, you know the one with the really hot guy! Damn, why can't I remember the name? It was really good! And they had that other hot guy come over from that other show they got rid of! Now, that right there, I knew something had to be off." Aslyn nodded in relief as Emma acknowledged her reference.

"The Goddess of Balance tells you about signs of an apocalypse, and among them she lists a deadly, fatal virus, a virtual world war, and a TV show's cancellation makes you say 'Oooo'? What is wrong with you people?" snarked Layla.

"Hey! When the Cardinals lost the World Series that was a definite sign of coming doom!" Jimmy corrected. Layla rolled her eyes and rested back onto the couch.

"Even so, that spells emanate danger for you and a deadly virus doesn't?"

"Hey, you're not from here! Being a local sports fan is something that is bred here! And besides, no one from Missouri ever actually goes anywhere where they could contract a deadly disease."

"Sheryl Crow," Emma said plainly. Jimmy blinked and looked at her.

"Huh?"

"Sheryl Crow, she's from Missouri, Independence actually. And Brad Pitt, he's from Springfield and then there's Kate Capshaw, she's from Ashland."

"Ah, yeah. You forgot about Nelly. He's from University City, right?"

"Yeah, but we don't like to claim him." Jimmy looked agitated.

"Alright! So some have left, but it's not like they ever come back." Jimmy looked at Emma to make sure he was right and she nodded in approval.

Aslyn had been standing back listening to all of this, shaking her head. She placed her fingertips onto her forehead and addressed the group.

"Enough! I am weary from this dimension and of your quibbling. I must go and rest now. Layla, if you have enough energy try to put up an alarm system so you can be ready if he attempts to return." As she uttered the last word she faded into nothingness, but the scale remained. The three looked back and forth at each other in confusion. Emma walked over to it and tried to touch it; she got close but lost her nerve. Jimmy stalked over to her and huffed.

"Are you telling me that you can touch a two-day-old dead body, but you can't touch a floating, imaginary scale? It's not real, it's just a projection!" he said as he looked at her grinning and started to walk through the image. At the same time Emma looked down at the floor, puzzled. As he encountered the left tray of the scale, it "encountered" his face. He yelped and then fell to the ground. At this time Emma had been just standing up from squatting down to retrieve something. As Jimmy stood up, rubbing his face, she smiled and raised her right hand and in between her thumb and index finger was a white pearl. She simply smiled as he furrowed her brow.

"Eh, lady! I think you forgot something!" Layla bellowed. Nothing happened. The scale remained.

"How is that really there?" Jimmy asked, somewhat perturbed. "And why does it feel like I just got hit by a ton of bricks?" Layla stood up and stepped casually over to the two.

"She's a Goddess, Jimmy. For the most part she can do whatever she wants. That includes leaving her crap lying around!" As soon as she finished the sentence, a flash of light came from the scale and then it was gone.

"Thank You!" Layla huffed as she looked toward the ceiling. Emma grinned and nodded her head as she held up the pearl that remained in her hand. But then, like the scale, it flashed into nothing. Emma grimaced and then pouted.

"Well, I think after that I could use some sleep. Goodnight, all." Layla turned to walk down the hall. Jimmy tilted his head and watched her rear as she sashayed toward her door. Emma slapped his chest and straightened up. He looked over at Emma in shock when he realized she was in her underwear, too! He threw his hands over his eyes in shame and whipped away.

"Oh GOD! You, too?" he yelled. Emma just brushed it off and looked down the hall.

"Hey, Layla! Why didn't you tell us about this when you got here?" Layla turned around and faced her.

"Would you have believed me? You barely believed what I did tell you."

"That's true. I don't think I could sleep if I wanted to. Too much has happened in the last twenty-four hours. I think I am going to patrol some more." Jimmy chased after her as she went to change for patrolling. He wanted to go with her. He didn't want either of them to be alone.

"No, Jimmy," she answered before he could ask. "I want to be alone. I have some things I need to absorb."

She sat on the edge of her bed and pulled a pair of jeans on. She didn't feel like putting on a skirt or culottes tonight, she figured that she wouldn't need her gadgets. All she wanted was the clarity the night air can give a confused mind. She grabbed a black tee shirt off the chair at her desk and pulled it on over her shamrock tank top. She stopped for a moment and thought about how many other girls around the world were doing this now. How many were being trained by those who created this "Slayer Army." And, how was it that she got missed? The bitterness began to rise; she tried to force it away. She sat down to put on her boots. As she struggled to manipulate one onto her right prosthetic foot, the bitterness and anger began to grow. She hated this. She hated that fate had dealt her such an unfair card. Why her? All she wanted was to be normal, and all this plastic thing made her feel was like a cyborg. She ripped the boot away from her foot and threw it into the wall where it stuck. She rubbed her hands vigorously and bit down hard. She growled in her throat and tears began to glisten in her eyes. She didn't like this feeling; she believed that it made her weak. She was supposed to be so strong. "Oh you are so brave!" people have said. "I wouldn't have even noticed! You walk so well!" They have "complimented." Emma always felt that it was condescending. She didn't need their goddamn pity. That's all that was. Their attempt to make themselves feel like good individuals for being nice to the crippled girl. Of course she walked normal! It's not like you lose your foot and you become an invalid! She thought sometimes that maybe she should just chuck it all and ride around in a fucking wheelchair. Maybe then their pity would make sense or even be validated. When they would make those comments to her she wanted to respond with something other than, "Oh thank you!" She wanted to say, "Oh you poor thing! How do you go on day by day with that giant honker of a nose on your face?!" Because of this stupid thing, people now define her by it. "Do you know Emma Hogan? You know, the girl with the fake leg?" Why not the really pretty girl, or the girl with the twin brother even. It's not fair that this happened to her! Losing her family was enough! Why couldn't this slayer thing have happened earlier, maybe she could have saved her family and her foot! She wiped her face with a discarded shirt from the floor. She shoved on her boots forcefully and threw her hair up into a ponytail. The hallway was dark as she kicked the broken bits of wood that littered the floor as she headed for the front door. Emma grabbed her jacket off of the coat tree and darted out.

As she walked, the thoughts in her head began to multiply. One thought led to another and another until she didn't know how one was connected to the other. She tried to retrace her mental steps but then gave up.

"WHAT AM I SUPPOSED TO DO?!" she yelled to the stars. A dog started barking from one of the yards behind a planked privacy fence. She continued down the alleyway. It was very narrow and very crammed with garages and houses. They were all so close they seemed to be connected. Emma kicked at the loose, broken pieces of pavement as she shuffled. She thought to herself about how much this all sucked royally. Onward she went. Passing crumbling sheds and derelict bicycles, she began to see the end of the alley. Emma heard the sound of something heavy hitting one of the dumpsters. She perked her ears and followed the bangs and bumps to its source. Silently she stalked toward a rusted green dumpster. As she moved closer she noticed a broken crate and picked up one of the sharpened pieces that was well suited as a stake. She hunched down a bit and slinked to the side of it. There she squatted with her back against the filthy dumpster, gripping her stake tight.

"Maybe it's just a stray dog?" Emma whispered to herself. She could feel the movement from inside. It rocked the metal box violently. As it rocked,

Emma felt a kick from inside the dumpster in the middle of her back, and along with it was a muffled whimper. "Nope, not a dog," she muttered.

She clenched her stake tight, closed her eyes and took a deep breath. She jumped up quickly, stood on her tippy toes and looked down into the cavernous dumpster. It was hard to make out at first; her pupils had trouble adjusting to the darkness inside it. But there it was, a filthy long-haired male vamp chowing down on a young woman. She had been bitten on the neck; Emma could tell by the way the blood glistened in the small amount of light that was able to penetrate the area. Her eyes were wide open and no longer blinking really. The woman's whole body twitched every once in a while, but it just prompted him to hold her down tighter and bite down harder. She would just stiffen her neck and try to blink. But it wasn't her neck he was feeding on right then. He had her thighs around his neck with his hands on top of them. He was feeding vigorously on her inner left thigh, close to her groin. Her clothes were nowhere in sight and her underwear was in shreds and hanging off her right leg.

Emma held her breath so as not to gasp, but unconsciously, she had shot her right hand to her mouth, thus dropping the stake she had held so tightly. She froze and rolled her eyes, shaming herself for her stupidity and ruining her advantage on the greasy beast. He jerked his head up and growled at her. His yellow eyes gleamed brightly in the darkness. The woman gasped for air, and it seemed that the vamp slapped her face and busted her lip. Emma could see blood dripping down from her mouth and off her chin. He leapt upward and grabbed Emma by her throat. He reeked of garbage and coagulated blood. She tried not to vomit. He jumped down off of the edge of the dumpster and led her backward into the middle of the alley.

He lifted her up off her toes and squeezed tighter.

"I know you," he said accusingly in a gravelly voice. "You're that chick who claims to be the slayer. Well, I got news for you, sister, there's only one and you ain't her!" He pulled her close and licked her right cheek. The sweaty filth from his nose rubbed off onto her face. She shuddered and the sensation.

"Your face tastes pretty." He looked her up and down. "I wonder what the rest of you tastes like?" He looped his finger around one of her belt loops and pulled her hips closer to him and tried to look down into her jeans. The thing leaned over to her ear and whispered gleefully, "I can smell it from here." She reeled in the comment. Her spine felt as if it had slivered down and back up. She thought about the stake in the toe of her boots and went to click her heels, but she stopped herself. She was wearing her new Nine West boots and wasn't about to ruin them.

Damn! she cursed in her mind. And then it dawned on her that she didn't need anything pointy to make him at least drop her! She pierced her lips and looked at him violently. She tried to mutter but he was clenching her neck too tight.

"What did you say? Speak up, I like to hear you plead!" With that, her eyes widened with anger, and she reared her right leg back and followed through, possibly shoving his testicles into his throat! He dropped her promptly and fell to the ground, cradling his wounded manhood.

"I SAID," she yelled, "YOU HAVEN'T BOUGHT ME DINNER! Was that loud enough, I wanted to be clear!" She stepped forward and kicked him in his face, making him flip and roll in the air before landing on his stomach three feet away.

"And by the way, grease ball, and I mean that literally, I am a Slayer and there are now hundreds of us in the world!" He looked up at her, horrified. He definitely knew that he had made an awful mistake. "Oh yeah! You are so gonna be a pile of dust!" She walked confidently over to him.

"Cocky Bitch!" He growled as he reached up and grabbed her right ankle. He pulled upward and she fell back, knocking her head against the ground. Emma rubbed her head and mumbled, "Ow." She looked down and saw that her right foot was twisted around backward.

"Ah dammit! Now look at what you did?!" she complained as she reached down to twisted back.

"Holy crap, what is that?" he asked, confused.

"It's a foot, what do you think it looks like?" Emma responded.

"Well, I mean is it fake? Or a cast? I mean that's not normal for a foot to spin around like that."

"Yes it's fake! I have a prosthetic leg!" She huffed as she stood up and put her hands on her hips.

"Wow! I mean kudos! Good for you! I wouldn't have known if you hadn't told me! You walk normal and you're not retarded at all!" the vamp professed. Emma was furious! Now even the filthy creatures of the night were patronizing her with their undeserved pity! And just because she was technically considered by the government to be handicapped, that means she's retarded?

"What type of moron thinks that shit?" she said aloud. *Well obviously a RETARDED MORON!* she thought to herself.

"What am I supposed to do? Roll around in a wheelchair and yell 'EMMA!' like Timmy on *South Park*? You know it would be nice to be objectified for other parts of my body other than my plastic leg ya know! I happen to have very nice breasts!" The Vampire raised his eyebrows and looked down at her chest.

"OH GOD!" she groaned as she flung her head back and threw her arms up. The vamp furrowed his eyebrows and blinked rapidly.

"You have issues, man, maybe I should just go. Sorry about all that, uh…ok…bye!" he stuttered as he started to back away and try to run.

"Oh! I don't think so, mister!" she yelled as she went after him.

They ran almost the length of the alley when he turned around to spit insults at her.

"You'll never catch up to me with that plastic leg, fuckin' cripple!" Emma yelled a ferocious yell and ran faster and faster until she leaped into the air and landed on him, standing up right.

"FUCK YOU!" she yelled. She stepped down on his neck with her right prosthetic leg and held tight to his arms with both hands. She placed her left foot on the ground and pulled back on his arms. At the same time she pushed down and away on his neck with her foot. She did this for a few seconds; her face turned red, her teeth gnashed, and she grunted as she put all of her effort into the task. At last she had pulled his body away from his head and he exploded into dust.

"Now who's the fuckin' cripple?!" she yelled down at the pile of dust. She stood there for a moment, breathing deeply and rapidly. Her anger was still burning hot to where her ears felt like the blood inside them was burning. Why did she care about what some dusted vampire thought? Still, all he did was voice things that she felt inside herself. This was just one more violent outburst of her self-loathing.

Tears threatened to spill from her eyes. Emma decided to give in for once and plopped to the ground. There she sat right where the vamp had been, arms resting on her knees and her bottom lip turned under and quivering. The longer she sat the louder the voices got in her head, telling her she was worthless, ugly, CRIPPLED. Who would ever want someone like her?! She would be stuck living with her brother until the day they die! And if anyone did want to love her and be with her, maybe they would be some kind of creepy guy who had a fetish for amputees. That is if they could get past her freakish strength. What guy would want a woman who could beat him up?!

She let her face drop into her hands and she sobbed heavy and hard. The tears drenched her face and dripped down to the broken, craggy pavement. The thoughts continued.

And you had the ego to think that you were special because you were THE slayer! HA! You should have known that wasn't true! You should have known that all along you were still nothing! And now, reality as you know it is going to fall to pieces like a dried-up dirt clod, and what are you doing? You sit here feeling sorry for yourself because life is unfair! Well at least you're alive for now! What about that poor girl in the dumpster? Do you think you're worse off than her?

The last thought made her snap out of her loathing and she perked her head up and realized that the woman in the dumpster was still alive, if not barely! She jumped up and ran back down the alley to the same dumpster and jumped inside. The woman no longer blinked and Emma couldn't find her pulse. She hung her head, ashamed of herself. More thoughts of "coulda shoulda woulda" raced through her mind. She slapped her forehead with her left palm and tightly shut her eyes.

"NO!" she grunted. It was an awful place to die. And probably no one would find her until trash day. "Poor girl," Emma whispered. "I'm so sorry!" Emma reached forward and slid her eyelids shut. She crossed herself, reached up and lifted herself out of the dumpster.

Emma continued down the alley in the direction she was headed before the vamp fight. She touched the back of her head where she fell and felt the sizable lump. It felt hard and wet. When she brought her hand back she could see that there was blood and she knew Jimmy would have a fit and insist she see a doctor, even though he knew well that by the time they got there anyway it will have healed up completely. She sniffled and wiped her nose with the back of her hand. She looked at her watch and saw that it was four a.m. She figured that she had better start heading home; soon it would be dawn.

Emma walked on and turned right at the end of the alley and out of sight. Once she had disappeared, two tall figures stepped out of the darkness and into the stuttering light of a street lamp. The first one was tall and broad and had short, brown curly hair. He had a firm, square jaw. His eyes were fierce and intense. His lips were thin and his mouth wide and slightly frowning in disgust. The second one stepped forward and was slightly shorter than the first; he had long blond hair and a narrow jaw. His eyes were wide and filled with a psychotic gleam. He grinned menacingly and lay his right hand on the first one's left shoulder.

"Why didn't we grab her, Leo?" he asked.

"Don't you smell that?" Leo asked the blond one in an Italian accent. The blond one sniffed the air and then breathed in deeply through his nose.

"Yes, desperation, mmmm, anger, and fear!"

"Si, Jerome. She's marinating in it. Give it time and she will be drenched in it! Then we will take her."

"They say the blood of a Slayer is like a shot of heroine! Makes you feel like you can conquer anything!"

"Why do you think they are always so self-centered and isolated? They are swallowed whole by this feeling. They push all others away because of it. But this one is special. She has battered herself beyond the matters of slayers. This one will be a delicacy to savor!" Leo smiled as he lifted his hands to his face and lit a cigarette. Jerome tilted his head as he watched.

"Leo, how is it that we can smoke if we ain't got no breath?"

"Idiota." He huffed as he rolled his eyes. "We can choose to or not to take in and expel air. Your moronic questions in your broken English wear on my patience. Get the girl, we have work to do." Jerome stepped over to the dumpster that Emma had been in with the "dead" woman. He leapt in and back out with her slung over his right shoulder. When his feet were firmly on the ground, he pulled her off of his shoulder and held her in a cradled position. Leo stood over her and lifted her eyelids and breathed in deep.

"She is not dead yet as the Slayer thought," he announced. "But she will be if we don't act." Jerome looked up at him thoughtfully.

"Are you saying we should start now?"

"Just enough, il mio amico. Just enough for her to last until we get there." As he ended his answer, he rolled up his right sleeve and sliced his wrist on a protruding nail on the electrical pole. Leo did not flinch. Pain was a gift to him. He welcomed it. The blood from his wound rolled around his wrist and dripped to the ground. His eyes narrowed and gleamed at the sight of the rich ruby red substance glistening in the moonlight. He lifted it to his lips and licked gently at the droplets. His eyes rolled back and he breathed in deep from his nose. Then he motioned for Jerome to open her mouth and he placed his wrist over her mouth and let the blood drip down into it. Her eyelids fluttered but remained closed; her tongue moved shortly and her lips instinctively puckered as a newborn searching for a breast. After just a few drops, it was evident that she was breathing normally again, but she was still unconscious. Leo brought his wrist back to his mouth and lapped the remaining blood up before the wound resealed itself. He rolled his sleeve back down and took a long drag from his cigarette.

"Let's go," he instructed. "We have only another hour before sunrise. They will be waiting for us." Jerome adjusted the girl in his arms and they walked off into the darkness of the alley.

Chapter Five

Keys

Two days had passed since the eventful night when Naberius and Aslyn the Azure made their presence known. While Jimmy was back home putting the finishing touches on patches in the hallway walls, and hanging a new bedroom door, she and Layla were here watching the book shop. Layla sat at the office desk slumped over some smelly old book and Emma sat in front of the TV at the register counter flipping through news channels. She had been hoping to find any coverage on a woman found nude and drained of blood in an alley dumpster. But so far for the last couple of days she was unsuccessful.

Layla emerged from the office behind the counter. She looked at Emma with her hands on her hips and sighed.

"How in the bloody hell am I supposed to find anything on this Naberius character if you won't help! Now, I have about fifty to a hundred GIANT books in there and I can't do this all by myself." Emma slowly turned around and looked down her nose at Layla.

"There is no way I am getting near those musty things! And what part of me leads you to believe that I can understand any of the ooga booga anyway?"

"Oh! Well, if that's all, then here." Layla gleefully produced a paperback book that was evidently fairly new. It was yellow and had some kind of character on the back. She flipped it over and was stunned by the title. *The Ancient Marduk Sumerian Texts For Dummies.*

"Are you kidding me?" Emma quipped. "Am I supposed to believe this is real?"

"Absolutely! You think that after thousands of years they wouldn't translate a copy or two with slayers in mind?!" Layla quipped back. Emma nodded her head once in agreement and then suddenly realized that it was meant as an insult.

"HEY! Just because I don't read Ancient Sumerian, or want to inhale God knows what from those fossils, doesn't make me stupid!"

"First of all your parents owned this place for years, you think you would have cracked a book or something. Secondly, sorry, love, but Slayers are not exactly known for their superior intellect. Mostly just for the brawn." Emma stood up slowly and walked over to Layla; even though she was still a couple of inches shorter than her, she still had a powerful presence.

"Jealous, girl?"

"That's WITCH girl, don't forget that! I may lack your Slayer strength, but I think you know that I can hold my own," Layla stated calmly.

"Look, there really isn't much else you can do to me that hasn't already been done. You could bippity boppity boo me into pot-holder hell and it still wouldn't compare to hiding in a closet while your family is turned into Happy Meals, and then your own foot becomes dessert on the go. But you are staying in MY house! Therefore, I think you need to start getting your attitude into check or you will find your ass thrown back across the pond." Emma stood back and sat back down on her stool. Layla remained where she was with her arms crossed, still emanating the air of authority.

"Are you off your trolley? If you sent me away you would be

making a stonking cock up! Don't you remember what Aslyn told us earlier? And oh yeah, THE GIANT SCARY GUY! The one who tore up your hall and could have killed you?"

"If I remember correctly, Mr. gray was there for you!"

"That's total pants and you know it! He was there for all of us; he just got to me first. We have a job to do and apparently you're too shirty to deal with it! You're more worried about your self image! You really need to get over that! There are more important things at stake here, than if you will be able to wear those fancy schmancy boots you saw in a shop window." Layla turned around and headed back to the office.

Emma sat slumped on her stool and scanned the book shop. It was dark and wooden. That seemed the only way she could describe it. The walls and the doors were all wood. There were rows and rows of wooden bookcases full of old and rare books. There were also tables covered in linen and also stacked with books. She got up and shuffled around in and out of the rows of cases. She reminisced about the past, thinking of the many times she sat tucked away in the back corners thumbing through various texts and leather-bound books with yellowed pages and elegantly inscribed vellum. Sometimes her mother would come and cuddle her as they thumbed through them together. Her silky dark hair would drape over Emma's head and shoulders as she leaned on her mother. Emma couldn't really understand most of the texts, but they had beautiful pictures and she could look at them for hours.

"Ah, Mom, this isn't me?! I'm not this bitter person. It wasn't supposed to be like this! I wish you were here. You were stronger than I could ever be."

"You underestimate yourself." The voice came from Emma's right. She recognized right away but could not allow herself to believe such a preposterous notion. But sure enough as she turned there she was. Her mother, Katherine. She stood leaning against the very corner that they had frequented over the years. "You are the bravest soldier I know."

"Mom? Is that really you? Mom?" She walked toward her mother but stopped short. She was afraid of the possibility.

"Emma, there are things in this place that you need. There are things that we kept from you and your brother and your sister. We wanted you to have an ordinary life. We thought, out of sight out of mind. But reality came knocking one night and changed your lives forever."

Emma bowed her head and pushed away the flood of violent memories from that wretched night: flashes of her listening to the screams and cries of her mother and sister while she was hidden in the closet under the stairs.

"If there is one thing you learned from that night it's that you cannot hide forever. Sometimes, you are going to have to come out and fight in order to survive! This is what you must do now!" And then she was gone. She had vanished as if there was nothing ever there. Emma's eyes grew wide in panic...

"Mommy! NO! Come back, come back, I need you!" Emma cried over and over again. She fell to her knees and sobbed. "Mommy, please come back! Please, please, please come back!" She knelt there with her head in her hands and let her pain out in sobs. Layla came from around a corner and looked at Emma, very put off.

"What are you on about? I didn't mean it! I'm not going to poof you anywhere. I need you to drive me around, I don't have a license yet."

"My mother was here! You idiot! I thought you were some kinda powerful witch or medium or whatever. Didn't you feel a change in the force or some shit like that!" Layla's face softened immediately and she joined Emma on the floor.

"I'm sorry, pet, I had no idea. I didn't notice anything. What happened?"

"She was standing over there. She told me that she kept things from me and that I need to fight to survive." They both looked in the direction of where Katherine had been.

"Wait a minute. What's that?" Layla pointed out a small metallic object glinting in the low-lighted room. Layla nudged Emma and she got up and walked over to see what it was. She bent down and picked up a small silver key. She sat down with it and inspected the key closely. The handle was ornate and fascinating to look at. It was a

Celtic knot with the capital letter "B" elegantly inscribed in the center in Celtic fashion. There were only three teeth at the end of the shaft and they also seemed to be in the shape of a "B."

"I've never seen this before," Emma said, sniffling and wiping the tears away.

"Someone could have dropped it while in the store," Layla suggested as she came nearer. They both looked at each other and then promptly shook their heads at the ridiculous notion. Emma handed the key to Layla to let her inspect it.

"I think my mother wanted me to find it, like SHE dropped it there just now," Emma said. Layla looked at it intensely.

"What do you see? What is it?" Emma prodded.

"It's brilliant. I don't know," Layla answered softly. "But I know I have seen this symbol before, and I am definitely getting a vibe from it." Layla placed it back into Emma's hands after turning it over and over in hers. "I wonder…" She trailed off as she got up from the floor. She turned and headed for the office in a bit of a hurry. Emma looked confused and jaunted off in her direction. Layla exploded into the office and sifted through stacks of her books that she had brought from England and Indiana. Her arms were flying above and behind her as she tossed books aside, followed by a series of "nos" and "bollocks." Emma entered the doorway and stared at the raving Layla. She dodged an airborne leather-bound book that looked like it might have taken her head off.

"What are you doing??" she asked urgently. Layla didn't stop to turn and answer her. She kept rustling through them more and more anxiously. Emma found herself questioning her ability to see straight when she saw Layla going down deeper into the trunk to where all that was visible of her was from her calves down. "How are you doing that?" Emma questioned.

Finally, she stopped and produced from the depths of her giant steamer trunk, an old tattered, dusty, worn book. It was the biggest book Emma had ever seen!

"How in the hell was that hard to find?" Emma asked. "And once again, HOW were you doing that?"

"The trunk's enchanted," Layla answered without looking up.

"En-wha-hoo-ha?" Emma staggered.

"ENCHANTED, are you deaf? Or am I speaking Spanish?" Layla spitted. "It was my father's trunk. Passed down from his father and so on and so forth. All of these books have belonged to my family since they first were initiated as Abgal Das."

"And when was that?" Emma asked.

"Since the beginning," she stated. "They even wrote a few themselves."

"Well what's with that one? We found a key; that doesn't look like a lock, Layla, that's a book," Emma condescended.

"Look, you're the muscle, I'm the brain. Trust me or just shut up. You know what? Just shut up anyway and let me talk, ok?"

Emma folded her arms and reached up with her right hand to wipe the remaining tears away from her encounter with her mother. She figured that if Layla was here to help then she guessed she was about to find out.

"This book is among the oldest of my family's Abgal Da Journals. It dates back to feudal times when my ancestor, Brahma Siddig, was an Abgal Da to the Slayer of that time in India. This chronicles his passage as an Abgal Da and a student of the mystical arts." Layla pushed past Emma into the front of the store and laid the book out onto a large display table. She flopped open the heavy book to about a quarter through, to a page that had a portrait of a tall man standing over scrolls in old Hindu style. It was very ornate and elegant. Emma reached forward and lightly ran her fingertips around the page and felt the raised and recessed hills and valleys of the ink. He wore a simple turban and wrap. Behind him were shelves filled with scrolls and books and to his right there was the trunk looking a little less modern. A monkey sat on his shoulder and it looked like it was stroking his mid-length beard. Looking at his eyes you could see the family resemblance. Brahma stood behind a simple desk with many papers laid out on it. In his right hand he held what seemed to be a writing implement. Emma continued to study the page when something he held in his left hand caught her eye. She tried to squint her eyes harder to focus. All at once it came together. He was holding the key! She couldn't believe her eyes! She looked down at the key in her hand and back to the one in the picture.

"That's my key!" Emma exclaimed as she pointed to the picture.

"No," Layla stated. "That was his key."

Emma looked back down at Brahma and at his key.

"When the Brotherhood transformed the Ba Musal, they soon realized that when a new one awoke, she was not always in their part of the world. Real bloody geniuses eh? Slowly they seeded their order throughout the known world. It was about this time that they decided they needed a way to keep their sacred texts and chronicles secret. There were very few of them in the world and they didn't have many means of defending themselves and their secret. So, they came up with this key! The Celtic knot represents continuity, or eternity. A knot itself represents a tie that binds. And, well, you know what the B is for." Layla stopped and looked up at Emma.

"What are you trying to say? That my mother was a brother? Don't you think I would have known?"

"Not if she didn't want you to! And I am not saying that your mother was a member of the Brotherhood, I am telling you that your whole family line were Abgal Da! These keys were passed down from generation to generation in a family. They were enchanted and could only be used by members of that family. But their use was short lived. After a while the Brotherhood's numbers grew and so did their wealth. They didn't need special keys to lock up their texts and journals anymore. They had an enormous network of Abgal Da throughout the world, including council houses strategically placed. Some of the keys were lost, but some families kept the keys and passed them down as a family heirloom; it became a tradition. Most Abgal Da these days don't even know about the keys. Only the old families have heard of them, let alone actually having one! We were one of the families that had lost the key and had forgotten it. If it wasn't for Brahma's journal, we might have never known about it! Until we found this one in your shop just moments ago, I had completely forgotten about it! What I am trying to make clear to you is that your family was one of the oldest Abgal Da families! Your parents really kept things from you!"

"An ordinary life," Emma mused as she stared off into nothing.

"A what?" Layla asked.

"It's what my mother said. She said that her and Dad kept things from us, that they wanted us to have an ordinary life."

Layla lifted an eyebrow. "What's ordinary?"

"I think it's safe to say that you are not it." They stood quietly for a long moment. They were both pondering where the lock to this key could be, when the silence was broken by the evening news blaring to a start on the TV.

"Good evening, I'm Tanya Jacobs. Tonight on our top story, a local family pleads with the public to help find their missing daughter. 24-year-old Veronica 'Nica' Todd, disappeared three nights ago from the parking lot of Mega Records downtown. The young woman had been closing the store that night and was last seen by a fellow employee headed for her car. If you have any information as to the whereabouts of Veronica 'Nica' Todd please call the number on your screen." As the reporter addressed the number, a picture of the missing woman flashed on the screen along with the number. She had short black hair and large eyes. As Emma stared at the TV she knew exactly who it was. It was the girl the vamp killed in the dumpster two nights ago! She finally found something on her on the news and it's that they haven't found her yet!

"It's been two days. Why haven't they found her yet?"

"Is that the girl you were talking about?" Layla asked.

"Yup that's her alright. I'll go by there tonight and make sure she's still there and call in an anonymous tip."

"I really think you should leave that to the authorities. We have more pressing issues at the moment."

"Don't you think her family needs to know what happened to her?! How is that not important? I have a responsibility…"

"Your job has already been done. There is nothing more you can do for that girl. She's dead and you dusted the bugger that killed her." Layla held up Emma's hand that held the key. "This is all that matters right now! This may very well help us fix that balance."

CHAPTER SIX

Sing for Me

The tiny flame from his lighter illuminated the darkness. Liquid shadows drifted on his face along with the movement of the flame. It gave an eerie aura to an already monstrous individual. He brought it up to his well-sculpted lips and lit the self-rolled cigarette that was clenched there. He drew in deep and puffed the excess smoke back out into the open and let go of the lever on the lighter. While his right hand went up to retrieve the cigarette, his left slid the silver lighter back into the pocket of his tailored and pressed black slacks. Now all that was left was the burning embers of that cigarette. He leaned back in his chair and felt the soft friction of the suede. He leaned his head back and ran his fingers through his curly brown hair. Just as he had allowed his eyes to roll back and his lids to close, a knock on his door broke the silence. He sighed and slowly padded to the door. After crushing his smoke out on in an ashtray near the door, he pulled it open.

Jerome stood there with his hands behind his back. His blond hair was pulled back into a ponytail and his eyes were serious.

"It's time, Leo," he said simply. Leo stepped out into the lighted hallway and led Jerome downstairs. Being who they were meant that a low profile was necessary. This also meant that they could not live in the normal luxury they were accustomed to. Although Leo had filled his room with beautiful and opulent things, the manor itself was derelict and infested with various pests. It was located on the outskirts of Walnut Grove in the farm district. This area was remote and prime reality for the wealthy populous. The land was riddled with large hills and valleys and was lush and green. Leo had spotted this place a couple of months ago when it was deemed condemned by the county due to severe wood rot, termites and ultimately neglect by the owners who had inherited the place. Apparently they were displeased with the inheritance and never stepped foot onto the property. For now it belonged to Leo and his cohorts.

Leo and Jerome made their way down the rickety stairs and past the great room into the kitchen. Jerome set his candle on the dilapidated counter and a rat scurried away from the light. He mumbled something about filthy vermin and proceeded to the door to his right. Leo glanced around the room and sighed. The rusted porcelain sink, the abandoned 1950's style refrigerator with its doors hanging from its broken hinges. He looked down at his feet and noted the peeling linoleum that presented the rotting wooden frame beneath it. He spoke aloud to Jerome.

"This place is not worthy of me. Not this house, not this town, not this country! I should be back in Europe, my home, but that damn slayer and her little club have infected it! I have been reduced to living in filth. In the very armpit of the United States! Il figlio di una Femmina! He keeps saying wait wait! It is not time yet! I have waited for months! I have been away from la mia casa for over a year! This all better be worth my patience! He better prove all of this to me stasera!" Jerome had become used to this. Leo's spontaneous ranting monologues of his displeasure. For the most part, Leo was one cool individual. He had displayed a certain amount of patience. But being vampires, their patience was limited, and Leonardo De Luca was not used to being the one taking orders instead of giving them. As most vampires do have distaste for authority, Leo was no exception. Jerome on the other hand was much younger than Leo and had realized early on that if one were to survive the life of the non-living, one must choose their allies and learn to take orders form older ones like Leo. Being his virtual butt monkey would teach him all he needed to know about circumventing unpleasant situations such as an encounter with a Slayer, and then also teaching him what he needed to know when it came to killing a Slayer. Jerome was grateful for this, but he, too, had his moments of doubt and mistrust. Mostly in the Master, though. Never in Leo. Sometimes he thought that maybe Leo should start his own order. HE was old enough, wise enough, and was certainly a very skilled killer. But Leo was too much against anything organized. He only went along with this because he thought he had a chance to wipe out these Slayer bitches and go back home!

It was two years ago that Leonardo was forced from his home. The Slayers came and basically cleaned house. Leo saw that Imperator herself one late night in his beloved city of Rome. He watched her from afar as she took five brethren of the Forsaken in one fight by herself! Soon after that The Army started stalking the night stalkers, setting a new order of the night. Like a pestilence they swarmed through Italy, sending the message that the presence of Forsaken would not be tolerated. Leo had slain a couple of Slayers in his day, but he knew even he was no match for an army of them. So, he and Jerome fled. It didn't take them long to realize that the Imperator and her captains had overlooked a small area of the mid-western United States while traveling the globe, adding newly born Slayers into their collective. It seemed only logical that this meant somehow this place was not on their radar and they wouldn't be bothered here.

It was on their trip from New York to St. Louis that they were approached by one of Naberius' monks and propositioned. With the promise of ridding the world of the Army and returning home again, they agreed.

At least Leo knew that Italy was in fact his home. He wasn't sure of much else. His name for instance. Was that really his name? I guess if you speak of something frequently it makes it more difficult to forget.

So maybe it really was his name. But Leo couldn't remember ever being human. He didn't know how he was brought into the fold of the Forsaken. It's not that he had gaps in his memory, it was that the further he went back, the fuzzier things got until there was no recollection of anything at all. But above all things he KNEW Italy was home. It was something that burned in his chest with fiery passion when he spoke of it. It was the cultural epicenter for the entire world wasn't it? When Leo found Jerome in New Jersey in the early nineteen seventies, he felt pity for him as brethren or more poignantly a brother would and took him back with him to Italy where he taught him about the world and the life he now had.

Leo himself didn't have to struggle for his nightly feeding hardly at all. His smoldering good looks, suave nature and aristocratic presence seemed to do all of the work for him. He was debonair and quiet, giving him an air of mystery. Even though he sought his prey mainly at local hot spots and clubs, he had no taste for discourse and was usually able to make his conquest without nary a word spoken. His steely eyes spoke volumes and that was all that was needed. In most cases it was easy enough for him to feed to the point of his victim's death with none the wiser. To observers, it was simply two lovers necking in a corner booth, against a wall, near the restrooms, or near the stage. All that was left behind was what seemed to be a young girl who drank too much and passed out. It wouldn't be until her friends decided to leave or last call before anyone would discover she was dead.

For him it was the hunt! The stalking and then their quiet surrender under his well played charms. For Jerome it was all about the theatrics and he enjoyed the art of the kill. The thrill of defiling a sweet flower of youth before ripping her to shreds was the point of all of this.

Jerome, himself, was quite the accomplished psychopath when he was alive. He enjoyed stalking young girls home from the grocery store he worked at as a janitor. He made their deaths into art. In a way that is how he saw himself, an artist of torture and death. Fitting that he would meet his end in a dark alley while stalking his latest prey. He had seen her in her pretty pink mini skirt in the produce isle squeezing tomatoes. He imagined what he would enjoy doing to her later. He had followed her that night from the store and down an alley she had turned into. He went to reach for her when someone beat him to it. The dark figure emerged from behind a dumpster and in her shock she dropped her paper bag and those tomatoes she had been inspecting so carefully, rolled forgotten on the broken pavement. She took a step back and squished one of them with her right foot and found herself stumbling backward into Jerome. She looked up at him somewhat relieved. But it was short lived. He grabbed her by the back of her hair and yanked her to his face. He smoothed her wisps of hair away from the right side of her face and licked it from her chin to her forehead. Then he whispered into her ear.

"I'll make you sing for me!" Jerome leaned back to gaze at her psychotically. But when he did, he realized that he wasn't the only killer in this embrace. He was taken back when he saw her face. It had been transformed into its hideous vampiric form. Her yellow eyes seemed to glow. When she grinned, her elongated eye teeth shown through. Jerome came to know that HE had been lured into a trap not the girl. She reached forward with her left hand and grasped his throat tight.

"But I was so hoping to hear you sing! Come on, you know the words!" With that she tilted her head to the left and bit down hard on the right side of his neck. He screamed in pain. She relented and looked up at him. "There you go, lover! That's my favorite song!"

The figure that had come out from behind the dumpster approached and spoke.

"Quit messing around! I'm hungry, too!" He was a large and somewhat dim individual. He looked very put out by all of this.

"Come on, kill me. Don't stop now! You're almost there!" Jerome gurgled and grinned. The vampiresse looked at him thoughtfully.

"You serial killers are always so much fun! Normally your kind squirms and pleads for their lives when confronted with their own torture. They claim to relish torture and worship death, but when it comes time for their turn, they do their best to run from it like scared children. You on the other hand, I smell potential. You don't fear me, do you?" She leaned in and sniffed his neck up to his chin and licked his lips. She grinned slyly. She felt down with her hand and found his erect manhood and grasped tightly. He moaned against the engaging pressure.

"And I can tell that you all but fear me."

"Come on! Quit fucking around and let's go! Finish him off and toss him in the dumpster so I can get something to eat before dawn! I'm dying here!" She rolled her eyes and let go of Jerome's crotch to retrieve a pencil in his jacket pocket.

"Here, let me help with that." And without looking behind her, she flung the pencil over her shoulder and it lodged right into the other's chest, penetrating his heart. He looked up in total shock, amazed that she had just done this to him. "There now, you're dead. I know how impatient you are." With that, he exploded into dust. "Now that that little annoyance is out of the way, where were we?" She pulled him closer and sunk her teeth in once again. He gritted his teeth and moaned as she gulped great draughts from his artery. He put both hands on her hips and pressed his body tightly against hers. She relented and threw her head back in ecstasy. She licked her lips and finally let go of his neck. She then kissed him on his mouth hungrily. When she pulled away she gazed at him and gave him her proposition.

"I could give you what you need to perfect your craft. You could stay young and vicious forever." He tilted her hips toward his and looked down ravenously at her skirt. The soft pink linen tortured his senses. All he could think about was ripping it from her thighs and conquering the soft, wet pink that lay between them. She sensed his desire and thrust his hand under her skirt and to the object of his desire. He gripped his fingers tightly inside her to cause her pain; she grimaced then laughed as she enjoyed the violent play. "Think of it! You could torture beautiful young girls for all time! Take them, make them yours, and make their bodies your playground! Then rip their hearts out and feed off of their very own souls! Every night you can feed your endless hunger as the god you are!"

He looked up at her and removed his hand from the tender and raw flesh of her genitalia and pressed his hand against her face, feeling all of her vampiric ridges and, ultimately, her sharpened eye teeth. He pressed his thumb into her left fang and pierced it until it drew large droplets of blood. He shoved his thumb far into her mouth, forcing her to suck the blood from it.

"And what if I say no?" he asked without expression.

"Then you die."

He removed his thumb and wrapped his hand around her throat, turned, and shoved her against a brick wall. Her head bounced off of the dense surface and she laughed maniacally. He grabbed the hair from the top of her head and slammed it against the wall a few more times. She continued to laugh. Blood ran down her neck and he leant forward to lap it up. He reached down to his tattered, dark blue work pants and undid them to liberate his carnal muscle. Her legs wrapped around his waist as he pulled her down toward him and thrust upward as hard as he could. The vampiresse let loose a deep, guttural sound and smiled largely. Jerome repeated his thrusting, slamming her again and again into the wall he had her against. She grabbed his head and pulled it close to her face and licked his cheek down to his neck where she bit down once again, pulling into her mouth the hot, thick, rich and salty nectar from his now weakened fount. Her feeding from his neck elevated his excitement. As his life's blood ebbed from him, his gratification became complete and he slowly let loose of her and began to slump.

She followed him down to the ground until she had taken all she could from him. As he lay in her arms and drifted into dizziness, she reached over and picked up a piece of glass broken from a discarded liquor bottle. She then brought it to the right side of her neck and sliced it deeply. She lifted Jerome to the wound and bade him to nurse from it. He started slowly but then when the shock of the highly charged liquid hit his throat, he latched on like a starved leech. He growled spitefully as he fed. It became too much for her and she tried desperately to free herself. She pulled at the hair on the back of his head, she pushed at his shoulders. Finally, he fell backward and allowed his head to swim. The vampiresse, herself, had fallen back against the brick wall and swooned.

"I underestimated your hunger." She gasped.

As Jerome lay on the crumbling pavement, he felt a piercing lump under his hip. He slid his left hand under and produced a piece from a broken wooden palate. He gripped it firmly and slowly sat up, concealing it next to his thigh. To his right his sire scooted over just as his head began to wobble.

"Easy, lover. In about ten seconds you are going to pass out and won't wake up until tomorrow evening." She brushed his greasy blond hair from his face and kissed his forehead. As she was doing so, Jerome brought the stake from his side and drove it into the left side of her back. She immediately shot up with her eyes wide and her mouth agape. She slowly turned her eyes to meet his in total astonishment.

"Did I do it right?" he asked sarcastically. She fell to dust.

That first night Jerome barely made it to a nearby dumpster to shelter himself from the coming dawn. But when he awoke the next night, he learned that a whole new world had opened up to him. With his newfound vampiric strength, it was easy to reach into a young thing's chest and explode her heart like a piece of rotten fruit.

But nowadays, it had become more and more dangerous to be one of the Forsaken, as Leo had called all Vampires. With the hundreds of Slayers running around, more and more are being dusted every day. That was until they met with the Order. Apparently, due to the overage of Dudley Do-rights, The Master of this Order found his way to tear back into this dimension. And brought with him a wicked plan! It was hideously terrific! He had discovered a way to tip the scales into their favor, and all he needed was their help. A few more Forsaken for their cause and a couple mortal sacrifices, bada bing, bada boom, you got yourself one hell of a tipped scale! Super-Evil! The only problem was Leo was insanely impatient and neither of them cared for taking orders from anyone, especially some wigged-out, self-proclaimed "Demon King" slash Vampire Master who got himself zapped into another dimension by some Slayer over a thousand years ago. But here they were. Standing in the middle of the run-down house's run-down kitchen about to make their way down some rotting stairs to finally begin the ritual that would bring forth the "Inanna," "She Who Is the Arm of the Damned."

As Leo began to wrap up his little tantrum, a vampiric Priest swung open the scrappy basement door and stood before them. His face was twisted in the demonic form and he wore a long red and black robe adorned with large talismans and what looked like the atef crown that was worn by the pharaohs of ancient Egypt during religious ceremonies. He carried with him a black staff with a decorative silver spear at the head.

"The Chosen is prepared. It is time to awaken the Inanna. Master Naberius awaits you," the Priest instructed with a gravely voice. He bowed, took a step back and gestured for the two to go along down the stairs. They looked at each other and, with hands in their suit pockets, they made their way down the rickety stairs to the dank, dim basement.

As they turned the corner, they saw a multitude of vampires encircling a stone table. It seemed that this basement went on forever. You could see where the original basement stopped and where they had tunneled out farther. There were at least fifty vampires standing around this table and chanting lowly in monotone. Several of them wore the same black and red robe, but only the one with the staff wore the head dress. The Priest made his way to the center of the circle just above a very nude and dead Nica Todd, the girl who had gone missing two nights ago, who lay on the stone table. Leo and Jerome took their places among the chanters.

"Gube uzu avec mud. Sudu ama tud adda musal lirum, Inanna."

"What took you so long?" a deep, husky voice demanded. Leo looked up and over his shoulder to the towering dark figure from whence the question came.

"Is it not bad enough that it took you almost a year to find the girl who could contain the great Inanna, but now you have been dragging your feet to bring her forth from the pits of Nibiru?"

"Naberius, we are here, we are chanting with the almighty chanty ones. The Inanna will be brought and I will be allowed to go home! Na di will never have to listen to your annoying sermons again!" Leo spat.

"Whatever brings you to the Blood Goddess." Naberius stood next to Leo and began to chant.

Chapter Seven

Out of the Closet

    Jimmy was stunned by what he heard. How could HIS parents hide something that important from them? He studied it carefully. For something this old, it was still very shiny. He ran his fingers over its elegantly etched surface. He couldn't hide the smile from his face! This was so exciting, and oddly made sense! It explained why he found that Legacy book in Dad's book closet. DAD'S CLOSET!

    "Emma! Dad's closet! It has to be in there! That's—"

    "—where we found the Legacy book!" said Emma as she finished his sentence. They all three jumped off of the couch in the basement and took off for the book closet in the back right corner. Jimmy flung open the door and started pulling books off of shelves. Emma and Layla were not far behind, tripping over various tools and Emma's "spare parts." When finally they reached the closet, they each took a wall, and all three were searching violently. They tore through the tiny library with such force that within seconds the shelves were bare with their cargo suffocating the three's feet. They furrowed their brows and squinted their eyes as they searched the walls high and low on tippy toes and haunches. After several minutes the group looked at one another and plopped to the ground on top of an old, discarded book. Layla shifted uncomfortably and pulled a large volume out from underneath her rump. They sat disappointedly, and drearily looked above themselves at the surrounding walls. Nothing seemed to glint in the darkness of the closet that would suggest to them a mystical lock of any kind. Hands on knees and heads on hands, Jimmy spoke, breaking the tense silence.

"Well, where else would they put it?"

"I don't guess it would have to be in the house, maybe there's a hidden doorway somewhere in the book store," Emma suggested. Layla looked up as if deep in thought. She strained her eyes and tilted her head.

"What? I can barely hear you; you're going to have to speak up! Yes, yes, GO ON! I know that much! If you have something that we can use…" Layla trailed off, still looking, unyielding off into the basement. The twins became aware that this was Layla speaking to some lost soul again. They looked at each other, both feeling that this was not the time to appease the talkative dead.

"Yes, the books, we took them off of the shelves, what about them? We couldn't find a doorway! The walls are solid!" Jimmy and Emma knew that they were both coming to the conclusion that this was not one of Layla's random conversations. This "spirit" knew something about what they were looking for. Layla slowly turned her head and looked toward Jimmy.

"It's your father," she said plainly. "But he's fading in and out. I am having trouble understanding him. He said you would know. 'Jimmy will know, Emma never had the love'? What does that mean?"

"I didn't love books like Jimmy. Dad always said that Jimmy got the love from him." Emma bowed her head.

"Well your father says that it's the love of books. I can't hear you! Something about all you need is to love a book, to opening a book, and I can't make it out! Where did you go?! For the first time I want them to stay and they disappear."

Jimmy stared off into blackness; he was remember something his father used to tell him. He was lost in a memory. He was seven years old and his father had given him his first "Encyclopedia Brown" book. Jimmy sat on his father's lap as he slowly opened the cover and slid his large calloused index finger down along the inside spine of the paper to flatten it. "All you need, son, is to love opening a book, and it will open the doors of your imagination to hidden worlds!" Jimmy mouthed his father's words out loud. The two girls looked at him, slightly stunned.

"Of course!" Emma exclaimed. "The key IS mystical right? Who says it HAS to be an actual door? I mean a DOOR!" she said as she reached up and grabbed the closet door knob and swung it to and fro.

"Well, if it's a book? Which one is it?" Layla seemed to voice what everyone was thinking, then immediately started grabbing up books and rustling through them.

"How are we supposed to know which one it is?" Emma asked, frustrated. All three looked carefully at each title of each book. There seemed to be a thousand lying strewn on the floor of the cramped closet. Jimmy became frustrated, straining his eyes in the darkness so he reached above his head and found the pull chain attached to the light above. But when he pulled nothing happened. He puffed a little in aggravation when he realized the new upgrade he installed on Emma's leg. Jimmy reached forward and grabbed her foot.

"Hey, asshole! Do you not understand the concept of personal boundaries?!" Emma spat.

Jimmy just rolled his eyes and pressed her second toe down like a switch. When he did, her whole leg lit up and let of a soft glow that illuminated the small room. Everyone sat and stared wide eyed at the glowing appendage in awe.

"Cooooool," they all moaned.

"When were you going to tell me about this one?!" Emma asked.

"Oh hey, I turned your leg into a glow stick. You'll be the envy of every rave. There I told you."

"How does this help me wear high heels???!!!" Emma demanded.

"How do high heels help you slay???!!!" Jimmy reciprocated.

"It looks good!!!" she yelled.

"How is this conversation finding the right book?!" Layla

protested. Emma fumed, folded her arms and stuck her tongue out at her twin. Jimmy did the same. He thought to himself what an ungrateful brat Emma could be. Emma looked up with her mouth agape and thought how Jimmy could be self righteous and sometimes a know-it-all. Jimmy narrowed his eyes at her.

"Look let's agree to disagree later. Ok?"

"Fine," she said sharply.

Layla rolled her eyes and went back to searching through books.

"I thank Goddess every day that I am an only child." As all three continued to look, Emma chuckled at Layla's comment.

"So you are one of those people that believe that God is a woman?"

"I believe that things aren't always what people necessarily say they are. Not everything is so cut and dry. I believe in the duality of all things obviously. That is why my patron deity is a Goddess of Balance. How and what you believe is all a matter of perception," she instructed.

Jimmy looked up as he had a wild thought. He thought to himself.

"What if we are looking for the wrong book?"

"You could be on to something," Emma spoke out loud.

"Hey, clue me in. I can only hear your inside voices when I am tuned in; my antenna wasn't pointed at you just then," Layla spoke.

Emma looked over at Layla and explained what was shared between her and her brother. "We are looking for some old and important book right?" Layla squinted as if in thought and nodded. "Who says it has to be some smelly old library book?"

Layla's ears seemed to perk at the notion. "If you really wanted to hide something wouldn't you put it somewhere that no one would think to look? Somewhere seemingly unimportant?" She looked up sharply out into the open basement. She stared intently, focusing on something the others could not see or hear.

"Did one of them come back? Who's there?" Emma asked.

"I'm not sure; I don't think it's anyone. It's more like a memory that's playing out in front of me." The saucy medium stood up slowly and began to walk forward, trance like. She moved toward the scene reacting before her eyes. There sat John Hogan on the old tacky couch and Katherine Hogan standing over him with a gray lock box in her arms.

"John, you are in your forties now. I think it's time we got rid of these things."

"Aw, c'mon, Kathy! I've had some of these since I was a kid! I still love to look through them now and again!" Layla moved closer and was able to see stacks of comic books on the coffee table in front of John. *Superman, Batman, Aquaman, Green Lantern,* and *Wonder Woman.* Lots of *Wonder Woman.* "You know you even like the *Wonder Woman* ones!" At this he stood up, took the box out of her arms and wrapped his around her waist and kissed her cheek. He leaned in and whispered into her ear.

"You're my Wonder Woman, remember? You even had the lasso, and you did that little…" She interrupted him.

"Ok!" She laughed at the memory. "Go through the ones that you can't live without and then the rest we will set up at the shop on a clearance table or something." He smiled and kissed her firmly on the lips.

"I knew you'd see things my way! Besides, I think I would like to save some of these for Jimmy. I think he'd like that."

"Alright, but don't take too long down here…Superman!" She winked and blew him a kiss as she skipped up the stairs. He smiled back at her and turned red. When she disappeared he went right to work, sifting through which ones stayed and which ones went.

As he began to fill the lock box with the ones he would keep and ones to pass on to his son, the vision seemed to fast forward and then return to normal as Layla watched John lock the box and walk straight through her and toward the closet where Jimmy and Emma sat staring at Layla confusingly. They were speaking to her, maybe even yelling, but Layla could hear no other sound than that of which was in her vision. She followed him to the closet where he walked through the pile of books on the floor and through his children who continued to watch Layla and call out to her. John stopped at the back right corner and slid the box under the shelf, which was now hidden by a stack of discarded books that made their way there in the tornado of searching that happened only moments ago. As John stood up and walked past Layla he faded into nothing, ending her vision. Suddenly her senses tuned back into reality and the calls of the twins pierced her ears.

"LAYLA! What is going on?!" Emma yelled.

"BUGGER! I can hear you fine now! I am standing right next to you!"

"Then what the hell? What were you doing?" Jimmy asked anxiously.

Layla furrowed her brow and pierced her lips. She looked at the twins, trying to think of a way to explain to them what had just happened without sounding like a complete loon. Then she remembered that she had told them she saw dead people and she got over her self-consciousness.

"I was watching your parents. Your mother was trying to get your father to toss out his comics and they were reminiscing about their super hero shag night." Emma and Jimmy both made sour faces and shook their heads as they tried to purge the disturbing imagery from their minds.

"Tell me that's not the important part, because I would care to just go on living life believing that my siblings and I were delivered by the stork," Emma said with her eyes tightly shut.

"Americans." Layla huffed. "Might I get back to my vision? OK, as I was saying, I saw your mother and father and your father said he wanted to save some of his comics to pass on to you, Jimmy. He put the ones he selected into a lock box and put it there under that shelf." She pointed to the spot where she saw John Hogan place the gray lock box. The twins looked at each other thoughtfully.

"I remember Daddy liking comics; Mom thought it was kinda silly for a grown man to read comic books. Especially a man with a doctorate in literature. But then again, Mom was a trekkie." Jimmy looked at Emma, scolding. "TrekkER! Sorry!"

"I remember when Pop sold those comics. He was so depressed. He looked like a kid who, well, like a kid who had to throw out his comic books!" Jimmy mused. Emma gave an exhausted look.

"Yeah strange how that would work out. Help me move these books out of the way." Layla stood in the doorway as the two began to stack some of books back onto the shelves above. As they came to the last few, they both squatted down toward the floor and reached under the shelf. Jimmy pulled out a dark blue sheet that had been covering it and then Emma pulled out the box. She picked it up and carried it out to the TV area and set it on the coffee table. Jimmy and Layla followed and placed themselves on the couch as Emma stood before them on the opposite side. Jimmy touched the dial of the combination lock. His index finger wiped away the dust that had settled over the years. He continued to inspect the gray matte, dimpled surface as Emma stood commandingly with her hands on her hips tapping her fingers and puckering her lips.

"You know all I need is to…" Before Jimmy could complete his sentence he saw Emma's glowing right foot come smashing down onto the lock box. Layla instinctively leapt back and huddled in the corner of the couch to prepare. He was barely able to lodge his protest and get out of the way, when the top of the box folded around the bionic limb, whose light now fizzled and then went out, and the coffee table fell and splintered under the force of the blow.

"I could have opened that the normal way," he said as he dropped his arms.

"Yeah, but it would have taken forever." She slowly lifted her leg off of the now steel taco. A couple of sparks popped as she lowered it back to the ground.

"That's just great, Em! Perfect! Do you know how long that is going to take to fix?! I keep telling you to take care of these things! I've asked you not to kick any concrete, steel, or brick. Why don't you understand that this shit is expensive and is a bitch to fix?! And not to mention, our coffee table is now two boxes of tooth picks!" Jimmy exploded.

"Oh take it easy, boy genius! You know you love it. Gives you a hobby!"

Layla sat still moving her eyes from Emma to Jimmy to the bent box on the shattered table. "That was bloody brilliant!!" she squealed. "Do it again!" she begged, leaning forward and wide eyed.

"You are a lunatic!" Jimmy affirmed. Emma shrugged and flashed a crooked, confident yet bashful smile. Just then a tiny flame burst out along her plastic ankle and shocked Emma to where she jumped slightly and started slapping at it to put the flame out. She looked back up at the two on the couch, a little embarrassed. Jimmy just shook his head in frustration and exhaustion.

"That can't be good," Layla blurted. "Sorry."

"Ok, now that we have successfully destroyed a safe, a table AND a leg, can we please at least go back to doing what we are supposed to be doing?"

Emma rolled her eyes as Jimmy tried to pull the door off. He looked at the girls and then tried again. This time he used all of his strength and bit down. The girls could see him straining. He looked up and saw Emma staring at him with raised eyebrows. He stopped and gestured for her to try. He looked away and up toward the ceiling as his sister effortlessly reached down and pulled the door from the box and tossed it aside.

"Why don't you just cut my penis off while you're at it," he stewed and rolled his eyes. Emma leaned forward and held his chin in her hands, squeezing his cheeks and smooshing his mouth.

"Aw, I would if only you had one!" she cooed.

"God, I wish I could still kick your ass," he retorted through his squished lips.

"Ok, you're a bad ass and he has no penis, got it, can we now find the door?" came the demand from the siren on the couch. Jimmy's face turned bright red. Emma let go and looked at him a little surprised as she realized his crush on their new psychic house crasher. He sharply and shortly shook his head, pleading with Emma not to tease for fear of further embarrassment. She gave him a reassuring glance as she sat on the littered carpet and they all began to pull out the comic books. They sifted through what was a majority of *Superman* and *Batman* comics. Toward the bottom they came across a stack of *Wonder Woman* books. Emma took half while Jimmy took the other. All, like the rest of the comics, were sealed in cellophane. All three of them looked at each book, studying the titles and cover art. Layla, who had a stack of *Batman*, spoke up.

"Oooo this one is beautiful! What's it doing with these? They were all in order until this one." Jimmy leaned over, accidentally brushing his chin against her bare shoulder. The softness of her skin and warm perfume made him feel that he would soon need to adjust himself. He looked up at her uncomfortably and she smiled back. He looked down at the comic she held. It was the 1987 *Wonder Woman* comic. *Wonder Woman: Gods and Mortals.* It was Pop's favorite one. It told of Diana's beginnings. From the hidden island of Themyscira to "The World of Man." From Amazon Princess to American Super-Hero.

Emma stopped what she was doing and looked over at the comic Layla and Jimmy were spying.

"Hey I know that one! Daddy read that to me a few times when I was little. Remember he used to call me his little Amazon! That always made Shea jealous! He would tell her that she was his Princess and that would make ME jealous!" Emma mused.

"Yeah well, all I got was Little Buddy. Might as well of given me a white floppy hat and bell bottoms." Jimmy took the book out of Layla's hands and shared it with Emma. They both held it and looked at the fantastic artwork of George Perez that graced the cover. Beautiful Goddesses and an elegant and statuesque Wonder Woman right in the middle. Emma ran her fingers over it. The siblings looked at each other, both having the same thought. Jimmy reached into his pocket and produced the silver Abgal Da key. Layla scooted to the edge of the couch. Jimmy's heart was racing, and in his anxiety he didn't even notice that her leg was touching his and her hand had rested on his knee.

The other comics fell from their laps and landed unnoticed on the floor. Jimmy and Layla instinctively moved to the floor with Emma and they all huddled together around the book. They laid it gently on the carpet in the center of their circle. Jimmy looked at the small, silver key in the palm of his left hand. He looked to the girls for an idea.

"Well, now what? Do I point it at the book, or lay it there? Do I do the hokey pokey or something?"

"I don't know. Don't ask me. Mine has an actual lock that goes with it! My parents believed in respecting the tradition their ancestors provided them." Layla sneered.

"Do you feel it's absolutely necessary to be a complete bitch at every inopportune moment you can?" Emma asked.

"It's what I do," Layla added without looking up.

"Trial and error, Jim. Start with laying it on the book."

"What makes you the boss? Why do you get to choose?" he posed.

She gestured for him to take the reins. "Go ahead, 'Big Brother'!" she mocked. He straightened himself and squared his shoulders. He looked at the key and glanced at the two women. He cleared his throat uncomfortably, furrowed his brow, and hesitantly laid the key on top of the book, and quickly took his hand back. Emma folded her arms and looked at him with a sneer.

"Well, don't think that one worked. What else?" Layla spoke up.

"For starters, let's take it out of the plastic," Emma said smartly as she carefully slid the paper book from its protective covering. She grabbed the key up before her brother could get it and pointed it at the book. "Open sesame!" The others snorted and laughed. "You got any bright ideas, smartass?"

"Here, give me the book," Jimmy demanded.

"No! You've had your chance! It's my turn! Just tell me what you want to do!"

"You just want to be the one to open it so you can walk around saying, 'Ooo look, I opened the secret door to the mystical library! I'm special!'"

"I am special, you nerd! Now, get back!"

"Oh my God how old are you guys?" Layla observed. Both twins grabbed the book and Emma dropped the key onto it as she reached out with her other hand to get a better grip. When she did the comic began to glow. However, they didn't notice because they were still bickering over who would get to open it. But Layla noticed. She tried to get their attention as she stood, backing away and tripping over a broken table leg.

"Uh, guys, could you stop please? GUYS!"

The squabbling twins stopped and looked down. Confusion quickly turned to shock when they realized that the key had pretty much fit the lock. Their eyes grew larger as they dropped it and furiously scooted backward. They stood up as the light grew larger and began to give off energy. Wind blew and made the broken bits of wood swirl around. They reached out and grasped each other's hand.

Layla became aware of her own fear and apprehension building inside her, and became desperate to be with the others. She mustered her strength and ran across the short distance from her to Jimmy. She was halfway there when one of the up-heaved bits of wood flew over and stuck into her right thigh. She toppled from the shock and pain, but was caught by Jimmy. He held her up and covered her head with his arm as he held tight to his sister's hand. The light seemed to fill the basement, and the growing tornado forced them to continue to back away. As suddenly as it began the wind stopped. The three let out their breath in relief just as a bright flash of light startled them. They all screamed in surprise and fell back against the wall. The last thing Emma remembered was the White Lady crouching down in front of her.

Chapter Eight

Birth

The cellar was dank. The smell of wet earth and rotted things filled their nostrils. But through it all they could smell the blood, rich and metallic; intoxicating. There she lay in the center of their great circle of vampiric monks and acolytes. She lay naked and unconscious, her shiny black hair still perfect in a short bob. Her bangs barely touched her beautifully arched eyebrows. Her lipstick was still unsmugged and rich ruby red. The altar she lay upon was solid stone and three feet high. There was no cloth of covering that protected her perfect white skin from its cold, unforgiving surface. At the head of the altar, just before Nica, was a black marble effigy of the Inanna herself. She stood commandingly with arms extended and a sneer across her wretched lips. She held the silver spear in one hand and a golden goblet in the other. Rubies were beset for her menacing eyes and snarling fangs. Her head was thrown back and her hair, which flowed to the carefully etched base, was carved elegantly around her shoulders and waist. The body itself was nude as Nica was, and just as perfect. As he looked down to the statue's feet, he saw that she stood upon a world of death depicted by a pile of carved corpses.

Leo was so taken by Nica's beauty. He wanted to reach out and stroke her cheek and brush her long, thick lashes with his fingertips. *Snow White in all her glory*, he thought to himself. He noted the hundreds of dead and dry black roses that encircled her frame. Flawless she was. Nothing marked her body. No tattoos, not even earrings. Her breasts sat in absolute symmetry and needed no assistance to defy gravity with their erectness even as her body lay flat. Never was there a more perfect vessel for the Inanna. Even Leo felt it was so, and he really didn't care about "The Empty One" or "She Who Is The Arm of the Damned" or even "The Blood Goddess." He only cared about having his un-life back to some form of normality. With all the Slayers around, he and his companion were more hunted than hunters anymore. And Naberius promised him that this "Inanna" would be able to set the scales into their favor.

So here he and Jerome were, in this giant circle, participating in the Ritual of the Inanna. They were now fully members of the Order of Naberius. And even as the Priest stepped forward to the head of Nica to place the wedged black silk pillow under her head, Leo still marveled at her pristine condition.

The Priest gently lifted her head with his left hand while sliding the wedged pillow under, making sure the thicker end was under her neck. All the while he chanted with the others.

"Gube uzu avec mud. Sudu ama tud adda musal lirum Inanna."

As he finished placing the pillow that now tilted her head back, he took a step backward and lifted the effigy of Inanna above his head.

"We call you to awaken! Please accept this vessel to be filled by your black emptiness, and to feed your unending hunger. Take this form to be the Arm, to control the pestilence that plagues the existence of your faithful children! Come to us and set right the balance that has been tipped against us! Accept the offering of nourishment we give willingly from our own unworthy bodies and set us free!" He lowered the statue and produced a very old looking flask from his robes. He mumbled something unintelligible as he tipped the flask and anointed Nica's head, hands and feet with its contents. From what Leo and

Jerome could tell it looked like black oil. It began to run and drip down from the places he had anointed. He then opened a compartment in back of the effigy and placed the flask inside.

"That is her blood," Naberius whispered to Leo. "It calls my queen to the vessel and binds her to it."

The Priest placed a finger on Nica's chin and gently pushed down, opening her mouth. He then presented his wrist and sliced it upon the spear he had held before. As the blood began to run, he held his wrist over her mouth. When he did this, he gave an instructive look to the others to do the same. Each vampire then produced a dagger they had been given earlier and slashed their wrists. They then formed a procession and, one by one, fed the vessel from their wounds. Because of the number present and the regenerative properties vampires possess, some had to continue to slice to re-open their wounds while waiting for their turns to present their offering. Finally, it came time for Leo. He sliced hard and deep as he walked up to the blood-soaked beauty that lay before them. He stretched out his arm and let his blood flow down into her gaping mouth.

"Accept this gift, and allow me to touch your elegant face." He reached up with his left hand and went to stroke the cheek he had been aching to touch. But just as he was about to do so, a hand that felt like rock grabbed his. He looked and saw Naberius looking down at him, scorning his presumption.

"You are unworthy of touching the vessel," he drilled. "I think you have given enough, you needn't give more." Leo stepped back and scowled at the great gray beast with deep black-red eyes. Leo was powerful, but he knew when he was outmuscled and outpowered. He sulked back and watched as Naberius placed his massive left hand on Nica's forehead, almost covering her face, and then ripped open his right wrist with his teeth to offer his dark blood to her as well. When he was satisfied he returned to the circle that had reformed itself and resumed its chanting.

"Child of Many Devils, awake and be host to the Empty One!" the Priest cried out. The torch light flickered and the cave grew colder. An icy wind brushed through the multitude to the center of the room. The group watched in amazement as the blood they spilt upon her body and face slowly absorbed into her skin as if nothing was there at all. The last to go was the Black Blood of Inanna herself. As the last of the black oily substance had disappeared, the ruby eyes of the effigy began to glow bright. Her fingers began to twitch, and then her head started to roll from side to side. The growing anticipation in Naberius was apparent to Leo. He could see his steely face twist into a sort of crazed smile.

Nica's body stopped twitching and began convulsing. Leo thought to himself how if the pillow hadn't still been there that her head would have been cracked wide open, ruining her perfect hair. She continued to flop and her eyes fluttered. He could just make out their rich blue color. Suddenly, she stopped moving altogether and her head rolled to the right, her eyes open wide, staring right at Leo. With his vampiric senses, he saw her body's last breath escape from her lips.

Leo adjusted his jacket and looked to Naberius. "Well I must say that was a lovely service. I take it now we bury her and then wait for her to rise?"

Naberius grinned, showing his gunmetal teeth. His blood-soaked eyes gleamed in delight. "Oh, to be so naïve! We are not simply siring a fledgling girl! We are awaking in the INANNA! The Empty Goddess! She does not require sleeping through a day to assimilate this vessel. What you have just witnessed is the soul succumbing to her will!" As the words exited his mouth Leo saw the change overcoming Nica's eyes. Blood rushed from the whites of her eyes to the irises where it was soaked in totally in a quick, bright flash. Their color was permanently transformed to a dark, rich purple. Her lids closed and then opened again. Her pupils dilated and her left hand reached up and touched her head. Naberius smiled greatly in satisfaction at the sight of his resurrected queen. She rolled her head back and sat up. She held her head in her hands as if waking to a hangover. Leo spied her naked back; it was speckled with bits of dust, tiny pieces of stone and broken rose petals from her ceremonial wreath. Her perfect porcelain skin seemed somehow defiled by the presence of the altar's debris. He wished he could step forward and dust it away for her. But he knew Naberius would never allow it. He saw her as belonging to him.

The Dark Goddess looked up and straight ahead and righted herself upon the altar. She turned her legs to the side, brushing away the dead flowers that had encircled her, and slid down, touching her exquisite toes to the grimy dirt floor. Leisurely, she continued down, placing then the balls of her feet, arches and then heels. She studied her digits as she dug them into the mud and muck. Her head rocked back, her eyes closed and a smile graced her divine face as she moaned in enchantment of the sensation. Her sighs were all that was heard, for the moment she sat up, everyone in the vicinity fell silent in awe. Finally, she slid completely from the altar, stood firm and glanced around the cellar, smiling wickedly. It was almost appropriate that the black petals fell to her feet as she rose from her stone bed.

"All hail the Inanna! The Empty One! Our Dark Goddess has come to reclaim this realm, to drench it in blood!" the Priest announced. Upon this, all in the room dropped to their knees and fell forward, face down in reverence. All, except Leo. He stood unmoving and unable to take his eyes off of the bare splendor before him. She looked back at Leo, smiling all the while, confidently and chiefly. The mutual gaze seemed to last an eternity, until it was interrupted by the deep gargle of Naberius' voice.

"If you do not show humility now, I will rip your legs from your feeble corpse and force you to lower yourself in her presence!" The Goddess winked at Leo teasingly. He did as he was instructed.

She turned to her attending Priestesses: three scantily clad vampiresses with black scarves covering their long hair. Each was clothed in black, sheer silk wraps tied at the waist with a red silken cord. Each attendant held below her supple assets, an article for the Goddess. The first held a golden bowl filled with rose water and sponge, and a large cotton towel draped over her left arm. The second held a silver tray on top of which were various oils and perfumes. And the third held a red silk garment.

The first approached the Inanna and knelt before her. When she was given permission to rise, she began to cleanse her with the sponge and the rose water. Leo rose his head just enough to spy upon this act. The Priestess began by rinsing away the debris from her sullied backside, starting at her shoulders, buttocks, and then her artfully sculpted calves. He watched a globule of the water roll down from the nape of her neck, down her spine and then absorb into her right firm and ripe buttock. As the Priestess went to cleanse her front, the angelic figure turned to facilitate her. As this were, she was now facing Leo and smiled as she noticed him watching this ritual. Once more the attendant dipped the sponge into the golden bowl, pushing the many floating rose petals away. She squeezed the soft ball and then released, allowing it to absorb the soft perfumed liquid. She brought it to the Goddess' shoulders and began to rinse her skin. Leo's eyes left her intoxicating gaze and followed the water as it ran down her chest, over her pert breasts, and dripped off of her coffee-colored nipples. The Priestess continued down to her abdomen and then the tops of her thighs. Leo couldn't help himself as he watched the water disappear into the small patch of curly hair that rested between her white thighs. When he caught himself, he shot his eyes back north and locked back with hers. She smiled slyly back at him to show that she enjoyed his eyes caressing her naked frame. Without taking her eyes away she tilted her head to the right, allowing her hair to touch her smooth shoulder, and lifted her right foot from the ground, bending her knee so that the attending Priestess could wash away the filth from the dirt floor and then place a red velvet slipper on it. She then did the same with her left leg, watching Leo watch her the entire time. When she had done this, the Priestess bowed and then hurried back to her place against the wall, thus summoning the second attendant.

 The second Priestess brought forth her silver platter of oils and perfumes and began anointing her Goddess with them. She chose a red Egyptian glass bottle first, pouring its oil contents in her palm and then rubbing her hands together. She smoothed it through her hair and then wiped her hands clean. Next came a large blue bottle in which she did the same but it was rubbed into her porcelain skin. She massaged the perfumed oil into her shoulders, arms, stomach and even her pert breasts. She persisted down her thighs and calves and then back up to her unyielding buttocks and back. He could feel that his arousal was becoming so imminent that, in all of his years on this earth, and all his attention to controlling his most animal of urges, this ritual was proving to be too stimulating for him to control these things. His gaze again was taken by her. It was as if her eyes commanded him to catch them. The second Priestess had finished and the third came forward. She unfurled the garment and draped it over her Goddess' shoulders. She pushed her languid arms through the sleeves and allowed the attendant to belt it at her waist with a matching sash. The Goddess waved the Priestess away and then walked forward, never taking her eyes from Leo and never once stopping her wicked smile. She stopped in front of Naberius and offered him her right hand. The massive demon king raised his head and then held her hand in his. He kissed it eagerly and rose to his feet.

"It is marvelous to have you at my side once more. I remember when we tore the southern dimension to shreds and danced as it bled! My hordes still hold a rigid grip over its pestilence. Once again, your expertise is required. Come, let us retire and we shall discuss our reign of these vermin over a few supple virgins. Shall we?" He gestured toward the stairs. As he turned with her at his arm, she looked down and smiled again at Leo's intrigued gaze. As they left, her attending Priestesses followed and within seconds the procession was gone.

The High Priest stamped his staff thrice upon the stone altar to signal all to get up from the muck floor. Leo and Jerome stood and dusted themselves as best as they could to try and remove the remnants of their time face down in the dirt. Jerome looked twice at Leo and noticed his thoughtful expression.

"You're not thinking about how you will soon be able to roam free back at home, are you?" he posed.

Leo didn't look at him; he just continued to adjust his jacket and watched the multitude of Forsaken exit up the stairs and off of the property.

"No, il mio amico. It is safe to say that I am thinking about something else entirely." Leo turned and headed up the rickety staircase with Jerome not far behind.

"Our task is done now right? Are we leaving this piece of shit place now or what?" Jerome prodded.

"No, I believe we will be extending out stay in the Heartland. At least for a while."

"What?! You're shitting me right? We are in the middle of nowhere! We have been suffering in this sink hole of redneck hell for over a year now! I am wasting my un-life here! I'm ready to leave!" he persisted as they reached the top of the stairs and entered the kitchen. Leo spun around on his heel sharply, making him virtually nose to nose with Jerome, if only Jerome were a few inches taller.

"You may leave if you wish. I will not stop you," Leo calmly commanded.

Jerome was dumbstruck! They had been together for thirty years! Not once had Leo ever uttered anything close to that to him before! He had never, ever suggested that Jerome set off on his own! They were as brothers, proven inseparable since Leo took him under his wing those many years ago.

Leo turned back around and continued into the parlor and then out of the front door to the wrap-around porch where he rested on the fragile railing and gazed up at the twinkling stars above.

Jerome stayed in the same spot in complete shock. But old habits die hard. His temper rose like a bonfire inside his chest and he stormed out to the porch.

"What the fuck?! I have stuck by your side for over thirty years! And when you asked me to follow you out here to this middle of nowhere state, to this back water town to help in some bullshit ritual just so you could go back to your precious Italy, I agreed! I stayed out here for almost two years! And now you are basically blowing me off without explanation?! You're just gonna tell me to go?! FUCK YOU!" Jerome spat the words in his face.

Leo spun around quicker than Jerome's mind could calculate and before he finished a blink Leo had his hand around his neck and had forced him up against the wall. Leo's frustration manifested itself by his face twisting into its demon form.

"Listen to me, idiota! I care not for your childish needs! You are a creature of darkness not an infant suckling from my tit! Start acting like it! If I wish to stay then I will stay! Whether or not you continue to tag along doesn't matter to me! Your delicate emotional state doesn't affect existence!" Jerome could do nothing but stare into Leo's yellow eyes. Leo closed his eyes and breathed deep through his crumpled nostrils. "Do you smell that, il mio amico? I do. It's fear." Leo dropped him and allowed his face to return to its human state. Jerome coughed and held his neck tenderly. He slowly looked up at Leo who had turned back around, staring at the stars. Jerome walked past him down the porch steps and turned to look at Leo.

"You've lost it, Leonardo." And then he slipped away.

Leo closed his eyes and replayed the images of the Goddess. Her elegant shape, her soft, milky skin, her perfect, supple breasts. And then there was her eyes, large and slightly almond shaped yet rounded. Her lashes were full and long and complimented her dark purple irises perfectly. He mused about her silky black hair, how it shined and lay flawlessly bobbed just under her ears. He knew it; he was fascinated by her. Completely enamored. He just didn't understand why. He had met thousands of beauties in his lifetime. Seduced them and ravaged them. He had tasted the souls of hundreds of gorgeous and exquisite women. Why, suddenly, is this one different? He rubbed his face vigorously.

"I'm tired, maybe that's it. I just need to get some sleep." It was true, dawn was approaching. He stood up straight and turned to enter the house, but when he looked up SHE was standing there. He was shocked! He began to take a knee when she waved him off. He stopped and returned to his upright position. She smiled and walked past him, to the very railing where he had been just before. She leaned on it and looked up at the lightning sky. Leo didn't know if it was an invitation to join her or if he should leave her alone.

"Tell me, does your master know of your wandering eyes?" This was the first time he had heard her voice. It rang in his ears sweetly; hypnotically.

"I have no master, mio caro."

"Italian." She let her head roll back. "Such a seductive language! I have wanted to learn it since I was little girl."

"You were ever a little girl?" Leo asked

"Of course, weren't you a child once?"

"Of course I was. But aren't you the great Empty One, the Arm of the Damned, a Black Blood Goddess?"

"Yes, but like you, I retain my human memories and persona. I am the Inanna but I am also Nica Todd."

"So what do I call you? Goddess? The Empty One? Inanna?"

"Oh no, those names are for Priests and lower beings, and Naberius. He refuses to let go of ritual and all the pomp that goes along with it. He's a child of the old ways. Me, because I am always brought into a world in a new form, I am always 'born' to that age. But that doesn't mean I start over each time. I am still the Blood Goddess, The Inanna of what you call the Forsaken." She unfolded her arms in a presenting gesture. "But for others, who I see are worthy, may call me Nica."

Leo looked at her, confused. "Am I assuming correctly that you do not see me as a 'lower being' and that I am worthy of using your name?"

"You assume correctly. You don't fear me. You don't worship me either. But you are definitely intrigued. And honestly, so am I." She took steps toward him and touched the lapel of his jacket. He felt himself quicken. It took all of his strength not to wrap his arms around her shapely waist and kiss her neck.

"Very nice, you're very stylish aren't you? I bet you have no trouble luring some sweet young apple into a dark corner, do you?" she cooed.

"Vermin!" came the thunderous growl from behind him. "You are not worthy of hearing her voice!" It was of course Naberius. Nica rolled her eyes.

"I speak to whomever I choose. And I say he is worthy. If you don't like it, then go play with one of the Priestesses, I'm sure they would be willing to fulfill whatever depravities you could conjure up." Her words seemed to wound him though he would not show it in his face.

"Do as you wish, Goddess, but remember, I called you here for a purpose."

"And it will be met, be at peace with that. But otherwise, allow me my space."

Naberius grunted and glimmered into nothing.

Nica turned her eyes back to Leo. She looked him up and then down. She ran her fingers along his lapels and then grasped them in her hands.

"You know, I am intrigued by you as well. They call me the Empty One, but do you know why? Because I hunger and can never be satisfied. But I am always looking to try. Wanna help?" She pulled him to her and kissed him forcefully. He let go and felt a kind of release he hadn't felt in a couple of centuries. He was finally able to touch her skin and crush her against him. And in that moment as they locked together under the brightening sky, he felt the darkness that lie ahead. The world would tremble before her feet and he would know what it meant to be truly wicked.

CHAPTER NINE

The Burden of Knowledge

How long had she been out? She had no concept of time at this point. She held the back of her head that had hit the basement wall from when the comic book threw them backward.

"Taken down by a comic book," she grunted as she rubbed her eyes. She blinked to try and focus her vision but it was still blurry. Emma strained her eyes, searching the room for any clue as to what came from the book, and where the White Woman went. She looked to her right and saw that Jimmy and Layla were still unconscious. Just as she was, they were covered in bits of dust and splinters of wood from the broken coffee table. Emma brought her hands to her opposite shoulders and began to push the debris to the floor.

"Geez, a simple 'no one's home' would have sufficed. Even a buzzer would have gotten the point across. Didn't need to blow the place up," she mumbled to herself.

"I don't think that that meant 'no one's home,'" moaned a now conscious Layla. Emma remembered that Layla had been hurt during impromptu tornado. She looked over at her leg and saw the small piece of wood jutting from her right thigh.

"Are you alright?" she asked.

"Yeah, I don't think it's serious, but it does sting a bit," Layla answered as she gently touched the bloody skin surrounding the oversized splinter.

"Well, I see you have actually gotten something accomplished." The girls looked upward to see where the voice had come from. There stood Aslyn in all her glory. She wore the same draping liquid dress as she had before. Maybe it wasn't really a dress; maybe she herself was just a projection of sorts. Either way, Emma thought that her colors seemed brighter than anything else she had seen in this world.

Emma could almost feel Layla's aggravation mounting with the presence of Aslyn, her patron Goddess. Layla let her hand drop from her wounded leg and huffed loudly.

"And where in the bloody hell have you been all this time? Aren't you supposed to help your faithful servants? Isn't that why they, oh I don't know, WORSHIP you?"

"If I just hand everything to you, how are you going to learn and grow?"

"Well, I would think that when it comes to things as important as the fabric of the universe, you might give us a heads up!" Layla barked at the glowing Goddess as if she were nothing more than an inept supervisor. "All you did was tell us who Naberius was! You have said NOTHING about how we can find out what he is plotting and how we can stop him! At this point you have proven absolutely useless and absent!"

With this last insult Aslyn flew across the room in the blink of an eye to where she was nose to nose with the injured, yet mouthy, Layla.

"You insolent, little ill-tempered child! Don't you think I care! If reality goes off balance then I cease to exist as I am! Without balance there is NO Goddess of Balance! I become nothing more than another sniveling, fragile mortal! Because of this Awakening, my powers have been limited, and as each day passes I become weaker and my sight becomes shorter! Don't you think that I would have done something by now if I could have? The truth is I cannot SEE what Naberius is up to! And it has become more and more difficult for me to anchor myself in this plane. So, if you don't mind, shut your flapping mouth long enough for me to say what I came here to say before I lose my grip and get tossed back into the ether!" Emma and Layla both were frozen in place. However weaker she may be, she was still very capable of making them nonexistent. Through the whole ordeal, Jimmy, who lay between Emma and Layla, stayed unconscious. Aslyn now turned her sights to him and made a confused face.

"He's alive, right?" She hesitated. Emma shrugged and nodded. She reached over and poked him in the shoulder.

"Hey, Jim, get up, c'mon, wake up."

"NO! NO! The cows! The Cows! Stop! I don't want the feather…" Jimmy jumped awake, sitting up against the wall and looked around.

"What?" he asked uncomfortably as the others stared at him, bewildered. "Uh she's really there right?" he asked as he poked Aslyn on the forehead. Her left eye twitched slightly and she slapped his hand away. He jerked his hand back and cradled it. Emma flashed him an appalled look and slapped his shoulder.

Aslyn stood and glided a few feet back.

"It's not like we are sitting around tickling each other's asses…" This, for obvious reasons, got a few strange looks. "We're trying alright! Our resources are limited, too! I mean we tried to open this comic book with the magic key the spirit of our mother left us, but it all just blew up, literally. Ok, now that I hear that out loud, I can see why you wouldn't believe us," Emma stammered. "But we tried; I mean I don't know how to get this thing to work! They should make instructions for these mystical comic book thingies!" She crossed her arms and pouted against the wall.

"What do you mean it didn't work?" Aslyn asked. "What were you expecting to happen exactly?"

"Well, isn't there supposed to be some secret stash of knowledge accumulated by our family over the years?" Jimmy suggested.

"Yes, that's exactly what it did," answered the statuesque figure before him. The group looked around their surroundings searching for anything new or out of the ordinary. Or anything resembling a mystical bookshelf. The only thing that looked out of place was the lustrous Aslyn the Azure standing before them amidst the scattered debris of wood, paper and couch fluff. Her blue light echoed off the paneling and concrete walls. It shone through the dangling prosthetic legs that hung above Jimmy's workshop, and through the railings of the banister to her left. With a shake of her head or wave of her hand, fluid shadows were cast, making the ragged threesome feel like they were sitting in the bottom of a pool. They continued to scrutinize the area, squinting their eyes to focus harder on every detail. After a while of checking the walls for a new crack to indicate a secret doorway, the moving shadows made Jimmy motion sick and wobbling; he turned his head back down toward the floor and moaned in discomfort. Concerned, Layla laid a caring hand to the back of his head and rubbed it gently.

"Did you hit your head when the book exploded?" she asked in genuine care.

Emma rolled her eyes and chuckled out loud as she began to stand to further inspect the room. "No, he's…" Emma stopped short as she turned and looked at her ill brother. He gave her a desperate look, pleading with her not to make him look any weaker than he had already done for himself.

"He's just frustrated." With her brother's ego intact, she turned her eyes to Aslyn, who stood at the opposite wall. "Maybe you could help us out a little and tell us exactly where this cache of knowledge is, because I don't see it anywhere."

"Why does it have to be 'seen'?" She smiled coyly.

"Why do you have to always be so gratuitously mysterious? I mean, why can't you just tell us where these books poofed at so we can dig through their smelly pages to find out how we can stop Naberius from raising the Blood Goddess, and Oh my God where did that come from?" Emma stood in utter shock and she turned slowly to her brother and Layla who stared back at her equally as shocked with their mouths agape and eyes wide. "WHERE DID THAT COME FROM?!" Layla asked again. "And what is a Blood Goddess?"

"The Inanna. Called forth by the sacrifice of a pure vessel and sired by an entire order of vampires. She is also referred to as the Empty One, because she harbors a constant hunger that can never be satisfied, thus making her a vicious and monstrous threat." Jimmy rattled off the definition without fracture, in one breath, and then gasped for air. Layla's hand had stopped rubbing the back of his head and sat perfectly still in amazement. Emma's jaw went slack.

"See, that right there!" She pointed at Jimmy. "What the hell was that?"

"How do you know that?" Layla asked in a mumbled voice. Jimmy looked into her large black eyes and shrugged.

"That was your magical bookcase you referred to," Aslyn spoke up.

"What?" Emma asked aggressively.

"For a creature of supernatural power and such incredible insight, you're very small-minded, Emma Hogan." Emma's mood was not improving. She did not take criticism well in any respect. Her arms folded and her lips tightened, ready to attack even a Goddess if she continued to step on preverbal toes. "You said yourself, 'a mystical bookcase; a cache of knowledge.' If it's mystical, who says it has to be tangible?" Aslyn moved toward the hardened slayer. They locked eyes and Aslyn continued to smile even though Emma refused to reciprocate. Aslyn breathed out, reached out with her right index finger and tapped Emma on the forehead. Emma's composure relaxed slightly as she began to understand Aslyn's point. The Goddess had already turned away, and with hands held behind her back, began to walk past Layla and Jimmy who were still huddled on the floor.

Emma whipped around and caught her twin's eye. He patted Layla and stood as well to meet Emma as she walked toward them. He put his hand on her shoulder and squeezed to show his support.

"Are you telling me that, when that comic book exploded, it shot all the info that their parents had into their melons? That's bloody aces!" Layla exclaimed.

"And painful," groaned Emma, as she grabbed her head with her left hand and, with the help of a conveniently placed brother, dropped to the floor. Jimmy held her tight by the shoulders as she crumpled into a smaller and smaller ball. She grunted and squeezed her eyes shut firmly. A flood of images rushed past her eyes at such a pace Emma was barely able to recognize them as words. Faster and faster they came, bombarding her senses until she could not hear, feel or even smell anything else around her. Jimmy gripped his sister tight, becoming more worried as the tears began to drip from her clenched eyelids. Suddenly, it was as if someone had hit Jimmy in the back of the head. The force of it knocked him off his haunches and he fell forward, holding himself up with his hands. Images and words came at him over and over again.

Layla sat in distress at the sight of the twins rutted in pain. She wanted to get up from her spot, but her leg was still hurting from the wood lodged in it, and she had a sense of apprehension about the decision. She looked to Aslyn in angst, pleading with her eyes for the Goddess to do something or at least give her an answer as to what was taking place. She just stood and held a hand up to let Layla know not to interfere. Their cries grew louder and as Layla looked at Jimmy, she could see his eyes were watering intensely and drool strung from his mouth to the floor.

The sight of Emma crouching on the floor holding her head was equally as disturbing. Her face, too, was wet from tears, snot and drool. Layla became frightened and wanted to help, and when she noticed that Jimmy's nose had begun to bleed, she resolved herself to do what she could to find out what was happening. She started to climb to her knees and crawl toward the now weeping twins.

Jimmy's head felt like it was going to burst from being filled too much. He couldn't even make sense of what was barraging his mind. Slowly, he became able to comprehend that a voice was speaking to him from the din. It took all he could muster to pull the words into focus. He howled as he forced them into the forefront of the assault in his head. Then there they were; in whisper they came and drowned out the montage if only for a fleeting second.

"She is the Rose. Give her light to grow," cooed a woman's voice that he could not place. As soon as the message was delivered the flood returned, rendering him an invalid once more.

Layla crawled through the pain to reach the twins. She tried to reach them through her mind's eye, but something kept pulling them just far enough away from her. Her anger with Aslyn mounted. How could she just stand there and watch them suffer?

"LAYLA!" Aslyn commanded.

"Get Stuffed!" Layla spat back. Suddenly, as Emma rocked, she began to yell out.

"The Arm must be severed! Severed, severed! SEVERED!"

With that, Layla fell forward and grabbed Jimmy's hand as it clutched the puce green shag carpet. The shock of the collapse sent shockwaves of pain from her wounded thigh up to her brain, telling her that she needed to move fast. She bit through it and clenched her eyes to focus on reaching Jimmy.

"C'mon, Jimmy, let me in there, and show me what's going on so I can help you find your way back," she mumbled.

"Layla! Get back! This is beyond you! You have to stop!" Aslyn begged.

"Just a sodding minute," Layla grumbled. In her mind she was racing through a red and black tunnel. But she was blocked at every turn. Finally, she punched her way through, and in a rip and a flash of light her mind was exploded into the torrent of information that had been tearing through the twins' minds. She cried out in agony. Maybe she should have listened to Aslyn this time. If she didn't get a grip now, she herself would be swept up in the surge and be lost in Jimmy's subconscious.

"How do I filter this?" she questioned herself. "All this couldn't be meant to fit in a person's mind. If I could just get him to focus. On what? ME! JIMMY! Focus on me! Listen to my voice!"

Another voice rung out in the distance. He thought it was another woman, but he couldn't be sure. He was sure that it was calling his name. Throughout all the other hushed and mounting voices quoting definition and prophecy, he felt that among them was someone calling out to him. Focus, yes focus. It called for him to focus. Jimmy held tight and used all of his strength to focus on the voice calling to him. Jimmy felt cold. It came from between his eyes: sharp, wet, and cold. Still, he forced himself to concentrate. He could make out the words now: "Jimmy, focus on me, listen to my voice and follow it." It was like he was drowning and someone had thrown out a preserver that was floating fifty feet above him, and the more he swam toward it, the more the undertow fought against him.

"I hear you!" he called out to the voice that was instructing him.

She heard him through the din. She wondered what the point of all of this was. Why couldn't his parents just have a secret room or magic box like any other self-respecting scholar of mystical studies? Slowly, she became aware that through all the quick, flashing images, she could just make him out; Jimmy doubled over, clutching the carpet. He was small and far away, but it was him. This was her opening.

"I'm coming! Jimmy, hold on! Keep holding on to my voice! Don't listen to anything else!"

He knew who it was now. It was Layla! He was pretty sure that his boyish crush on the spicy bronze beauty was turning into love! She was coming to his rescue. "Oh crap!" he felt. "I really have no penis." Still he focused. She was there and she was going to help him find his way through this and get control of his mind. But what about Emma? He couldn't help but think of his sister who was no doubt suffering the same fate as he was. "Ah God, Emma!"

"No! I'm losing him!" Layla cried as the image of Jimmy began to flicker. "Jimmy, no, come back to me!"

Hundreds of voices rushed through Emma's brain. She tried to fight them and she tried just letting it come, but nothing could stop the pain. Pictures, words and memories it seemed took her over completely. She couldn't take much more, she thought; soon her brain would give out and she would die. "Stop, stop, stop!" she howled. "Just stop." She let go and fell to the floor. She rolled to her back and let the tears come.

He heard Layla again pleading with him to come back to her. Jimmy's body began to shake as he was going into convulsions; it was beginning to shut down. "If I die now, I'll never get to Emma!" he cried out and reached for Layla with all that he could.

~~~~~

Suddenly he came back into focus. Almost shocking the way the image of Jimmy flew into clarity and pushed everything else cluttering his mind out of Layla's way. She reached out and grabbed hold of him, making sure this time he wasn't going anywhere without her. "You hold on, Jimmy boy, I'm not done with you yet, we're getting out of here!" And with that she pulled him and herself back into reality, agonizingly but effectively.

~~~~~

He rolled over, gripping his head. It was so good to be able to feel that old crusty carpet, and be able to smell how musty it was. His face was wet and when he went to wipe it, he found that his nose and ears had been bleeding. "That can't be good," he said out loud. He remembered swiftly that his sister was still lost in that same blinding maze. He flopped over and slid over to his sister. She was beginning to twitch and he knew that her brain was on the verge of shutting down as well.

"Sis, no, don't let this happen, you're too strong for this! Fight your way out, push past it, and come back to me!" Jimmy pleaded in a hoarse voice.

Layla began to come around and make her way toward the unconscious slayer. She looked around the room for her ineffectual Goddess, but she was nowhere near them that she could tell. She saw Jimmy hovering over Emma, trying to wake her.

"Jimmy, use it now, your connection, use it to find her and pull her free."

Jimmy looked down at Emma and grabbed onto her left hand. He spoke to her in the voice only they could hear.

Come on, Emma, you're too good for this! Listen to me, push it out and come to me! Push it out of your head!

She could hear him. And she knew he was squeezing her hand; if she could only squeeze back, she knew she could get out.

Jimmy jumped. Emma had squeezed his hand. It was slight at first, but then he was sure she was coming around. The pressure was increasing and her eyes began to flutter.

The noise was gone; all she heard was Jimmy now. The relief was immaculate. Her head felt fifty pounds lighter. Emma blinked her eyes and looked up. It was blurry at first, but then there he was. Her brother; bloody and smiling at her.

"Damn, I thought I was finally rid of you. Then I could have the bathroom all to myself and finally be able to score with hot chicks!" Jimmy joked.

"Yeah well, I was never the reason why you couldn't score. For starters, do you bathe in *Old Spice*?" she defended in a raspy voice. She leaned up and rested on her elbows. Layla smiled in relief and dropped her head down.

"What the hell was that?!" Emma forced as she sat upright.

"I think that was the secret library we were looking for," remarked Jimmy.

"Well, duh. If that was what we were looking for, why do I feel like it almost killed me?" Emma pondered as she held her throbbing cranium.

"Because, it wasn't meant to be contained by just the two of you. There's too much info in that blasted comic book of yours," moaned the sore and sweaty medium resting on the floor. "Bollocks, this really hurts." She reached down for the giant splinter that was still jutting out of her leg.

The twins made their way over to Layla to tend to her wound. Jimmy lifted her head and rested it on his lap. He looked down at her; her forehead was glistening and her complexion was becoming ashy. He did his best to smooth the hair from her face and dab the sweat with his t-shirt. Her head rocked and her eyes rolled back and closed. Jimmy was starting to panic.

"Layla, hey, stay with me! Wake up, I need you to stick around so I can awkwardly flirt with you some more!"

Her lids opened somewhat and she cracked a half smile for him.

"There we go, there's those beautiful chocolate orbs that make me stutter!" he cooed. He combed her hair with his fingertips. He marveled at its softness. He'd never felt hair like this. And it was the kind of black that seemed to have blue tints in it when the light hit it just right. It was like having pure black silk wrapped around your fingers.

"You didn't seem to have any trouble talking then," she stammered. "I'm ok, I'm just tired. Just need a ten-minute nap, love." She began to drift once more.

While Jimmy was making his best attempts to keep the waning Layla conscious, Emma examined her wound. She hadn't realized how large the impaled wedge was. By all definitions, it was a small stake lodged in her thigh. If Layla hadn't put any pressure on it, it may not have gotten this bad. But it was, and her blood was pouring down her leg. They didn't have time to call 911 now. Emma had to do something fast to make the bleeding stop.

"Jimmy, go upstairs to my room and get the bottle of pills from my night table. Then grab the stitch kit we keep in the bathroom along with a bowl of water and some towels. DARK towels." Jimmy gently laid her head back onto the floor and whispered to her that he would be right back. He began to dart up the stairs when he stopped and looked back at his sister.

"Which pill bottle?"

"What?" she asked, sounding put out.

"I'm not stupid, I know about your little 'sleep' aides. Which pills?"

Emma bit down and looked at Jimmy with half-lidded eyes. "The oxicodone. The big bottle. Now hurry."

Emma held Layla's hand and coaxed her to open her eyes. It took so much effort, and she was so tired. But she knew that it was important that she stayed awake right now.

"Layla, are you with me?" She nodded the best she could. Emma slapped her cheeks to get her to rouse. She knew she needed a tourniquet so she began to look around. She felt her waist to see it she had a belt on, but no luck, she was still in her pajama shorts she remembered. When she went to remove her shirt to tear it to make a tourniquet, she noticed Layla's peasant skirt and the rope belt she wore with it.

"Sorry, chica, I'm not getting fresh, I just need this to slow your bleeding."

"Yeah, I knew you were funny when you saw me in my knickers that night. Not that I blame you," Layla mustered.

Emma scoffed and continued to remove the belt and then raise the red and black gauze skirt just above the wound. "Ok, this is probably going to hurt." She slid the beige macramé belt under her blood-soaked thigh and tied it tight and then knotted it. Layla faintly arched her back and groaned as the belt squeezed her. By this time Jimmy was bounding down the stairs with his arms full of supplies. "You're lucky that my occupation requires that I learn field medicine. You try explaining to an ER doc how you get four broken ribs and a crucifix sticking outta yer ass!"

"Yeah that was hilarious; I took pictures I'll have to show sometime!" Jimmy chimed in.

Layla attempted to laugh, but gagged instead. Jimmy propped her head back up, this time with a pillow. He soaked a rag with the water he brought down in the blue glass bowl, rung it out and then dabbed her face with it. Emma also took a rag, but after placing a towel under her injured leg, she rung it out over the wound. Blood and water mixed together and ran down onto the awaiting dark blue towel.

Emma opened the bottle of synthetic morphine, and dumped out two tablets. Jimmy lifted her head and explained to her that they were going to give her something for the pain and that she needed to swallow. It took some effort, but she was able to get them down. Emma then opened the converted toolbox and prepared alcohol, prepackaged needles, gauze, scissors, tweezers, and a hunk of smooth wood to bite down on. She took the cigar-shaped piece of wood that was covered in bite marks, and tapped Layla's cheek with her hand, coaxing her to open her mouth. She positioned the wood between her teeth and Layla understood what this meant. This was REALLY going to hurt. Emma nodded to her brother and in response he placed his hands on both of Layla's shoulders.

Emma placed her left hand on the patient's thigh, above the wound, and gripped the impaled piece of wood and swiftly yanked it out. Blood shot out along with the wood and Layla grunted in agony as she bit down on the bit in her mouth. Emma took some of the gauze and sopped up some of the blood to get a better view of what she was working with.

"Well, I think it just missed your artery. Ok, I'm going to clean it off now, keep that bit in your mouth." It wasn't a large opening, but it was deep. Emma looked at the quivering Layla empathetically as she opened the full bottle of rubbing alcohol. "Don't worry, kiddo, those pills are the best of my personal stash. They'll kick in soon and you won't feel anything but floating." With that she poured the cleaning liquid over the wound and quickly dabbed it with a fresh piece of gauze.

Layla let loose a guttural moan and bit down on the wood in between her teeth. The burning from the alcohol was far more intense than having that stake removed. It was too much for her. And where did Aslyn go? So much for majestic deity; she was proving more and more useless. At least she led her here to find the Hogan twins. Layla let herself go and she drifted into unconsciousness.

~~~

Layla's arm rested above her head and her hair laid disheveled about her shoulders and pillow. Her bladder ached, nagging her to rouse from her blissful slumber and relieve it. She hated waking up; it was the worst part of the day. There was nothing more unsettling than stirring from an intriguing dream and forcing yourself to shake free from a magnificent rest into the blaring reality of consciousness. And this was a magnificent rest! She smacked her lips and clumsily began to rub her eyes. She knew the next step would be to actually open them but she wasn't ready for that. She knew what would be there when she did. The same thing she saw every morning. And the worst of it was she wasn't sure if it was real or just a waking dream. She got those a lot. Of course, one of the first troubles one has when they realize they are a medium, is the inability to decipher reality from fantasy.

She remembered what it was like when she was a child. It was horrifying for her. Turning the corner of their home in London could mean an assortment of things. She could see an old man smoking a pipe, a harlequin clown in oxford print holding a large axe while jumping and laughing manically, a singing teddy bear, or another spirit begging for her assistance. At first, she would run to her mum every time something like this occurred. But she soon grew tired of exciting her mother and father. There was nothing they could do to stop the inconsistent visions anyway. At least them being Abgal Da was an advantage to where they believed that she wasn't mental. They actually knew what she was and eventually requisitioned lessons for her from the resident coven.

For fifteen years she studied with the gentile women. She began to amaze even them. Her parents couldn't have been prouder. Her Abgal Da training was different, however. That began at birth as with all children of Abgal Da. They did their best to take their darling daughter with them on every expedition they could. The more dangerous always meant that she was to stay home with her vigilant and plump nanny, Aunt Dorrie. As furtive as she was in her childhood, Aunt Dorrie was no fool and foiled her every plot. But even Aunt Dorrie wasn't able to see what the future held for the Fellows and the rest of the London Motherhouse.

Layla had been training with the Coven of Musal. She was studying a book on transdimensional demon relocation, when she heard her father call her name. She had looked up from her book and seen both of her parents standing before her. Before she could utter a question of why they were there, she knew. She knew they were dead and that they were saying their farewells. She remembered dropping the books and her face quivering until tears fell without a sound. She had said no, trembling and reaching out to them. They had simply smiled and told her that they would be around, with her always. So cliché, she had thought, but true.

And now, as every morning since their untimely fate, she knew that when she opened her eyes she would see them sitting there at her feet, if only for a fleeting second. As much as it warmed her heart to see her parents' smiling faces, it hurt to know she couldn't wrap her arms around them and kiss their cheeks. The dreadful part was, she wasn't even all that sure if it was really them or just another waking dream. After two years, it was beginning to feel like torture. With all her power and talent, she could never bring them back. Where they were they were happy, and at peace.

She took a deep breath and opened her eyes. Sure enough there they were, smiling. And as they faded she came to realize that someone else was really there and they sat sleeping with their heads propped up by their hands. Jimmy, sweet Jimmy. He kept watch over her.

"So sweet," she whispered. "And so painfully adorable." She pushed down with her hands and scooted herself upward. As she moved she felt something roll up on the underside of her right thigh. She pulled back the red and blue quilt to reveal her bandaged right thigh. She touched the dark red spot on top and discovered it was still wet. She must not have been out for too long. She saw Jimmy begin to stir and looked as if his head was about to fall from his hand. Layla quickly pulled the covers back and pretended that she was still sleeping. No sooner had she closed her eyes than, sure enough, Jimmy's head slid from its prop and jolted him awake. He looked around abruptly and then back at the phony sleeping Layla. He smiled to himself as he gazed at her.

"God, what is wrong with me? A girl like this would never have anything to do with me." He stood up from the bed and turned to leave the room. Layla immediately shot her eyes open and faked a waking yawn to get his attention. Jimmy stopped in his tracks, turned around and hurried back to her side.

"Hey, I was wondering when you were going to come back around!" he greeted her happily. "How ya feeling?"

Layla promptly made a pouty face and gently touched her injury. "Oh, ok I guess, I am a little sore still. How long have I been sleeping?"

"A couple of hours now. You passed right out when Emma dumped the alcohol on your leg. Probably a good thing you weren't awake for the stitches. Emma is many things, but well, let's just say she wouldn't have made it through medical school, or sewing school for that matter. Do they have a sewing school? I bet they have a better name for it. Maybe something like seamstress academy or…" He rambled on. His discomfort was becoming apparent.

"Do I really make you that nervous?" Layla asked frankly.

"Uh, well, yeah, I mean most beautiful women do." He stopped and smiled awkwardly.

Layla smiled, largely flattered by his comment. "You think I'm beautiful?"

Jimmy blushed and looked away from her intense dark eyes. "You know that you are."

She smiled softly and touched his arm. "I didn't know that you thought so."

He turned back to her and looked her face over. "I've never seen anything so beautiful. You scare the hell outta me."

She picked up his hand and held it in hers. "Trust me; you've got nothing to be nervous about." She leaned forward and Jimmy's eyes grew wide. Was this really happening? Did she just say that she was attracted and was going to kiss him?

"Oh good you're awake, where's that book about Marmaduke you showed me the other day?" A very badly-timed Emma interrupted. The two jerked around and stared at the intruder in the doorway.

"You mean the book on the Ancient MARDUK Prophecies?" Layla asked, agitated by not only the interruption, but Emma's failed attempt at pronouncing the name of the book.

"Yeah that one, whatever, where is it?"

"You left it in the living room, on the floor I believe!" Layla spat.

"Oh yeah! Thanks!" Emma began to disappear down the hall when she caught herself with her right hand on the doorway and turned back. She looked puzzled back at Layla.

"How are feeling? Didn't I tell you those things would knock you out!"

"Uh, yeah I'm aces. Thank you, they were hunky dory. Give me a tick and I will help you get up," Layla stammered.

"Sure, take your time. Jimmy, do you think you could stop drooling enough to fix my leg? I would like to patrol when the sun goes down. You know, tonight, in like eight hours."

Jimmy slowly turned and glared at his evil twin.

"What are gonna do? Glare me to death?" With that she walked away down the hall.

Jimmy bit his lip and lowered his head. He looked back at the object of all his desire and smiled uncomfortably.

"I have to go to work. She has a pretty bad temper, and she likes to start trashing my *Star Trek* collectable figurines when I tick her off. And I just completely ruined a chance at ever getting back to that moment didn't I?" he spluttered.

Layla just raised her eyebrows and smiled. "Well, just don't tell me you have *Chewbacca* bed sheets and I think we'll be straight."

"Actually, *Chewbacca* is *Star Wars*..." Jimmy stopped. "And I'm doing it again."

"Kinda are. Let's just get to work and maybe when there is time we can get back to that conversation." She grinned and batted her eyes.

Jimmy smiled back and walked away. As he made it down the hall, he thought that with the way things were going they would never have another free moment. And here he was and little Jimmy was ready for action. He spoke out loud to himself.

"Thank God no one's in the bathroom." He turned into the bathroom and locked the door.

CHAPTER TEN

Always Trust the Sassy British Girl

Emma flipped through the translated prophecy book. She remembered something from her ordeal about "The Arm must be severed." She somehow knew that they weren't actually talking about someone's arm. But she couldn't be sure. The same nagging feeling also prompted her to write down what she could remember. But when she finished all it said over and over again was: "The Inanna! The Empty One, Everlasting Hunger. The Arm must be severed!" Over and over again throughout an entire notebook. She fought to put together the fragments from her violent experience.

"Goddamn comic book!" she mumbled to herself. "Why the hell couldn't they just have some books in their sock drawer like normal parents?"

"Because they weren't normal parents. They had seceded from the Brotherhood of the Abgal Da, probably because you were a compatible vessel, and they knew what that would mean if you were ever called. And probably also because a slayer had never had a twin! They knew what that would mean for the two of you. Research and testing, the Brotherhood very well may have intended to take you from your parents 'for the greater good' of course," interjected Layla. She hobbled toward Emma who sat Indian style on the floor of the living room. "And being that they left the Brotherhood with a vessel and her twin brother, who had a mystical connection, they would have been sought after by the other Abgal Da and would have wanted to stay as hidden as possible. Therefore, the extreme lengths they took in hiding their family knowledge."

Emma furrowed her brows and contemplated the idea. It made sense. Perfect sense actually. They wanted a happy, normal family.

"But why this way? I mean it almost killed us! Shouldn't it be 'rigged' to know who we were?" Emma posed.

"That's true, but what you are forgetting is the volume of information here. It only opened when you both touched the book and the key, so it 'knew' who you were. What I believe you're missing is, you two were never meant to have all of that in your heads."

"Yeah, you said that before you passed out. What do you mean by that?"

"There are two options here that we need to look into. One, maybe your entire family is supposed to be present to 'share' the load. But since they are obviously not around, it was too much for the two of you to handle. Or option number two. This is what I would do, and what I think your parents thought of in case of a situation just like this; there could be a sort of template around here that the information could be transferred to. That way it would be accessible only to you, but it also wouldn't be punching a bleeding hole in your noggins," Layla explained.

Suddenly, a crash came from the bathroom down the hall, followed by a thud. The girls perked up and looked in that direction.

"Are you ok in there?" Emma asked.

"Yeah, fine," Jimmy answered back in a cracking voice.

"Are you sure? Did you break anything? I swear if you broke my jewelry dish...!"

"PLEASE, JUST DON'T TALK TO ME RIGHT NOW!" he yelled, stuttering.

Emma and Layla looked back at each other and shrugged. Layla continued.

"Do you see what I am saying? Think, do you remember anything in your parents' wills, anything at all that could be associated with this?"

Emma stared off into space and thought hard. She closed her eyes and tried to picture the words themselves. Nothing.

"No, the only things I can remember were the house and estate, and the book shop." They stared at each other thoughtfully from across the room. Layla leaned back on the flowered couch and Emma rested back on her haunches on the cushy blue carpet.

"Emma, what's the name of your book shop? I don't believe I ever caught it. Even when I was there, I didn't bother to read the sign."

"Oh it's stupid really. It's not exactly the kind of name that really makes you think, *hey, this must be a book store*. Hogan's Vault." Emma raised her hands in the air as she announced the name.

"Yeah, the only people we get anymore are ones who think that we're some sort of storage facility." Jimmy walked casually in the room and sat in the brown corduroy easy chair next to the kitchen doorway. He smiled at Layla and she stared back at him with eyes wide.

"Blow me!" she exclaimed.

"What?" he asked awkwardly, hoping she didn't realize what he had been doing. "I think you've got that backward!"

"What? No," said Layla, shaking her head. She whipped back around and looked back at Emma. "We need to get to that shop!" she exclaimed.

"If you just tell me what book you need I can go get it for you; you should probably stay off your leg for a while," Jimmy offered.

"No, I think the WHOLE shop could be the template!" Layla justified.

"Oh my god! Yes! Hogan's VAULT! Why didn't I think of that?" proclaimed Emma. Jimmy and Layla both rolled their heads toward her and raised their brows.

"Like I said before, Slayer no read good, Slayer like hit!" Layla grumbled mockingly. This received a snort and a chuckle from Jimmy. Emma flashed a menacing glare, letting him know she was not amused.

"You take yourself too seriously, woman." Jimmy turned and headed for the basement. "I'll go get the comic book and the key; you wanna help her into the truck?"

"Oh, I'll be fine; I just didn't have the strength earlier to heal myself. I think I can manage now." The twins were once again astonished by the ever surprising Layla.

"You can honestly do that?" Emma asked, dumbfounded.

"Well, yeah. Any witch can if they have been practicing long enough."

"Can you heal other people?" The question came from Jimmy who had stopped in the doorway to the basement.

Layla rolled her eyes. "Of course I can, if I can heal myself obviously I can heal others; it's just not easy, though. It takes a great deal of energy and concentration. So, do you mind, you two get what you need and I need a few minutes to meditate. By the way," she started as she realized she was only in her shirt and cotton underwear, "where's my skirt?"

~~~~~

An hour later, the group pulled up to the shop in Jimmy's truck. After Jimmy got out, he chivalrously lifted Layla down from the high perch of the cab. Meanwhile, on the other side of the truck, Emma lost her footing attempting to lower herself, slipped on the curb and dropped to the sidewalk, unseen by the other two. She directly jumped back to her feet and commenced to scold her brother for his choice in vehicles.

"Jimmy, why in the hell do you have to have such a huge ass truck? It's not even practical to have something so freakin' high off the ground!" He just shook his head and walked past her.

The sun was high and bright. People occupied the sidewalks of downtown Walnut Grove. They passed from dress shops to cafes to the bargain stores and drug store. A happy young couple walked arm and arm out of the First State Bank and into the local children's consignment clothing store. Everywhere Emma spied happiness and contentment. Even her brother and the new addition to their household seemed to be sparking some new romance. *Not me*, she thought to herself. *Never me.* It was something she would never admit to anyone, even her brother. Every day she tortured herself with thoughts of rejection and loneliness. She felt that even if she did meet someone who accepted her physical appearance, namely her fabulous plastic accessory, she would still question their moral code in whether or not they had some sick amputee fetish they looked to fulfill with her. Or, maybe they would just be so desperate they would have to screw the crippled chick. *And if that doesn't scare off the guys, my freakish, underground superhero life will!* Even her brother was uncomfortable with her Slayer abilities and felt completely emasculated by it.

Always alone. She was destined to lead an empty existence. There was no one else to share it with other than her brother, who, although she teased him regularly otherwise, was destined to make some lucky girl very happy and leave his tortured soul sister all alone to her vices. And, by the looks of it, he may have already begun to head down that road with the lovely, but feisty Layla.

She felt her heart skip and beat and then sink. *Everyone but me. Alone in the crowd. That's it, forever alone in a crowd.* She let everyone around think she was so strong, that she was so brave and tough, when the reality was she felt broken inside, like her colors were fading and had been ever since the night she lost the majority of her family and her foot. Normality had been lost to her forever that night.

The only thing that helped was the slaying. It was a release of all her anger and frustration at the hand fate had dealt to her. Every kick, every jab, every vamp that erupted into a cloud of dust was every bit as therapeutic as an hour-long session with a shrink. But the problem was, when the job was done and the vamp was dust, there was nothing left to punch or hurt but herself. That's why she took the pills every night. To quiet the evil little voices in her head that tore her apart inside. She knew that eventually she wouldn't be able to take it anymore, and she would explode all over everyone. *Like soda*, she thought. *Like a shaken can of soda, I'll open up and spill over everywhere.*

She had been standing there a while staring off into the busy street, shaking her hand and chewing on her lip. Jimmy had seen her do this many times. He had tried to pick her brain when she went into her silent revelry, but she had put up a wall, hiding whatever she was thinking from the only person in the world she ever even spoke more than a sentence to.

~~~~~

"Em, you coming in or do you want me to bring you a chair?" She looked up sharply as if she hadn't even realized that any time had passed at all.

"Uh yeah, bring me a chair and I will keep watch at the door, you know make sure no one comes in!"

"Yeah, like we have any problems with people actually coming in here!" Jimmy joked. She smiled back at him. He could tell she had done so to appease him, so he wouldn't ask what she was thinking about. He smiled back to let her know he wouldn't bother her about it this time. She entered the store and walked past him to the office where Layla had disappeared to. Jimmy lingered by the shelves of books, slowly running his index finger down the spine of every other book. Memories of him and his sisters playing hide and seek and chasing each other around the shelves passed through his mind. He missed that. He missed Shea. She would be seventeen now if she were alive. "No use thinking on that now," he spoke to himself. "If we don't stop what is coming, there will be many more kids who won't see seventeen."

"Jimmy, come here! We need you for this!" It was Layla. He would fly if he could, just to get there sooner. Whatever it took to get to her, that's what he would do. He had never met anyone like this girl. She was smart, funny, lively, not to mention powerful and damn gorgeous, too! And the best of it all, she pretty much had waved the go signal in Jim's direction! If Emma hadn't walked in the room, she would have planted one right on him! That was ok, though. The anticipation and suspense of what was going to happen next and when that might be was intoxicating! It was like Christmas! The waiting and waiting for Christmas day, the staying up all night imagining what would be under the tree in the morning and desperately trying to make time speed up so you could open them now! That's what it was like for him. The waiting was Christmas and she was the present. He stopped and pondered the idea of Layla being a gift, and that led to her being a wrapped gift and of course that led to her wearing nothing but a large bow, and then that obviously led to unwrapping and a nude Layla. It seemed another bathroom break was imminent, when once again she called for him to make himself present, but this time it was not so pleasant.

~~~~~

"Stop fanning around and get your arse in here!"

Jimmy moved himself from his spontaneous daydream and hurried to the office behind the cash counter.

"Did you get lost, Jimbo? Or did you spuriously decide to catch up on some light reading?" she teased.

"Well, I won't be taking that bathroom break now," he mumbled.

"What was that?" she asked. Emma had heard it and, slack jawed, snorted and covered her mouth in an attempt to stop her laughter. Jimmy looked at her sternly.

"You two are barmy. You know that?" Layla tried to accuse, but to no avail; the twins had no idea what she was saying. Layla placed the *Wonder Woman* comic on the large desk in front of her and the silver key next to it. "Ok, *Wonder Twins,* activate!" she commanded. The siblings looked at her in dismayed confusion.

"Wonder what what?" Emma asked.

"You know, the superhero brother and sister twins, with the rings and the *'Wonder Twins Activate'* and then there was morphing. Oh come on! You two prats can yammer on about *Star Trek* and various other geeky prerequisites, but I can't make one comment about an actually popular children's Saturday morning series? And you two don't even know what I am talking about?"

"Layla, we NEVER know what you are talking about!" Emma clarified.

"It's not my fault you people don't understand proper English in this country! Now, belt up so we can suss this out."

Emma plopped down in the oversized leather desk chair and looked down at the comic.

"Ok, we touched the key to it and then we both were touching the book right?" Emma asked aloud. Jimmy reached for it; just as she was holding it she quickly yanked her hands away. "Alright can we wait until we know exactly what to do, because I really don't want my head to implode this time?" Jimmy retrieved his hand as well and they both looked at Layla.

"Well I'm not going to touch it." Layla pondered for a moment. "Normally, when working with templates, it already has the information stored; it's just a matter of calling it up. But this is very different. Hmm, maybe, maybe when you two opened it earlier, it simply had nowhere else to go, so it tried to transfer to you directly. And the reason you were able to spit out facts about this Blood Goddess is because that is what was on your mind when you opened it. So this time, when you open it, it should be able to automatically transfer to its original destination." Layla folded her arms, pleased with herself.

"Well, that's just great, Layla. Very astute. But where exactly are we to FIND the original destination?" Emma sassed.

Layla rolled her eyes. "I swear, Slayers! Don't you remember? I said that the whole shop could be the template! You could very well pick up any book and be able to call up whatever it is you are looking for!"

"Alright, then let's give this another try. If my head goes wonky again, then you better be sure that you can get your ass back to the other side of the pond, 'cause I'll kill you!" Emma threatened.

Layla rolled her eyes.

Jimmy squatted near his sister and together they placed their hands on the comic and held the key in the other. They all three braced themselves, but this time the book simply glowed and then returned to normal. Jimmy slowly opened one of his clenched eyes and peeked around. Emma did the same and then just opened them completely and relaxed.

"Did it work?" she asked

"I don't know," answered Layla as she looked around. "It's your shop, so you see anything different?" Jimmy stood up and walked into the main shop.

"Well, you said that we should be able to just grab a book." He walked over to the first shelf and selected a copy of *The Odyssey* and opened it. "The Slayer Legacy," he commanded. "That's simple enough, right?" he asked the on-looking girls. Nothing happened. He shut the book and held it up.

"It didn't work," he grumbled. "What am I supposed to say, PLEASE?!" Emma walked over to him, took the book and inspected it. Jimmy looked to his left in frustration, when something caught his eye. Way in the back of the store, he saw a cabinet. He had never seen this cabinet before.

"Emma, look. What's that?" He pointed at a tall mahogany armoire. She looked up and squinted her eyes.

"I don't know. I've never seen that before." They all three walked to the back and stood before the new furniture piece.

"Open it dammit! I hate suspense!" Layla had clenched her fists and was absolutely alive with anticipation.

Emma was the first to try it out. She reached forward and turned the tarnished metal knobs and the doors creaked open. There, by itself, was a large leather-bound book. It looked as if it were four inches thick at least! Emma had to use both hands to lift it out of the shelf. She opened it and allowed it to lie across her forearms. All the pages were pure, pristine, white, and completely blank.

"Now what?" Emma asked Layla.

"Ask for something!" she instructed anxiously.

"Inanna, the Blood Goddess." Emma spoke the words clearly and precisely. Immediately, the pages began to fill, line after line. The twins' eyes grew with amazement. Layla simply smiled.

"I told you! There is your template!"

Chapter Eleven

So Much for Super Nerves

The night air smelled like campfires. That hint of woody smoke and fresh air. The wind was cool on her face. She was regretting that she had worn her old jean jacket; she could have enjoyed this cool weather a little more. She looked up and shook her head, making her ponytail flop from her collar and fall down her back. Not a cloud in the sky was there to block the magnificently large, bright moon and billions of twinkling stars.

"I guess that's one of the good things about living out here," she said aloud to herself. "You can always see the stars."

She pulled her hands from her pockets and played with the swaying ponytail. The sound of her black leather boots hitting and scooting on the broken pavement was all to be heard. Pebbles that had been kicked aside by her steps echoed tiny, bouncing dribbles from the sides of the derelict sheds and garages. She was alone.

Emma needed this right now. She needed the clarity that only the quiet night could give. It gave her time to think about the events that had taken place over the past few days. But it also gave her inner demon's voice a chance to torment her without interruption.

"Come on, there has to be some vicious blood sucker out here tonight! I need to kill something!"

She continued down the next dark and forbidding alley, hoping for someone to take the bait and jump out at her. She reached down and smoothed her hand over her exposed right plastic shin. "Thank God for culottes! Stylish and functional!" she mused. Jimmy had had enough time to make some quick repairs to her "bionic" leg. Right now he and Layla were taking notes at the book shop from the newly discovered template. Emma's head still ached from their first attempt to retrieve the family knowledge last night. It was easily the most painful experience of her life. It was worse than when the vamp ripped her foot away from her leg!

So far, they at least had an idea of what Naberius had been planning to tip the scales in his favor. He planned to raise up some sort of "Super Vampire." Emma considered it to be their answer to a Slayer. But the only thing they could find to stop it was some gibberish about an arm being severed. Had he done it already? Is that why she was having so much trouble finding something to kill tonight? They were all busy? Or is it this Goddess had scared them all off?

"Speaking of Goddesses, what in the hell happened to our oh so very helpful helper, Aslyn? Thought it was her business to know who was doing what to the balance!"

Emma seemed to talk to herself more and more these days. She thought as long as she didn't answer herself, then it was ok. She walked on. Her thoughts started to drift toward her brother doing research alone with Layla. They seemed to be getting along better and better. This made Emma nervous. Or was it jealous? It was most likely both. She was afraid of Jimmy falling in deep with the exotic mystic and then leaving her alone. And this is what made her jealous. He would have someone, and Emma would be alone. These thoughts made tears well up in her eyes. She was so lonely. She had her brother and now Layla. But it wasn't the same. She went back to earlier today when she saw the couples walking happily together through downtown. When would that happen for her? Would it ever?

"It's not fair!" she mumbled.

You are such a child! the inner voice accused. *So selfish! That's all you worry about. "It isn't fair!"* it mocked. *Why can't you just shut up and get on with your life! Nothing is ever fair! You take what you get, sometimes you luck out and sometimes you get dumped on. Either way grown-ups learn to deal with it! So stop your whining and grow up! You should be happy for your brother! And you should encourage him! Did you really think that you two would be living in the same house forever? HA! Not only is that beyond being a ridiculous notion, it's crazy to think that anyone would want to stay with you in the same house for more than a week, let alone a lifetime!*

"GOD SHUT UP! Stop it! Why can't you just stop?" she cried to herself. She stopped to wipe her face with her jacket sleeve and scold herself for being such a baby. Then, she heard it, the distinctive growl of a vamp about to pounce. She faced forward and shoved her right arm, palm facing out, out in front of her just in time to knock the quickly approaching beast backward.

"It's about damn time!" she announced. She took her stance as he leapt to his feet and began his attack again. This time she kicked with her right leg straight up, connecting with his chin and forcing him to stagger while splattering blood from his mouth all over the both of them. She immediately spun around and clocked him with the outside of her right foot on the right side of his face. He struggled to get balance and she went to give a nice left crossover, but he grabbed her fist and hit her with his own right fist. This only fueled her anger and she smiled as she head-butted him. But he still clasped her left fist tight. She stamped her right foot on the ball and the hidden dagger came jutting from the toe of her boot. She swung her leg upward and swung it right into his groin. He finally let go and dropped to the ground.

"Sneaky Bitch!" He howled in pain.

"Like there was anything there to actually do any damage!" she taunted, as the dagger slipped back into its position and she kicked him with her left leg right across the face. He lay on the busted black and gray pavement, clutching his shredded manhood. Emma's heart was racing! She was feeling much better now. Slaying always put things into perspective. She knew what her place in the world was when she was pummeling the undead.

"Oh come on. Get up; I have more issues to work out." She rolled her eyes and squatted next to him. She pressed down on her right heel and the stake popped up for her to catch. She spun it in her hand and placed it right at his heart. His eyes opened wide as he awaited his fate. "Tell me where all your little friends have been?"

"I don't know what you're talking about," he grumbled

"Come on now, we're buddies! You can tell me!" He looked at the tiny slayer very perplexed.

"What?"

"It's share time, tell me where Naberius plans to raise the Inanna and I will consider allowing you to continue on with your pathetic existence."

"Uh, really?" asked the thoroughly confused and beaten vampire.

"Really, now, tell me. Where's Big Gray going to do the ritual so I can stop it."

The vamp laughed and then grabbed his destroyed gonads and moaned.

"You don't know!" he taunted.

"What don't I know?" she asked, becoming angry with his teasing.

"Naberius, he already called her up! HA! Last night! The sacrificial host was taken over by The Blood Goddess last night! Ha ha! You're too late!" He continued to laugh and cough.

Emma pushed the stake slightly into his skin. His eyes grew wide with terror. She gritted her teeth and flared her nostrils in fury.

"Tell me now, where they are and who the host was; tell me what I am looking for. NOW!"

The bloody vamp scrambled for words as the wild-eyed Slayer eased the stake slower and slower into his breast. "The FARM, the Farm, ok! The one just outside of town, the abandoned one. The one with the big gray barn. That's where they did it. I don't know if they're there anymore, though. I heard that the Goddess was displeased with it and wanted something fancy and shit."

"Who?! Who was the host? What do they look like?" Emma demanded.

"Uh uh, Nitro, Nero, Nike, Nica! That's it, she calls herself Nica! She's got black hair and..." Emma interrupted him before he could finish his description. She dropped him, stood up and stared down the alley.

"I know what she looks like," she said simply.

The terrified and agonizing vampire began to crawl to his knees and attempt to stand. "So are you going to let me go now? Can I go?"

"Sure," she said without looking at him. "I'll let you walk."

"Thanks!" He quivered as he walked past her and started up the alley. After he had made it about ten feet, Emma tossed her stake in the air, whipped around, caught it and hurled it at the limping vampire, lodging it into his back, his heart. He dropped into ashes onto the pavement. Emma made her way up to the pile and retrieved her stake and placed it back into its compartment.

"I said you could walk, didn't say anything about living." She kicked the dust with her foot and turned around to walk down the next alley.

She was stopped abruptly by the presence of another.

"I should know that your kind travels in packs." She looked up to find a face she recognized but couldn't quite place from where. He was tall, handsome and had brown wavy hair. He wore a sharp gray suit and fine leather shoes. He pulled the cigarette from between his lips and flicked it away. He smiled and seemed to study her intently.

"Such cruelty," his voice sang out with a rich and seductive accent. Italian. That's what it was. "I enjoyed your display quite thoroughly. You thrashed him with such—gusto." He grinned, allowing his eye teeth to show through a bit. He slid his hands into his pants pockets and rocked back on his heels, presenting himself in a casual manner. But the light from the street lamp that shown down on him cast menacing shadows across his face and she knew that he was not to be taken lightly.

Emma stood completely still, her brow knitted and her fists tight. She stepped backward with her right leg and prepared to twist the ball of her foot to unleash the spikes Jimmy had rigged it with. The smooth vampire pulled his hands from his pockets and waved them critically in front of him. His expression changed to disapproval and he voiced his position.

"No, no, no, caro, you are not ready yet." He leaned toward her and took in her scent. "You are close, but I think you need some more time to marinate in your despair before you will be ripe enough. Slayers are an exquisite delicacy as it is, but when you find one as dejected and as mentally unsound as you, well then, you have something truly exceptional. And you, mia caro, are one troubled little lady and shall prove to be an excellent meal worthy of my patience." He took a few steps back and snickered.

Emma relaxed and folded her arms. "Then, why tell me? Why show yourself to me now and let me know that you are waiting for me to ripen? What if I decide to stop 'marinating'? It would ruin your ultimate meal," she mocked.

"Trust me; you are too far into your desolation to ever come back out. First, you will alienate those who love you, and then comes the self pity, and then, Oooo then, your self destruction will culminate and explode all over! What the explosion will be is different for each one. I can't wait to see what yours will be!" He was almost giddy. But Emma felt that he was hiding something. That he was keeping her from something.

"Why are you hiding something? What is it? Is it about Nica? You know where she is, don't you? You know I'm getting close so you're trying to distract me!" The suave Italian vamp raised his arms and shrugged.

"Think what you like, Ms. Hogan. But I just wanted to introduce myself."

"You've hardly done that."

"Scusarme, signora. I am Leonardo De Luca. I am the one who will be feasting on you soon enough." He bowed before her. Then, he turned his back to her and disappeared into the shadows of the alley.

Emma continued to stand in her spot and watch down the alley even though he was long gone and had been for several minutes. She suddenly became aware that she was shaking. It wasn't that she was cold; she was afraid. The vampire with the expensive shoes had terrified her. And she was pretty sure he knew that. He knew her very well; knew about her self loathing and desperation. There was something about him; something familiar and unsettling. He said he was patient. That scared her more than anything. There was nothing worse than a mad, blood-thirsty killer, who was patient. It was easy to kill the random thirst-driven vamps that normally were found while on patrol. For the most part they didn't know anything about her. But if one was patient, took their time and studied her, that made her worry. That meant she needed to be more alert. Maybe there was something Layla could do, maybe a little hocus pocus and, poof, instant force field, or something else equally as sci-fi. Either way, she needed to get back to the book shop, but she needed to make sure she wasn't followed. So she stood right where she was and used her heightened senses to take in the night.

She closed her eyes and listened carefully. At first, it was only a dog barking a few houses down, then there were the tree frogs, then dishes clattering in someone's kitchen, and somewhere someone was watching *The Tonight Show*. But no evil undead stalking the streets of the living. She reached out with her being to see if her sixth sense could tell her anything. But everything told her that he was gone. She opened her eyes and scoped out the area. Once more, nothing. At first this was a comforting conclusion, but then came a thought. Maybe he wasn't going to follow her, because he didn't need to. It was now occurring to her, that since he knew so much about her, maybe he had already followed her home before. She tried pushing the thought from her mind, telling herself that it was preposterous. But the churning in her stomach told her that her assumption was right. He knew too much. He knew her last name! Well, at least she knew his now. Leonardo De Luca. It sounded so regal.

Emma pulled her black rubberband from her soft, wavy hair and ran her fingers through it. With the band in her right hand, she smoothed her hair with the other into a high ponytail and replaced the band. She adjusted her jacket and dusted her sleeves to remove what she could of the deceased vamp's dust.

This was all becoming too much for her. Too much was happening too fast. One day she thought she was it between the world and the forces of darkness, and all she thought that was, was a couple of vamps a night. Then the next day it turns out there was a whole world of oogidy boogidies that needed taken care of and she wasn't the only one anymore. There were hundreds of Slayers scattered around the globe.

But they are the ones who got the training and group support apparently. Not Emma and Jimmy, Missouri wasn't on the mystical radar of the Super Slayer Squad. All the Hogans had was a smart ass, know-it-all British chick, who had Abgal Da for parents, which as they were to discover, so were their parents. On top of all these revelations, the fact that all of these Slayers existed together had caused some sort of disturbance in the force. Too much good. How could that be? How could there be too much good? And now some crazy Demon guy has raised a vampire Goddess to tilt this out-of-whack balance to his advantage! How was anyone supposed to deal with all of this at once and be expected to save the world?

"God is definitely a man," Emma grumbled. She reached up to rub her eye and realized that another tear had fallen. Another voice told her not to worry, that it was the stress, it gets to everyone. But Emma just rolled her eyes and huffed.

"Some superhero I am. I can't even handle the threat of nonexistence." She turned around and started to run. She needed to make it to the book shop to tell the others about the events of tonight's patrol.

CHAPTER TWELVE

Revelations

She wrote furiously in her notebook. She wanted to make sure she got it all. It was a pain in the wrist, but after discovering that they couldn't leave the shop with the template or Xerox its pages, this was all they could do. Jimmy had asked her if there was some sort of mojo she could do, but she explained to him that this book was mojo protected. If she tried even a simple copying spell, the magics protecting it might put her into a coma.

Jimmy stood leaning against a wall on the other end of the room. He was flipping through one of the books that Layla had brought with her. It was all about the art of magical and mechanical weaponry. She didn't think he really understood Gaelic, so she was pretty sure he was looking at the pictures. He said he was looking for new ideas that might help them out. Not only to add to Emma's arsenal, but a little something that he could use to protect himself. Every once in a while she would catch him staring at her and he would quickly look back down at the book and clear his throat. She would just smile and bite her lip. She was quite taken by him she had decided. He was smart, handsome, witty, and very caring. She figured she would allow herself to indulge in this.

She looked back down at the large book and continued on writing.

"*She is raised from purity. When called, the essence of The Black Goddess will entwine and fuse itself with the soul of the host; never allowing it to crossover.*"

"Poor bastard," she muttered.

"Her immense hunger can never be satisfied. It burns within her, a constant need to feed on human life and satisfy her unending thirst. This continuous torture fuels her lust for cruelty; she acts out her arduous inner pain on the ones from which she feeds. It is not just their lives she takes, but their souls."

Layla sat up from the book in shock. She had never heard such a thing. No wonder things had been quite in the ether surrounding her senses lately. She placed her left hand to her forehead and closed her eyes. "How?" She continued to transcribe.

"*In an attempt to fill her dark emptiness, she devours their souls as she drains from them their life's blood. The more souls she takes, the more powerful she becomes. Thus giving her the name Inanna, the eater of souls.*"

"This is not sounding good," she grumbled out loud. Jimmy looked up from his magical weaponry manual and walked over to the perplexed witch across the room.

"What did you find?"

"Give me a moment. Because at this point, I don't think you want to know." She read on.

"*Her existence here is only temporary.*"

"OH thanks to the Goddess!" she exclaimed. As she wrote down the information, she saw that there was more and her relief may have been premature.

"*However, as her power derives from the souls she ingests, all she needs is a soul of a warrior of the people to have enough strength to hold herself to this plane permanently. Once she has accomplished this, she will begin sharing her dark blood with others. She and her children will then infest the Earth and, with their massive thirst, consume the human race.*"

"Oh balls," she said exhaustedly. "If Naberius thinks he can control this thing, he's a blooming idiot."

"WHAT?!" Jimmy demanded.

"Read for yourself." She rose from her seat and allowed Jimmy to take her place and read the passages she had just transcribed.

"How in the hell are we supposed to stop this?! It says here that ordinary means of defeating the undead are useless! It says, 'she will not perish by the light of day. Holy icons and artifacts do not affect her, and no stake can render her to dust.' So what then? Does this mean she is unstoppable and that there's nothing we can do?" He stood up and paced with his arms folded, deep in thought.

Layla turned the great book in her direction and turned the page. She ran her fingers over a black and white rendering of a statue of a woman with her arms outstretched. In one hand was a spear and in another a goblet. It was the effigy of the Inanna. There was a caption underneath it.

"The Black Effigy contains the black blood, which calls the essence of the Inanna to the Host."

Layla's eyes followed her finger to the right of the depiction and read the paragraph.

"It is the source of the Inanna's invulnerability. Only by destroying this will she be destroyed."

"Wait! Here it is! We have to find this statue! It's the key. It gives her life, it can take it away! All we need to do is find it and destroy it!" Layla exclaimed. She held her hands together and rung them. Jimmy stopped and walked back to the table to inspect the picture himself.

Layla began swatting the air and muttering. Jimmy looked at her absurdly.

"Then what? We destroy the effigy and she falls down dead? How does this work?"

Layla continued to push some invisible thing away, looking more and more frustrated. "I'm not sure! But it clearly says 'only by destroying this will she be destroyed.' Maybe it means she goes poof, or maybe it means it renders her a normal vampire. Either way, we need to get our hands on this thing and quickly. Oh bloody hell! Will you bugger off?"

"Who are you talking to?" Jimmy asked her.

"It's some loon who keeps poking at me, wondering if I'm real or not just because I can see them. I'm just going to ignore him if he keeps it up." She brushed her hair out of her face and leaned on the table.

"And what about this business about her needing the soul of the warrior of the people to stay here? What does that mean?" Jimmy threw his arms up in the air.

"Warrior of the People is another name for Slayer. She needs the soul of a Slayer to be strong enough to anchor herself to her host, and stay in this realm. A Slayer's soul is the most potent, the only one strong enough to sustain her."

"You mean, she needs Emma."

"That's precisely what she means," came the voice from their left. "So, why am I here?" Layla and Jimmy turned their heads to see who the voice belonged to. There she stood, elegant and statuesque. Her short black hair was cut in a blunt bob and it shined as the light reflected off of it. Her eyes were lined with black in an almost Egyptian way, making them look larger and her lashes more pronounced. Her full, pouty lips were turned up in a wicked smile, allowing her prominent eye teeth to show. She wore a red satin corset that pressed her breasts up high, almost to her collar bone. Her black velvet frock coat hid her porcelain shoulders but remained unbuttoned to reveal her navel. Her right hand rested casually on her leather-clad hip. The leather pants were so tight they left little to the imagination. Her pointed-toe, high-heeled black leather boots clacked against the stone floor as she made her way down the stairs toward the pair. A man appeared through the door of the shop. He was well dressed in a gray suit and leather shoes. He took a long drag from his self-rolled cigarette and flicked the ashes into the air.

"Uh there's no smoking in here, sorry. Guess you'll have to go outside!" Jimmy laughed uneasily.

"Scusarme, il mio amico." He subsequently flicked his cigarette to the floor and crushed it under his fine leather dress shoes.

Layla stood close to Jimmy and spoke to him telepathically. "It's her."

She pushed Jimmy behind her and outstretched her arms at her sides. "Na'aki Makikio Amen Nukti Ra!" A yellow light began to grow from her hands, creating an arch. She clapped her hands above her head and then pushed them before her with all her strength as if she were pushing a lead weight. With that, the arched light became a huge ball that flashed before them and created a wall between them and the intruders. Layla held her hands, palms facing outward, to hold up her mystical shield.

"Wow," Jimmy said quietly in amazement.

"Oh please," said Nica as she rolled her eyes and finished down the last step. She closed the distance between her and the glimmering golden wall. The threw her arms up in sarcastic fear and made an Oooo face. She cracked her fingers and waved her hands in front of the wall.

"Wax on, Wax off!" She dropped her hands to her sides, tilted her head and smiled shyly. Suddenly, her face changed dramatically to anger and she swung her right fist through the transparent wall. The shop shook as the shield crackled and ripped apart then disappeared.

The force of the blow shot Layla, who had been holding up the shield, sliding her on her back across the floor. Jimmy ran to her side and helped her up. When she was back on her feet and had dusted herself off, she held her right hand up by her right ear in a claw.

"Totlah Kum!" As she finished the incantation, a blue ball of flame ignited in her hand and she instantly hurled it at the raven-haired she-devil.

But in surprise to them both, Nica caught the ball and held it in her hand as she studied it.

"Nice. Not bad at all, sweetie. But unfortunately for you, futile." She held it up with her palm flat and blew at it, making it vanish as if it were never there.

Layla was dumbstruck and decided not to squander any more energy on this. She reached out for Jimmy's hand, clasped it and they took several steps back. A sharp click broke the silence. It was the man in the front of the shop; he had lit another self-rolled cigarette. He took a deep drag and blew it out in a soft gray cloud covering his etched features.

"Sorry, nasty habit I know. But what are you going to do, eh?" The man walked closer to Nica and continued smoking his cigarette.

"So, you know who I am, and what I am looking for, so once again what am I doing here?" Nica demanded.

"Uh, is this a trick question we are supposed to answer or should we just be awestruck by your commanding presence?" Jimmy quipped.

Nica laughed and then licked her teeth. "You're cute." She breathed deep into her nostrils and closed her eyes. "If you are a witch and you are a man, why do I smell a Slayer? Don't get me wrong, I'm still going to eat you; and you, witch, your soul will really be a boost. But it's the Slayer I need. And I can smell that soul as if it were saturating this place. So tell me, why have I followed my nose here, if the Slayer is not?"

"You can smell souls? What's that like?" Layla asked honestly.

"Like Pine Sol." As soon as Nica answered she closed her eyes and began smelling the air again. Jimmy took the opportunity to feel around behind him and grab a large stake from the table. He hurled the stake, but as soon as it had left his fingertips, Nica was there and had caught it millimeters from its launch point and grasped Jimmy's hand. Jimmy almost wet himself. They couldn't believe how fast she had closed the distance between them. She took the stake in her other hand and slammed it into Jimmy's left shoulder. He howled in pain as the blood ran down his back left side. Layla jumped in shock at seeing Jimmy hurt so badly.

Nica continued to grasp his right hand in her left. She studied him, perplexed for a moment, and then it became blaringly clear.

Layla held her right hand down low at her side and twiddled her fingers as she mumbled low to herself. Nica swung her head in her direction sharply and spat.

"Don't even try it, witchy. You know it won't work. It'll just irritate me. And I really don't want you to ruin this moment for me. Because I know why I came here. I know why I smell a Slayer's soul. This is something that has never happened before, do you know that?" She smiled wildly at the clarity. She brought her face closer to Jimmy's and studied him closely. His face was pure white and sweat glistened on his forehead and cheeks. She pressed into his face and kissed his right cheek, leaving a bright red lip print.

"There has never been, in the entire line of Slayers, a twin of a Slayer! You have the soul of Slayer! Isn't that funny?" She chuckled in delight. "But you don't have the cool super powers 'cause you're a man!" She laughed heartily. "That's just a hoot! I bet that just eats you up inside, don't it? Just nips that little pecker of yours right off! I bet it does. Watching her day in and day out, so much stronger and more powerful than you. She's the one who stalks and kills while you do what? Do you stay home and cook and clean?" She laughed more, right in his face.

"Nah, I make cool shit!" And with that he brought his left arm up, painfully, and slapped her neck with his stainless steel watch, delivering a pill-sized explosive into her jugular. Before she could scratch, it exploded, releasing Jimmy from her grip and knocking him and Layla into the bookshelves behind them.

When the smoke settled, Leo staggered and coughed his way through the debris to get to Nica. Before he could reach her she jumped up out of nowhere, holding her neck and flailing around. Her clothes on her entire right side were charred and torn.

"Mother Fucker! That little bastard! I am going to torture him extra painfully for that! This is going to itch for at least a week! And look at my clothes! This shit is expensive! Do you know how hard it is to find good shit down here in the sticks! They don't sell this at Wal-Mart! AHHHHH!" She howled deafeningly; it shook the shop and more books fell from the shelves and broke glass from doors and various décor. Leo sniffed out Jimmy's blood and silently signaled Nica in the direction he was in. They stalked ten feet forward to a toppled shelf and a pile of books. Nica reached down with her right hand and lifted Jimmy up by his foot, allowing his head to graze the floor. She grabbed his opposite shoulder with her left hand and tilted him upward. He was unconscious, so she grabbed the stake still sticking in his shoulder and twisted. He cried out and shot awake.

"You listen to me, you little shit, I don't care what you've cooked up, all you're going to do is piss me off, and trust me, you don't want that. You're coming with me, and come sunset tomorrow, your essence is mine! But so you won't be lonely, I'm going to leave a calling card for sister dear. Why have one Slayer soul when you can have the matching set!" She flicked him in between the eyes and he immediately was knocked back unconscious. She looked back at Leo and grinned. She dropped Jimmy and pulled Leo to her. "Leave her a message that you know she will get; have fun, handsome. But we need to go so make it quick." They kissed intensely and she retrieved the sleeping, bleeding Jimmy and sashayed from the building.

Leo bent down and shifted the books that covered Layla. She was also comatose. He placed his freshlyl-it cigarette between his teeth so he could use both hand to rip her shirt apart, exposing a white satin bra and an elegantly-sculpted tummy. He took his smoke back out of his teeth and held it in his fingers. "Like a blank canvas," he mused. He leaned down and kissed it gently, and slowly rolled his face over it, feeling its softness and its firmness. He licked it lustfully as he brought his head back up. He searched around and found a broken piece of glass under a broken wall sconce. "Now, this is going to hurt." He put the pointed end of the shard to her stomach and started carving.

Layla awoke with a scream. Leo forced her head back down with his other hand on her forehead. She cried pitifully and screamed more and more as he continued on.

"Now, now, you don't have to do that just for me. There, all finished. And I must say, my penmanship is tops! Now, you just relax, I'm not going to kill you yet. We need your new friend to get this message. So try not to move too much or you'll bleed to death."

Layla's eyes rolled back and sobbed deeply.

"Hey, you should feel flattered! If you were just anyone I wouldn't care if you bled to death. But you, you are exquisite! You are beautiful, and your body is so supple and fresh. And I haven't had Indian in quite a while. You can imagine how difficult it would be finding any here in the middle of nowhere. And I think you will have just the right amount of spice to tickle the senses! Am I right? I can wait for such a dish as you. Now you just stay put, mia caro. I will see you soon." He leaned close and kissed her quivering lips. He then rose and walked away, shutting the front door carefully as he left.

Layla cried out and sobbed profoundly. The blood from her stomach poured down her sides and onto her hands, so when she lifted her hand to place it on her face, she pulled it back in disgust when she realized she now had her blood all over her face.

"I'm sorry, Jimmy! I'm sorry!" she cried. "Where the hell are you? What kind of Goddess are you? You leave me when I need you! You're never around when you are really needed!" she screamed.

"If you keep that up you will bleed to death, Layla." It was Aslyn, late as usual. She stood over her in all her glory, glowing and blue.

She knelt down next to Layla and placed a hand on her forehead.

"I tried to warn you. But you never listen. I told you not to interfere with that book and you did anyway. And now, humanity is going to be wiped out because you have a soft spot for tall white boys."

Layla looked up at her patron deity in horror. "Are you saying I should not have helped them? That I should have let them suffer from that knowledge growing in their brains and then die?"

"You read for yourself in that book! The Inanna has a limited amount of time on this Earth if she doesn't take hostage the souls of a Slayer! If those two would have died, she wouldn't have had time to seek out another! And now, now she has one twin and that's all she really needs, but we know that Emma will go and try to rescue her brother, so then that devil will have two! And do you know what that means, Layla? She will start to populate the Earth with her own pedigree of vampire. Never satisfied and unstoppable. And there you have it! The balance of reality is permanently tipped!"

Layla sniffled. "And you cease to exist. That's what this is all really about isn't it? You. It's all about you. You're afraid of death. You don't care about what happens to anyone else really, or who gets hurt or killed in the process. You only care about you."

"And what is wrong with self preservation?"

"Nothing, as long as you don't purposefully cause the death of innocent people in that course of action!" Layla schooled. She glared at Aslyn. What once she revered, she now reviled.

"You are so simple and weak-minded. You could never understand the mind of a Goddess."

"Oh I understand perfectly. The years have twisted you, Aslyn. You are a Goddess gone mad! You've completely lost sight of those you were breathed into existence to protect and care for!" Layla spit in the glowing entity's face. Aslyn became infuriated and her aura quickly changed to red.

"You little fool! You think you know so much! You think you have the importance enough to insult me! You are VERMIN! All of you! I have spent eternity keeping you primates in check! Still, you never learn! You always throw the universe right back out of whack! You're right, I am tired. I am tired of babysitting such loathsome, unworthy, bumbling, unappreciative creatures. What exactly is a child like you going to do about it?"

Layla bit her lip and smiled. "Pray." She then hardened her face and began her prayer, all the while Aslyn screamed in protest. "Oh, great Ra, giver of light, your child has fallen from your sight. She has turned her back on your great will. Take this fallen one from us, I plead with you still!" Layla repeated her prayer over and over. Aslyn stood and looked up. Layla prayed louder.

"You have no idea what you have done! They should have died! You know I am right! How is it your place to judge me? I AM THE JUDGE! I am The Judge!"

Layla continued the prayer and closed her eyes. She reached to her chest and clutched a tiny gold amulet of an Egyptian hieroglyph depicting the sun god Ra.

Aslyn tried to fade out and away from Layla's pleading, but to no avail. Her face began to fill with fear as the room filled with white light. Layla opened her eyes to see light streaming from a portal that had opened just below the ceiling. She slowly trailed off as she watched Aslyn cower in fear. Her body began to stretch upward as she tried to hold herself to her spot. Her efforts were unsuccessful as she was sucked entirely into the portal. As soon as Aslyn was gone, the portal closed and everything went quiet and dark.

Layla let her head fall back against the pile of books she lay on…and sobbed on. She felt betrayed by the one thing she had closest to family in this world. She had been betrayed by her Goddess! She felt sick. She had placed them all in danger just by arriving in Walnut Grove.

"I should have stayed in Indiana!" she moaned. She stopped and thought for a moment. "No, it's not that bad of a situation." When she tried to sit up, she painfully remembered that she had been sliced open along her abdomen. She cried from the pain and from the agony of being used as a pawn and deceived. And she cried for Jimmy. She had lost him just as she had found him. Her heart was broken before she could even give it away. She wept for him. She had let him down. And if bleeding out didn't kill her here and now, she was sure that Emma would.

Chapter Thirteen

Who Needs a Hug?

She ran faster. She didn't think that it would take so long to get anywhere in this town. The blister she had developed on her inner thigh, just above her right knee where the top of her prosthetic leg met her flesh, was tearing open and blood was running down her stub of a leg and pooling in the bottom. The pain was burning and sharp, but it was easy to push away. Something was very wrong and she knew Jimmy needed her desperately.

Emma could feel him calling for her in the back of her mind. She had been jogging toward the book shop when it happened. Emma had already been nervous about the smooth vamp Leo knowing all about her, but shortly after she took off, it overcame her senses. She felt a throbbing pain in her left shoulder, the back of her head felt like it had been bounced off of a tile floor; her skin felt hot and singed and she could taste the salt of fear in the back of her throat. Her heart broke as she knew that these were all things Jimmy was feeling first hand.

The book shop, yes the book shop. She had run as fast as she could and that's when the hard, rough surface of the curve of her fake leg tore into her fragile flesh. She hadn't even allowed herself to react to the shot of pain. This sort of thing happened all the time to Emma. In fact, that particular section of her inner thigh just above her knee, had turned into a brownish, grey, and bumpy callous that was a constant irritation. She could see it now, in two days time, she would have a nasty, pussing blister that would require several days of ointments, fresh air, and rest. It's what every doctor recommended to her every time. She would raise her objections, but her arguments were always lacking. It's not like she could outright say she was the only Slayer in this midwestern area and rest wasn't exactly a possibility.

She was downtown now, passing the abandoned beauty school where they had dusted the vamps weeks earlier. The moon was large and full and shown down onto the street of the business district she ran fiercely through. In her peripheral vision she caught the various businesses and cafés she flew past. Jurgon's Drug and Dime, Walnut Grove Thrift, The Grove Four Theater, Special Occasions Dress Shop and Ed's Bait and Tackle. Emma thought to herself that only in a small southeast Missouri town would you have a bait and tackle next to a movie theater and a dress shop.

"Just a few more blocks," she coached herself out loud. She was scared for Jimmy and worried that her traitor limb would soon give out. This was bad. The feeling in the pit of her stomach was worsening because Jimmy's voice in her mind was weakening. She gritted her teeth and her feet pounded the pavement harder. She could see the light from the shop coming through the windows and bouncing off the dark and empty street. A sort of relief, albeit small in regard to her task at hand, came over limbs as she realized that soon she wouldn't have to push anymore. All she could see now was the door to her family shop; everything else just fell away. What once she saw as a commercial hub, crammed with one- to three-story brick buildings standing wall to wall, was now just a black tunnel, her small shop with its wooden, green and hand-painted sign swinging as if beckoning her to hurry.

Emma felt a crack in the bottom of her plastic foot but kept going; she didn't have time for this now. The distance became shorter until— she was there.

She swung open the dark wooden door and thrust herself in, breathing heavily. She almost lost the breath she was gasping to keep. Shelves were toppled over, light fixtures were shattered, and the ceiling, floors and walls in the back of the store were charred. Books covered the floor and a trail of blood led from the door where she stood to the burned portion of the shop. She slowly made her way, shaken, down the steps and followed the trail. She could tell that someone had been carried out by the fact that there was a lot of blood, but no footprints. And the sizes of the droplets were small and slightly elongated, indicating to her that they were moving fast. When she got closer to the now blackened back section that once housed their "world history and you" books, "Never a popular seller," Emma commented, she noticed something out of the corner of her eye to her left. A tan and bare foot stuck out from under a pile of books and another toppled shelf. Emma ran and quickly lifted the shelf and tossed it aside. She continued to throw all of the books covering her to the side. She kept digging, the books that were at the bottom of the pile covering whom she realized could only be Layla, were spattered and then covered in blood.

"Oh no." Emma winced. She carefully spread the books out of the way, revealing Layla completely. Her body lay discarded and crumpled on more books. Blood was everywhere. Her shirt had been torn and her stomach glistened red. Her hands were stained and sticky and there was even a bloody handprint on her face. Her beautiful, silky raven hair was ratted and stuck with clumps of blood. Emma felt the tears well up in her eyes. No matter how much Layla annoyed her with her sarcastic quips and her constant need to voice her opinion, she knew that she cared for her brother and that meant a lot to Emma. Layla's hands were laying up by her head in such a manner that it looked like she had tried to protect herself from the falling books and shelf. Emma had never felt like such a failure as she had now. Even when her family had died, she was able to justify her actions; she wasn't a Slayer then. But now she was. And she had left them alone.

She reached forward and moved a strand of hair from off her face. Just as she did Layla's chest heaved and she took a shallow breath. Emma jumped back and smiled with joy.

"Layla! You're still alive!"

Layla's eyes fluttered and she looked at Emma. Tears appeared in her brown and black eyes and then rolled down into her ears. "Oh no, I'm still alive, and it's you."

Emma blinked and was totally confused by her statement. "You're delirious. Can you tell me what happened?"

"She was here, she was here."

"Who? Nica? The vamp Goddess?"

"Yeah, I tried, I tried, but nothing could touch her. She found a way, she took Jimmy. She wasn't alone." Layla flopped a hand to her stomach and Emma looked down. Through all the blood she could make out some deep cuts. "He left a message. It's a trap. All my fault, all my fault…" Layla trailed off and her eyes rolled to the back of her head. Emma snapped her fingers in front of her face to call her into focus.

"Hey, hey, stay with me, you did all you could. Let me call for help and get you to a hospital and you can tell me what you guys found out while I was patrolling."

Layla snapped her eyes back open and looked up at Emma. "No, you don't understand. Aslyn, she tricked me, she led me here to help you find that comic and let you open it." She breathed as deep as she could and gathered her strength to finish. "She wanted you to open it like you did the first time, with, with no template. She wanted to overload your brains and kill you."

"What?! What are you talking about?"

"She wanted you to die so Nica couldn't get to you, to take your soul. That's what she needs to stay here."

Emma stared at her, not wanting to accept what she was hearing.

"But Nica, she was looking for you, but she found Jimmy. Because you are twins he, too, has a Slayer's soul. So now she has him, and it's all my fault." She let her eyes roll back.

Emma's eyes grew large with fury and her face turned bright red. Her body temperature rose until she felt that the blood was boiling in her ears. Jimmy was all she had left! However, her anger wasn't only projected at the ailing Layla, it was also pointed at her. How could she allow this outsider to enter into their lives and cause harm to come to Jimmy?! "I knew we shouldn't have trusted you! I knew it! You listen to me, if anything happens to him, I will kill you! Do you hear me?! I will kill you!" She grabbed Layla by her shoulders and lifted her slightly from the pile of books and shook her a little. "That's why you aren't going to die on me now. You will live long enough to make sure he lives!"

Layla looked at her fearfully, breathing shallow. Emma reached into her pocket and pulled out a cell phone. She started to dial 911, when Layla began protesting.

"I can do it; I just need to build strength."

"You'll die before then." Emma thought for a minute. "You need strength, use mine."

"I can't; you'll need it to get Jimmy back."

"It's ok, it's like sperm. I'm always making more. So, what do you need me to do, do I chant or do a little dance or what?"

Layla shook her head a bit and reached for Emma's hands. She gripped them and closed her eyes. "Normally I would be able to do this slower, but because I am so weak, well, this might hurt a bit."

"Just do it. If you die and Jimmy does, too, I will drag your ass from the grave just to kill you all over again."

"Ok, here goes." Layla closed her eyes again and concentrated.

Suddenly, Emma felt like she had been plugged into a light socket. But this time instead of filling her, it was sucking it straight out of her and fast. Her head was thrown back, her eyes were wide open and her jaw was slacked. She would try to cry out but all she heard was a gulping noise every once in a while. Emma felt like her skin was being peeled off one layer at a time. Waves of red and orange light flashed before her. It looked like fire washing over her. Before she knew it, a very bloody Layla was hovering over her, shaking her. Everything was in a tunnel. Her vision and her hearing. Finally, everything came shockingly into focus.

"It worked. Are you ok?" Layla asked her delicately.

"Yeah, I think so. My head feels like I stuck it in a vice and my skin is on fire, but other than that I'm good." Emma slowly sat up and adjusted herself. When her head finally stopped spinning she lunged and gripped Layla by the throat. She tightened her lips and stared at her with fire in her eyes. If Aslyn knew what was happening the whole time and kept it to herself, then she would make her pay.

"Where is that loony bitch of a Goddess you worship or I will snap your neck." She grunted through her teeth.

"I thought you wanted me alive so if anything happened to Jimmy you could kill me." Layla gagged, gasping for air.

Emma pressed in with her fingertips on Layla's arteries. She wanted to make it clear that she was not the type to make empty threats. "Ok, then I will just paralyze you, tell me."

"She's gone. I banished her."

Emma let go. "Am I supposed to believe you now?"

Layla held her bruised neck gently. "Damn. This town has not been kind to my neck. Look, I swear to you I had no idea that I was being used. And when I found out I banished her."

"What the hell do you mean you banished her?"

"Ok, when little Goddesses have been naughty, what do you do? You tattle! I simply rang her daddy and told on her."

Emma blinked. "Um, ok. How exactly could it be that easy?"

Layla reached down with a blood-soaked hand and lifted the golden talisman that hung from her neck. "You see this? My daddy gave this to me when I was a little girl. You know when Catholic girls turn a certain age they have their Confirmation where they choose a patron saint? Well, I guess 'little witches' have something similar. When I chose the path I wanted to follow, my daddy, being the Abgal Da he was, gave this to me on the day of my 'Confirmation.' It is the talisman of Ra. The ruling God of the order of Light."

"Ra as in ancient Egypt, The Sun God?" She was getting tired with being confused all the time when Layla spoke. Why couldn't she just say what she meant to say in the first place?

"Exactly, but the interpretation was a little different. Anyway, Daddy told me, 'Poppet, sometimes being very powerful can make some people go mad. And sometimes it can even happen to a deity. Even though they are very old and very wise and very powerful, they still possess some human failings. And being that they are very old, wise and powerful can make them tired and those failings can take over and they can lose their way. If that ever happens, and it may not, but if it does, take this. All you have to do is hold this and call to Ra and he will take your Goddess home straight away.' He told me to keep it with me to keep me safe. I never thought I would ever use it. But I did, and I thought it would be the last thing I ever did. But you saved me, even though it was my fault."

"Yeah, well if anything happens to my brother, I'll still kill you. But I don't guess it was completely your fault." Emma shrugged, mumbling through her pride.

"Everything Aslyn had said earlier. It wasn't about saving us. It was about saving herself. I couldn't believe it. She was the closest thing I had to family left, I worshiped her. And she betrayed me."

"Hey, if religion's what you're worried about, you could be Mormon," Emma suggested. They both looked at each other for a moment and then waved the idea off.

"They won't let you drink caffeine, I'm English I need my tea."

"Don't they make decaf?"

"Bollocks! Don't be ridiculous! It's not even tea then."

Emma waved her hands in front of her face and shook her head vigorously. "Ok, I need to know what happened. How did you end up there?" Emma looked around the charred walls. "And does Nica breathe fire?"

"No, that was Jimmy." Emma nodded in acknowledgment. "We were cramming over there and had actually found out plenty, when mega bitch came in with her boy toy in fancy shoes."

"Wait a minute; did he have curly brown hair, gray suit, smoke and have an Italian accent?" Emma asked, now knowing her apprehension from after her surprise meeting was well founded.

"Yes, how did you know?"

"I met him tonight, too. Called himself Leonardo De Luca. He knew a lot about me. Got me worried so I started back this way, when, when I knew Jimmy needed help." Emma lowered her head then raised it swiftly, fighting back her more feminine of emotions. "Keep going, what then?"

"She said that she 'followed her nose' here, she thought she would find you but instead it was me and Jimmy. I tried putting up a barrier, but she punched right through it as if it were Styrofoam. Then I tried throwing The Flame of Uritous, but she caught it and blew it out! I'm telling you this broad is no airy fairy! Anyway, she came up and Jimmy tried to stake her but she was so fast I don't even think we actually 'saw' her do it. I mean, the stake was in his hand, and his hand moved as if he had thrown it, but then it was in his shoulder. I couldn't do anything! She shrugged off everything I tried! She had him by the throat and was toying with him when he slapped her neck with his wrist watch and then BOOM! There was this massive explosion and we were blown over here into the stacks and they fell on us and everywhere. But it barely touched her. And she was quite ticked off! She jumped and howled like I've never heard before. Then she grabbed Jimmy and told Leo to leave you a message. She said that why have one twin when you could have a complete set. She plans on taking you both. Then after they left I carried on a bit and then Aslyn appeared and told me how I screwed everything up, that I was supposed to let you both die in the basement. That's when I called to Ra and had her banished. And the next thing I knew the shelf you pulled off gave way and fell on top of me. And then you arrived."

Emma looked off as Layla finished. It hurt her to see her parents' shop in such ruins. The entire back area was a disaster, its real wood paneling charred and blackened. The six-paned windows' glass was covered in gray film from the smoke. All of the beautiful Victorian blown glass and iron sconces were shattered, showing only wiring and hanging from their former perches. The corner where she and Layla sat now was completely covered in first editions and rare leather-bound texts. Emma scouted for the Persian rug her mother had gotten from her mother, and so on and so forth, and found it was where it should be, just half the rug it was. A black line of burnt and ashen thread marked where the missing half had been burned away. In fact, the only thing in the back of the store that remained untouched was the cabinet that housed the template. Emma scoffed to herself and shook her head in incredulity. If only her father hadn't let those vampires in that night none of them would be in this predicament right now. They could all be back at the house watching some *Star Trek* movie and Layla could be back in merry old England sipping her tea and eating whatever it was they ate with their tea over there. But this wasn't the time to have a pity party. She could do that after she saved the world. She just needed to know how.

"Message, you said that he left a message."

"Yeah, he carved it into my belly with a bit of broken glass."

"Wait a minute! If you healed yourself…"

"I saved it for you." Layla spread her tattered and bloody shirt to show the white scar tissue showing through the stain of red from her blood. It simply read one word.

Emma drew back as she saw how thick and deep the cuts had been. "Kender," she read out loud.

"Do you know what it means?"

"I sure do. The Kender Farm. It's this property on the outskirts of town. When we were kids we used to tease that it was haunted and dare each other to spend the night out there. Never did. We were too scared. It has a main house, a house for the farm hands and a barn on it. I can't remember a time when anyone lived there."

"Well, they are expecting you to show. She is going to ingest both of your souls and I think she has until sunset tomorrow."

"What makes you say that?"

"Because she told me she is going to do it at sunset tomorrow."

"You said she needs our souls to stay here?" Emma asked, looking for an explanation. Layla raised a hand and looked around the debris. The mountain of collapsed books and shelves made it impossible for her to find the large mystical book or her pad with all of her notes. She pulled this book and pushed that one, but it all seemed futile. Then she recalled that she possessed a quicker way to search. She closed her eyes and held out her hand. "What was lost is now found." And in a twinkling the large template plopped in her hand, tilting her forward. Layla caught herself and sat upright again.

"Wow, you're like the Swiss army knife of people!" Emma said in amazement. "Except louder and more sarcastic and Indian."

Layla opened the book and prompted Emma to voice her command. She asked it for the information on the Inanna and it appeared row by row as it had before.

"See here, it says that she not only drinks the blood of humans, but she takes their souls along with it. It is what fuels her constant hunger. A soul is too pure to ingest, no wonder she's gone wonky. Anyway, it also says that the normal ways you would go about killing a vamp won't work with her. But if we can get a hold of this," she turned the page and pointed to the rendering of the effigy of the Inanna—the slender coal black figure upon a heap of bodies, "and destroy it, she can be killed just like any other vamp. Kinda like making her mortal. This is her effigy. It's made of black marble and has rubies beset for her eyes and teeth. In one hand she holds a silver spear and in the other a golden goblet. It is used in the ceremony that calls her up. It also houses a vile that contains her black blood. When a host is chosen and the time is right, they pour this on the host's body and then fifty vampires sire her. And she doesn't just take over a dead body, no! The host is kept alive so its soul is still intact." Emma looked down. When she saw Nica in the dumpster that night, she had thought she was already dead. Her heart sank. "That way, she can infect and meld with it. In the end she is that person and the Inanna. But her time here is limited; if by two weeks she hasn't ingested a soul powerful enough to give her enough strength to anchor herself here, she is forced from the body and banished back to the ether."

"So me and Jimmy, we have the kind of souls she needs to anchor herself?"

"The book says that the only one powerful enough is that of the Warrior of the People. A Slayer. Turns out, you two are the lucky bastards she needs to eat."

"So, who's to say that if we get Jimmy and she somehow slips away that she won't go and find another Slayer, since now it's the latest trend."

"She won't have the time to track another one! She has until tomorrow night I believe. And, if I am wrong..." Emma's face tightened and her arm began to rise. Layla raised her hands in fear and continued. "...We will just have to make sure that we get her effigy and destroy it and kill her so she can't find another one."

"How do we get it? I really don't think she leaves stuff like that laying around. It would be like Superman leaving kryptonite hanging about all willy nilly. Oh my God I just channeled my brother." She looked at Layla and her faced softened. "It's her, Layla, she's the girl

I saw in the dumpster, and you know the one that was on the news. I thought she was dead. I really did. If I had only done the decent thing and…"

"Hey, you had to protect yourself, mate. How could you have known what was about to happen? The only one who did was Aslyn, and she didn't tell anyone. If you're going to blame anyone, blame her."

"Why now? Why not last year or five years ago? Why was she raised now?" Emma asked openly.

"Remember when Aslyn showed us the scale, and how when it was tipped it created a rip? That rip is sort of a doorway. I think that because of that doorway, the Inanna's essence was able to get through to our dimension and then it was possible to put her into a host body."

"Ok then. I guess we get up, get ready and go take out some pent-up aggression while saving my brother and the day in the process!"

"Whoa, first we need to know how to get past Naberius, pet. He's the one who called the Inanna so he could take over this place. He's a complete idiot if he thinks he can control this psycho. Anyway, this lunk head thinks that he owns Nica, so he is going to protect her. So, we better know how to take him out. And we should also find out if that effigy has any protective spells on it. We really don't need any surprises."

"Good point, we'll take the book with us. We need to get home so you can get cleaned up and I need to get another leg. I think I broke this one on the way here. I heard a crack and all of the sudden I have ankle mobility."

"That's a fantastic plan, but we can't take the book with us. Every time we would walk toward the door, the book would vanish from Jimmy's hands and reappear back in the cabinet. We'll have to write down whatever the book says and then we can take it with us." Once again, instead of sifting through the rubble, Layla closed her eyes and held out her hand and asked for what was lost to be found. And like with the template, her note pad appeared. She met Emma at the counter where she had already had the book reveal the information it had on Naberius. All of the lights did nothing but flicker and then fizzle out, so Emma was forced to retrieve various candles from the office, but before she could set them onto the counter, Layla had an alternative.

"Lumiesca, grant us your gift," she said simply. As soon as she said it, a hovering ball of white light erupted above them just below the ceiling, alighting the area around them and farther out ten more feet. Emma dropped the candles onto the counter in a "why bother" manner, and picked up a pen to begin transcribing the information.

The consistent light revealed the extent of the damage. Pictures on the walls had fallen and their frames shattered. Some of her mother's antique hurricane lamps had also fallen victim to the attack. She shook her head in disappointment. These things belonged to her mother and she had let harm come to them. Inside, Emma's heart was breaking over and over again. Every time she raised her eyes and spied the spoiled store, she felt her heart pang and drop into her gut. How odd that so many little things carried so much weight. The display table that spotlighted her mother's love of old gold-tipped pens that once stood against the left wall in the back was now in bits and the pens were no more. Even the Xeroxed copy of an old picture of an ancestor that had been burned affected Emma's palpitating heart. She wanted so much to just lay her head down on the untouched and pristine counter top and cry a thousand tears to relieve the crushing pressure rising in her chest. Even the thought of allowing herself to go in hysterics and wail and hyperventilate sounded like relief. But she needed to be strong, not for herself and not for Layla, but for her lost brother who had been tortured and stolen from this very room. She knew that she had to keep it together. Not to try her best, but to do it. If she let herself drown in her emotions and fall apart, that meant doom for him and doom for the rest of the world.

All that was heard in the devastated shop was the scratching of pens on paper. Layla transcribing the left side of the book and Emma on the right. For several minutes not even a mumble escaped their lips. Time was a commodity and that meant getting this done as quickly as possible. Emma became increasingly frustrated with the volume of information that needed to be transferred. Studying was never her strong suit; after all, Jimmy was the brains and she was the brawn, as Layla so often reminded her. Her hand started to cramp and her eyes started to burn, this was what she would consider cruel and unusual torture: note taking! Layla had explained that the book wouldn't allow itself to be copied by the Xerox machine. Emma had mumbled something unintelligible and started writing. But for now they wrote furiously, doing their best to finish quickly so they could rescue Jimmy.

"I can get you into the compound if you will accept my help." A male voice broke the silence, causing a still very jittery Layla to leap from her seat and spin around. Emma had already started marching in his direction. She stepped on a broken wooden chair; vaulting it upward and ripped a leg from it. She broke into a sprint and stopped nose to nose, well her nose to his chest that is, with him with the stake poking into his left breast. He was tall and had long blond hair. It was Jerome.

"And what makes you think that I would need help from a vampire?" Emma barked. He looked down at the tiny figure that threatened his unlife. He couldn't help but smile at her, but raised his hands to his eye level, being careful not to infuriate her further.

"Because I don't want the bitch to stay here any more than you do. My name is Jerome, and I can help you. I am one of the vampires in the Order of Naberius. It was that order that brought the Inanna here. I know the layout of the property and all of the entrances to the main and guest house. The Master has said he has dealt with her before. He even calls her 'My Queen.' But he has no control over her and she is ruining everything."

Emma took a step back and pulled the stake away from his chest. She still held it in view, though, to remind him he was not trusted.

"How did you know to come here?" she demanded. He dropped his hands and shoved them into the pockets of his black slacks. He looked down as if in thought and then again raised his face to look at her.

"We had been watching you for a while. We saw you in an alley, we have watched you hunt and kill. And we have watched you torment yourself all the way back to your home and to here." He smiled, pleased with himself, and ran his pink tongue along the front of his teeth.

This disgusted Emma and gave Layla goosebumps. So much so that she had made her way to behind the counter.

Emma dropped to the floor, stuck out her right leg, and spun around, catching Jerome's ankles and knocking him down. She jumped on top of him and shoved the stake to his chest. This time she allowed it to penetrate his skin just enough for him to know it was there and to draw blood. She placed her left hand on top of her right, which was pressing the fatal piece of wood over his heart.

"If you even twitch, I will shove this into your shriveled little heart faster than you can have second thoughts. Now, you are going to tell me who 'we' is and why YOU need my help. Because let me tell you, I have had it up to here with you pieces of dog shit, and after the last couple of days, I am just itching for some violence!"

The defeated vamp swallowed and looked up at the angry Slayer. He moved his blue eyes to his right and saw Layla cowering behind the counter.

"Looks like your little witch friend there has lost her nerve. You may want to send out for a new one. I think this one is spent," he ribbed. Emma slowly pushed the stake in further, causing him to grunt in pain. "Ok, ok. I'll stop."

"Oi, I'm not spent! I just wanna watch her do something for a change. I can't always be the one doing all the work!" she yelled, defending herself from across the way. Emma rolled her eyes and went back to questioning the blond intruder she sat on.

"You gonna answer me, or do I get to relieve some stress?" Emma this time forced her left knee into his groin, making his face turn purple and his eyes bug out.

"Ok! I'll tell you! It was Leo! Me and Leo! He said he wanted to watch you marinate in your despair until you were perfect. Then he was going to feed on you!"

"Would this Leo be Leonardo De Luca?" Emma asked as she held tight to the stake with both hands.

"Yes, that's him, been together for thirty-some odd years until she came around. After she rose, from the MOMENT she rose, he became obsessed with her. We were supposed to go back to Europe after we helped sire her, but he changed his mind! Said he wanted to stay here in the butt crack of the planet just to stay with her!"

Emma rolled her eyes and stood up off his chest. She folded her arms and scoffed as she walked back toward a smiling Layla.

"You want my help to get your boyfriend back!" Emma accused mockingly. Layla looked like she was going to explode. The humiliated vampire pushed himself to his feet and dusted his pants and shoulders of his indigo, matte finished silk shirt. He pulled down his cuffs at his wrists to straighten his sleeves. He walked with his head down, showing his humiliation at her off color comment.

"He's not my boyfriend! He's like my brother!" The two girls continued to snicker and snort. "She's got some sort of hold on him. Once she gets the soul of a Slayer, she will be able to make more like her! And I don't mean she will be turning humans, I mean she will be turning both! Starting with Leo! And you know what that means! The more of them and with that constant thirst, they will wipe out our entire food source! And I don't want to be one of them. I want things back the way they were. I need you to help me get my brother back and I will in turn help you get yours." He finished his speech and leaned forward on the counter. Emma was leaning back on it with her arms folded and her brow furrowed in deep thought. She looked back at Layla, and she nodded, letting Emma know she could sense he was sincere. Emma turned back and took a deep breath.

"If we were to agree to scratch your back, how are we to know that you will scratch ours, or how do we know you won't double cross us?" She looked into his eyes sternly and without blinking. She was looking for any signs of hesitation. It made her stomach turn and her backbone go cold to think that she was actually considering working with a vampire. But if he could really get them in and out to rescue Jimmy, it was worth it.

"I give you my word. That's all I have. If I double cross you, you can kill me."

Emma snorted and flopped her arms down. She looked at him cynically and put her hands on her hips.

"I guaren-damn-tee ya I will kill you dead if you do anything that I think will lead to a double cross or if anything happens to my brother. There's no question there!" Emma bit her lip and looked pensive over her right shoulder. The light that Layla conjured cast wavering shadows over the rubble of books and shelves and glass that now filled the back of the store. She closed her eyes and imagined it looked like a sunken ship with the white, glowing liquid light moving gently over the lost treasures. She imagined how her parents would feel about something like this. And then she thought of how Jimmy cared for this place out of obligation and love of their father. She had to get him back so they could restore their parents' livelihood to its former glory. And she would have to do whatever it took. This shop wasn't all that was at stake. She had to remind herself of the fact that the world as she knew it could be torn apart if she didn't stop this crazed vampire Goddess. She had two priorities now, and they were fighting inside of her to be her top one. She turned back abruptly toward the desperate vamp and rubbed her face as if she were cleansing herself for what she was about to say.

"Ok, we will work together. But on one condition, I run this game! You move when I say, you speak when I say and only when I say. You are simply a convenience for me, get it? We stick together at all times. Now, first thing we need to know to get this done is getting by or killing Naberius. We need to know what to do. Secondly, Nica's effigy; it's the only way you can kill her. If we destroy the effigy she becomes just an ordinary vampire who can be dusted. Do you know what I am talking about? It's a black marble statue about so high with rubies for eyes and teeth." Emma stopped and looked at him, waiting for his answer.

"I've seen it. The woman is holding a spear in one hand and a goblet in the other, right?" The two girls nodded in agreement. "We used it in the ritual. After it was over Naberius took it up to his chamber. It's his trump card. From what I have heard, he holds on to it in case she gets too out of control, but this time she plans on taking it from him. I think that's where Leo comes in. We may not have to get Naberius out of the way. They may do it for us." He scratched his head and then smoothed his hair.

"You're probably right," Emma added. "No one likes to have a leash. Especially a half-crazed vampire Goddess who has been swimming in the ether of a hell dimension for eons."

Jerome looked Layla up and down. She was exotic, half naked, and drenched in blood. He couldn't help but stare. He smiled at her slyly and winked. She gave him a repulsed look and became aware her bra and bloody midriff were exposed and awkwardly attempted to cover up. Emma saw Layla's actions and glared back at Jerome who was still gawking at the blood-soaked Layla.

"Hey! And definitely no eating us! No eating, period! If you want our help you better be on your best vampire behavior, buddy!" she commanded as she poked him in the chest where she had punctured him with the stake. He winced and covered the injury with his hand.

"What? She got her shirt ripped open and she's covered in blood. Hello! Vampire! I'm evil and drink blood. What do you expect?" he said as he waved his arms around and pointed at his face.

Emma rolled her eyes and put her face in her hands. She went over things in her mind, making a mental list of what needed to be done before they set off for the farm and saved the world. As stressed and frustrated as she was right now, Emma loved being in charge! There was nothing like being the boss of everyone! It meant she could control everything around her. The downfall of being in charge of everyone was being responsible for them, too. If anything happened to them during this fight, it would be on her. And she was barely stable enough to be responsible enough to ensure her own safety. What made her think that she was the one who could do this? Why couldn't they just call those big shots over in Europe? After all, they had the experience, the know how. And for that matter, why didn't they even know what was going on here? Or were they just too busy taking care of themselves, and oh yeah, all the other Slayers that they had picked up and offered assistance to. All except her that is. How nice for all those others having all the help and learning they needed. Must have been great not just being thrown into this whole new crazy world and then left there alone. But, here she was, alone as she would be for the rest of her miserable life. No cavalry is going to ride in and save the day for her. She WAS the cavalry. She opened her eyes and looked at the bloody and pissy Layla giving the malevolent and personality-challenged vampire Jerome the evil eye.

"And these are my horses."

CHAPTER FOURTEEN

It's Hard Being a Single Demon Father in This Day and Age!

One Week Earlier

She paced anxiously across the plush ruby carpet. Her black silk robe billowed and flapped across her legs as she constantly changed directions. She wrung her hands vigorously and tapped her elegantly-sculpted red fingernail on her lower lip, which was also painted a brilliant ruby red. Not a hair was out of place as she whipped around to and fro; it remained ever coiffed and as shiny as polished black onyx.

Nica's room was in stark contrast to the rest of the farm house. It was decadent, opulent, and cultured. The ceiling was black molded plaster, and large, lavish mahogany drapes dripped from the crown molding to the thick carpeting below. Black iron gothic candelabras were placed on either side of the windows and doorways. A large matching chandelier hung from the ceiling in the middle of the room.

The candlelight cast eerie shadows along the floors and up the walls, making the room look even more menacing. Unlit Tiffany oil lamps adorned the three claw foot cherry wood tables that were set against the front and side walls. The table at the front wall was book ended by two red velvet Victorian wing back chairs that were the resting places of some discarded black shawls and a new *People* magazine.

Nica stopped her pacing abruptly and grabbed one of the four posts holding up the red-with-black-trim canopy. She let her body swing back against the bed covered in silk pillows and let the fringe from the canopy run across her face. She grabbed her abdomen with her left arm and grimaced in pain. She felt her insides burn and toss. It was like they were being ripped apart and losing their cohesion. Her body shimmered and for a second it was as if she wasn't there. Nica dropped to the ground on her knees and held herself with both arms. She couldn't wait anymore; she needed something now. She could call some in here but there was no one here with a soul! Her hunger was becoming more intense. Where were they? She sent them hours ago to bring back with them her lambs. Naberius was yet to allow her to venture out of this house; his nightingale in a gilded cage. This time it would be different. She had an ally and she would finally be able to break free. Of course Naberius wanted her here permanently, as soon as it was "time" he would let her out of here and seek out that little slayer so she could have enough strength to keep her cohesion, but he would still have that leash around her neck. Whoever possessed her effigy controlled her. And Naberius had it, he had had it for more than a millennia. But this time, she was going to get it back. She was tired of being his slave. It was fun at first, but after a few hundred years and then being forced back into the ether of a hell dimension, it had gotten old. She had Leo now, and he was just what she needed to finally break free and do some real damage to this place.

But for now, all there was was the searing agony wafting through her insides. Suddenly, her door swung open and a couple of Naberius' lackies dragged in her repast and tossed them in front of her. The closest to her was an overweight man with glasses and thinning hair. Not but six inches from him was a younger blonde woman in a red jogging suit and an orange reflective belt. Both were bound at the hands and feet with gray duct tape. They also were gagged with the same tape wrapped around their heads. The vamps didn't even bother to move the woman's ponytail out of the way and so it, too, was taped to the back of her head. Hungrily, Nica crawled over and on top of the fat man. She reached up to his mouth and placed a finger to his covered lips and prompted him to hush as he was whimpering and quivering viciously. He blinked and looked relieved for a moment, but as soon as he felt the relief, it was replaced by the heat and sting of the tape ripping from his face and taking hunks of flesh along with it. Nica grinned manically at the reaction she had gotten from such a quick and simple gesture. He began to cry like a child at the knowledge that these were his last moments. She opened her mouth in delight and licked his bloody cheeks, lips and grazed her teeth just enough to scratch at the surface.

"Please," he whimpered, "I have a wife and kids! They need me! Please! I beg you!"

She smiled as she pulled out his wallet and produced his driver's license. She tapped at the personal information that included his address as she taunted him.

"Don't worry, baby, I'll take care of them!" She grew tired of playing as the pain in her stomach reminded her of her terrible hunger. She fell upon him and sunk her teeth in as deep as they allowed her to and drank deep. The blood was thick, sweet and hot. It rolled down her throat in droughts. The other two vamps watched as she gripped his abdomen with her left hand and what little hair he had at the top of his head with her right. Naberius entered the doorway and watched with a smile on his stony face with the rest of her audience. The glimmer in the man's eyes shown brighter for a moment and then quickly began to fade. At the same time, all of his coloring started seeping away into the direction of Nica's mouth. Once all of the color had drained into her, her coloring shown brighter and then flashed back to normal. When the man was empty, she flung her head back and reveled in the ecstasy that the man's soul had provided.

The woman on the floor, seeing all that had just passed, began a desperate attempt to break free of her bonds and get away from these monsters. Nica wiped the tiny droplet of blood from the corner of her mouth and shoved the empty shell of the man to the side to make her way to her next victim. The woman froze in sheer panic, wetting herself in the process. She knew she should have taken her run earlier that night and now she would die for her procrastination. Nica clutched the loop her taped-down ponytail had made and drug the woman toward her. The woman closed her eyes tight and began to cry. Nica rocked her in her arms and brushed her bangs from her eyes. She wiped her tears with her fingertips and licked them.

"Shhhh. It's ok, darling." She traced the duct tape covering her mouth with her index finger. "Oh, now, now. This won't do." Nica smiled lovingly and stroked the woman's face. She nodded reassuringly as she wedged her cold white fingers in between the tape and her cheek. The woman tightened her knitted brow and began to shake violently. In an explosion of pain Nica ripped the tape from the woman's head as hard as she could. With the tape came bits of flesh, the majority of her ponytail, and her lower lip. The woman twitched. Blood glistened, showing where the flesh had been torn away. Her once brilliant white teeth were visible and covered in blood.

"You know, I really think this is a much better look for you! Ponytails are so over anyway!" Nica said as she tossed the tape with the hair attached over her shoulder. "But you know what? With this face all torn up like this, even *The Swan* couldn't help you now! Oh well, might as well put you out of your misery! I do hope you had some fruit today, that guy was all salty. I need something sweet to balance it out." With that, Nica bared her fangs and sunk them deep into the woman's neck. For a moment her eyes grew wide and then lapsed. Her color drained and Nica let her body drop from her lap as she stood. She looked up and smiled at the attentive Naberius.

"You could have joined me if you liked," Nica teased.

"At my age, my dear, you know I don't need blood to sustain me. Besides, I like to watch." He waved the other two vamps to leave them and they did so obediently. Naberius stood up straight from his leaning post of the doorway and walked with arms folded toward the slightly satiated Nica. He placed his massive hands on her silken shoulders. They were so large, his hands, that they covered her shoulders, chest and half way down her bicep. He smoothed her hair and raised her chin so that her eyes met with his in a perfect line. His once jovial expression turned hard and angry.

"I am not dumb, Inanna. I know that you have been cavorting with that lesser being. You are tainting this gift of corporeality that I have given you. You have merely one week left here before you are expelled from that lovely shell into the nothingness once again. If you wish to stay here on this plane, you will comply with my commands." He wrapped his stony clamps around her delicate-looking neck and began to squeeze. He lifted her off of her feet to where they were nose to nose. Her face tightened and she glared at him angrily. She stayed completely still as he held her there so close to his face. "Because if you do not, your little marble action figure will be dust and you will lose all that makes you the Goddess you are. You will be nothing, a lowly lesser being. Just one of those 'Forsaken' as your precious Leo refers to it." He lowered her back to the floor and released his grip. He straightened her silk robe, combed her hair with his fingers and folded his arms back across his chest. "Now be a good little girl and you will have your Slayer."

She put her hands on her hips and looked at him defiantly. Her hunger began to grow once more, fueling her rage. Her purple irises flashed brightly with her steely gaze. "Let's not play this game, Naberius. I'm not stupid either. You won't get rid of me, oh no, at least not until you get what you want." She took another step closer and ran her index fingers down his chest and stomach. She looked at him playfully but her eyes were deadly serious. "So, maybe you should play nice, or I won't play at all." As she ended her ultimatum, she turned abruptly, allowing her robe to billow, and walked briskly to her large English oak four poster bed. She swung around and then plopped down among the down silken pillows. She lay there twitching her rounded toes and filing her well-manicured fingernails. She smiled coyly. This wasn't the first time they had had this discussion. To a point she enjoyed irritating him. And he knew it.

He closed his eyes and willed himself away. When he opened them once again he was down in the cellar of the farm house. He stood stalk-still staring off into the blackness. How she infuriated him. Did she not realize that she was simply a tool? A means to an end? An end to this prison that the new army of Slayers had put him in? Because of this new situation in the world, power was changing hand and the Old Ones, the Demon Kings and Coven Masters were becoming weaker and more and more of them returning to the Deep Earth to sleep until a time came for them to rise back up to their true strength. But Naberius refused to resign himself to such a fate. And the Inanna was the key. In another week she would be ready to take the soul of the Slayer and her essence would be powerful enough for him to confiscate. With that he would have what he needed to reclaim his powers and create a new legion of monsters. If only he could keep her under better control. This was easier said than done, however. The Inanna herself, alone, was volatile, perverse, corrupt, unstable and powerful. When coupled with a human being who had been tortured and robbed of life in the flower of youth, then what you got was one resentful, crazy and almost unstoppable Hell Goddess. Luckily for him all doggies come with leashes. As long as he held onto that black marble image of her, he had his leash. One false move on her part, and he could bust her down to a vampiric version of mortality and leave her floating around from dimension to dimension being nothing more than that of the consistency of air.

He had used her before. A couple of times actually. They enjoyed a brief love affair, but as with most office relationships, it soured quickly. But this time things were different. Normally, he simply used her as a general of sorts. He would keep her around long enough to aide in his conquer over a realm, and then allow her to return to her ethereal self until the stars allowed for him to call upon her again. But now he really needed her. And there would be no calling her back. Once she was at her true self he would open the effigy once again and devour her blood that remained in its vile. After that it was only a matter of smashing that statue and forcing her essence to anchor to the host that possessed her blood. And of course that would be him. With the power of two hell gods, he could go about his plan of building up an army to rival the Slayers and take over this realm once and for all. The only one who could foil this wasn't the Slayer, though. It was her witch. Only she could find and destroy the Effigy of the Inanna. Slayers are good for beating on things and sticking them with pointy objects normally made out of timber, but when it came to things of a mystical nature they fell a bit short. Naberius knew that he needed to get this over with before the sepia-toned medium could find him and stop all that he had so painstakingly put into motion.

"Master, your chamber is prepared. Do you require any further assistance?"

Naberius turned and awoke from his thoughts. His aide stood with hands folded at his waist, awaiting his instruction. He was white and bald with his face permanently fused into its demonic form, signifying his rank as subordinate. Naberius nodded in gratitude and walked toward the vampiric assistant.

"Thank you, Arturo. You may call for the guards now." He waved a hand in his direction and moved thoughtfully farther into the depths of the dank cellar.

"How was your address with the Goddess? I trust that it went well and all is still going according to plan?" Arturo asked genuinely as he stood at the bottom of the cellar stairs.

Naberius stopped short of the entrance to his chamber and turned slightly to face him.

"Arturo, you are no longer required. Your questions are inappropriate; if I need anything further I will find a circus monkey to do my bidding, for at least they lack the ability to question their masters. Send for the guards and make yourself disappear until I need you." He turned abruptly and walked into his chamber.

Meanwhile, back in Nica's suite, she had waited just long enough to be sure that Naberius had really gone when she called for her attending Priestess.

"Lunera, come." The Priestess entered the room dressed in the same sheer black fabrics as at the ceremony. She walked evenly to the side of the bed that Nica was lounging on and knelt before her.

Nica looked her over carefully. The beaded headdress that she adorned draped the luminous material over her long, thick chocolate curls. Nica smiled and sat forward to touch the milky white skin of her bare left shoulder. She ran her finger over her collar bone, up her neck and to her chin where she lifted it to raise her face to hers.

"Aren't you a stunner? Where did they find me such eatable Priestesses?" she purred.

"I was born into this sect, my Goddess. I wish nothing more than to serve and to please you. What is it that you require?" She smiled.

Nica leaned back on her pillows with her hands on her chest and mused out loud.

"What is it that I require?" She pointed to her left toe and used it to trace the attendant's frame. She then gestured for her to rise. "Go and get Leonardo for me. Tell him it's urgent."

Lunera rose and bowed her head before turning to leave. Nica bit her lip as she watched her leave.

"Woman cannot live by blood alone." She giggled. She rolled over onto her stomach and waited for them to enter.

Within minutes Lunera returned with Leo. Nica rose from the bed and walked wantonly to him. They embraced in a deep and ravenous kiss. The attendant began to leave when Nica noticed. She pulled back from Leo and addressed her.

"No, you stay." Lunera stopped and bowed, knelt and stayed. Nica turned her attention back to Leo who continued to nibble her neck and ear. "Naberius tried to ground me tonight. He told me that I better start playing nice or he was going to send me back."

Leo stopped his nuzzling and looked her in the eyes. "So now what, mio caro? Do we continue as planned?"

"Oh, baby, Daddy's all talk. Don't you worry about him! He needs me; he won't harm a hair on my head until he gets what he wants. And by then, it will be too late." She kissed him once more and took a step back. She untied her robe, slid it slowly off her shoulders and let it fall off onto the floor. The abandoning of her robe revealed a black lace under wire bra and panty. She stepped closer to him once more and started to take off his gray blazer.

"Now, what we have to concentrate on is finding that gimpy little Slayer. Once I have her, I'm yours forever. And we will spread across this earth like a wave of pestilence. We will devour it until there is nothing left, and then, we will continue on to new dimensions. And from there, we will rule virtual galaxies!" He grabbed her hip and the back of her head. He licked her neck up to her ear. He bit down on his lip, causing it to bleed and then kissed her with it, allowing her to suck.

She licked her lips and met with his eyes. "I have waited millennia to break free from this curse. And now that I have you, it's possible! Soon we will destroy Naberius and his order and I will be free!" Nica turned her gaze to the lovely Lunera and gestured with her right index finger for her to come closer. Lunera rose to her bare feet and came within inches of the pair. Nica ran her fingers through her hair and let her hand fall down, caressing her neck and then breast.

"Lunera, that clasp on your shoulder, does it hold all of that fabric together?"

"Yes, my lady," she answered dutifully.

"Maybe you should take it off so I can see it better."

Lunera did as instructed and when she removed the small silver dagger-like clasp from her shoulder, her sheer garb fell to her feet. Her body was perfect and firm. Though the rest of her skin was white her nipples were the color of her hair.

Nica smiled enough to show her fang teeth. "Now, show Leo your special talent."

Lunera nodded and smiled brightly.

Chapter Fifteen
The Advantages of Superpowers and Plastic Feet

The Present

Emma sat on the old yellow couch in the basement surrounded by ointments, peroxide, cotton balls, gauze and paper tape. The wound on her right thigh had grown to the size of a quarter and had begun to ooze yellow liquid and bleed. Her abused fiberglass and mechanical limb lay exposed by itself on the floor next to her. She grimaced as she cleaned the wound with a peroxide-soaked cotton ball. She hadn't had one like this before. She pushed herself too hard this time. It burned so badly when she put pressure on it; it felt like someone had stuck a hot poker deep into her leg. Because she did not have a foot, and could not walk in the conventional sense, the "ball" of her "foot" was now the back of her calf and on either side of her knee. So, under normal circumstances, any kind of walking would be out of the question and

Jimmy would have to confine her to the upstairs with a pair of crutches and a TV remote. But since this time he was in trouble, therefore not here to tell her to take it easy, she was going to have to find a way to suffer through to save him.

Blood ran down from the sore down the inside of her thigh and dripped onto the couch. She tossed the used cotton ball down to the floor. It bounced and rolled next to the tiny pile that had begun to build.

Jerome stood behind her in Jimmy's "shop." He stood casually with his hands in the pockets of his black suit pants. With the sleeves of his gray button-down shirt, he looked up puzzled at the sight of several of Emma's spare legs dangling from the ceiling. He reached out with his left hand and gently pushed the nearest leg, making it swing and knocking into the others.

"You know, people would think that some sick shit goes on down here if they saw this stuff, Slayer," he scoffed.

"You would know, psycho," she retorted. He shrugged and nodded in quiet agreement.

Upstairs, Layla dried her hair in what was once the youngest Hogan, Shea's room, now hers. She sat on the end of the bed, rubbing her head with the blue terrycloth towel. Closing her eyes, she tried to push away all the voices that cried out to her in the tiny bedroom. With just a small twin size bed, dresser, and closet, to the average individual it would seem quite empty. But to someone like Layla it was very congested. Several souls fought to gain her attention through the curtain of a blue haze. But after this evening's excitement she found her usual discipline lacking. What had normally become a pesky nuisance was now reverting back to the riot that consumed all of her senses. Without thinking, she had dropped the towel and brought her hands to her ears in an attempt to shut them out. So many things had happened, laying so much on her mind at one time. The attack on the shop, her inability to stop Nica from taking Jimmy, Leo's torturing her, and Aslyn's confession, which led to Layla banishing her. All of this compounded with guilt was causing her to lose the tight control she had worked so hard for so many years to get. Then gradually she heard a voice rising above all of the others.

"Layla Wayla Bumble Bee. Mummy's little cup of tea. I'm as happy as can be, with Layla Wayla on my knee." It continued to repeat the little poem and Layla began to recite it as well. It was something her mother had said to her since she was a baby, and when she got older her mother would use it as something for Layla to focus on when she was bombarded like she was now. Layla had recited the poem three times when she realized that the voice wasn't in her head but was actually there. She opened her eyes and saw her mother kneeling at her feet, reciting.

"Layla Wayla bumble bee. Mummy's little cup of tea. I'm as happy as can be with Layla Wayla on my knee."

Layla looked deep into her eyes and nowhere else and kept pace with her. Soon the din around her began to fade and she was able to hold on without the old "Apply Dapply" poem.

"Mum, it's happened! I've gone mad! It's my fault and now I've gone mad!" She was beginning to panic. Her wide eyes started to well with thick tears and her chin began to quiver. She wanted to reach out and hold her but she knew she couldn't.

"No, you haven't gone mad, poppet. It's just stress. You'll be fine. You'll see. Just remember that you're my cup of tea!" She winked and stood. Layla gripped the edge of the bed with both hands and tightened her entire body as she sat vulnerable in just a gray t-shirt.

"No, no, Mum, no! I can't do this! I'm a fraud, I know it! I let them down! I let Jimmy down! And I am pretty sure I fancy him! Emma is going to bloody kill me and there is nothing I can do because I have gone mad and..."

"Layla, none of what has happened is your fault. You were not made responsible for everything that happens to everyone. Hey! You're a Fellows! You have been training your whole life for this sort of thing and you are one mighty medium! Are you going to let some tiny incident with a switched-off Goddess, a kidnapping and a little torture throw you off? NO! That's not who you are! You have made being a pain in the ass an art form! No one gets rid of you that easy! They haven't even seen a fraction of the power you possess! Now, get up, wipe your nose and show them what Layla Fellows can really do! Go on, baby, go save the world!" With that her mother stepped away and blew her daughter a kiss as she faded away.

Layla stood up more confident than ever and wiped her nose with the back of her hand.

"I meant with a tissue. Really, darling, that's rather gross," her mother scolded as she popped her head back in through the veil.

"Oh sorry." Layla quickly picked up her towel and wiped her hands on it. That being done, she went back to her confidence and tightened her fists.

"Fucking right I'm Layla Fellows and I'll…"

"And I really don't care for this language here. I'm sure you could monologue without such crassness. It's not very ladylike at all," her mother interjected, shaking a finger; and that was all that was seen of her.

"Mother! You are killing my moment here! You give this big fantabulous speech and then you keep cutting in. Do you want to do this for me? I mean, be my guest. There you go, have the floor!" Silence proceeded. "Really, are we done then? Go ahead if you like. Good. When normal parents die, they, you know, DIE. They are no more in this realm." Layla opened her mouth to continue her war cry but stopped short. "You know I don't really know what I would have said anyway. I think you got it right when you said it." She grabbed the notebook off of the dresser and made her way for the basement.

~~~~

Emma finished up by packing her wound with gauze and wrapping it with ace wrap. Next on her agenda was seeing if she could repair her battered bionic leg. She picked it up from the floor and held it upside down. She watched the foot flop over as it was broken at the faux arch and hung on by a mere thread of rubber. She had somehow broken the steel endoskeleton cleanly in half!

"Wow, never seen that happen before," she mused quietly to herself. She flicked with her finger and watched it flop up and down like a fish.

Layla had come down the stairs in time to catch Emma playing with her foot. She stopped short in shock and then quickly recovered.

"I'm never going to get used to that," she said, shaking her head and plopping down on the couch next to Emma.

Emma continued to inspect the limb, spinning it around and checking all of the switches and hatches. When she checked the one at the ball of the foot, she hadn't taken into account that the foot itself and all its internal workings had been severed, so when the wooden dagger came jutting out of the toes it continued on flying out completely. Layla ducked just in time for it to fly past her and into the arm of the couch behind her. "Oops."

"Have you gone daft?!"

"That's why Jimmy is the mechanic," Emma said. "Well, safe to say this one is shot. As soon as we save him he's gonna kill me." She tossed it back to the floor.

Jerome stepped forward a bit more from the shop area and scratched his head. Layla flipped open her notebook and slid her pen from the binding.

"I need you to tell me what you know about what Nica and Leo are up to. And stop looking at my neck." Jerome stood up straighter and looked around the room conspicuously. Layla looked up at him and squared her eyes. "You are a brutal bastard aren't you? You certainly have your share of tag-alongs." She referenced the many tortured souls she sensed all around him.

Jerome smiled coyly and shrugged. With a swagger of confidence he spoke. "Well, you know, I do what I can." The girls looked at each other disgustedly and shook their heads.

"If I'm such a brutal bastard then why did you invite me into your home? I could just kill you now, or even wait until you're sleeping. What makes you think that I won't?"

Just as he finished his sentence the hatch in her leg malfunctioned and the stake inside came sailing up into the air. Emma caught it and without even blinking or looking in that direction, she threw the stake just to the left of his head. He flinched as it stuck in the wall. In the same manner Layla raised her right index finger and sparks crackled forth from it. She wiggled it up and down and then when right back to work.

Jerome coughed and adjusted his collar. "Oh, that's what."

Emma reached over and retrieved her beater leg from behind the couch. She bit down on her lower lip and forced the leg on. The extra padding made it all the more uncomfortable. She hobbled over to the shop and lifted open the stainless steel counter top and brown box.

"Jimmy's been working on this almost from the beginning. He wouldn't ever let me play with it, though. Caught me a couple of times so he hid it. He was afraid that it wasn't ready yet." Emma opened the box and pushed some of the packing peanuts out of the way.

"How did you know where to look?" Layla asked.

"It's where he hides my presents." And then she added as an after thought, "And his porn." When she pulled it out and placed it bare on the counter what they saw amazed them.

"Wow, he really did get the super smarts," Layla said with eyes wide. It looked like a perfect leg. From the limp synthetic skin at the top, that was meant to roll over her existing knee, creating a seamless transition from prosthetic to flesh, down to the artfully sculpted toes complete with toenails. "Emma, it's your 'Barbie Foot.' It's what you've always wanted. Don't tell me you've never tried it on and taken it for a little test run?"

"Aren't you afraid of finally having what you have been wanting? Some things are easier left as ideas."

"How sweet of him, he was making you a cosmetic leg, Emma."

Emma smiled. She thought of the kindness her brother possessed in his heart. They may tease and quarrel, but they were all that each other had and beyond that they loved each other greatly. The pain of one was the pain of both. There is no bond like that of a brother and sister. She knew that he was a little jealous of the abilities fate had bestowed upon her. He had insecurities, too. But she also knew that it broke his heart to see her struggle each day with the pains and inconveniences that having something like this causes. He could feel her squirm when a beautiful woman sashayed across the television in a short skirt and sexy strappy stilettos. As much as she fought to keep up her cover to the rest of the world, she couldn't hide it from him. The more she thought of her brother, the more her chest sank, knowing that he was lost, in trouble and afraid, the more the tears threatened to break their seal. She tore herself from her revelry, took a deep breath and continued on.

"Actually, it's more than that." Emma ran a gentle hand up and down the leg; when she got to the heel she pressed inward. Immediately it caused a reaction. The surface of the synthetic skin covering the leg began to spin around it. Within seconds it had disappeared to reveal a black shell. Layla reached forward and tapped it.

"What is that?" she asked.

"Ceramic Kevlar," Emma stated proudly.

"You're kidding!" Layla was amazed. This was impressive even for Jimmy!

Emma reached over to the big toe and tilted it up. A clicking sound was heard and then a familiar hatch popped open on the side. This one was slightly different from its counterpart. Instead of just a hollow spring-loaded door, this one was hydraulic and wasn't hollow. Emma gripped the inside of the door and pulled. It was a clip of sorts. It slid out from the interior of the leg to a length of about twelve inches. She laid it out flat and opened the drawer to her right under the counter.

"What's that for?" Layla asked, intrigued.

"Lipstick holder. Yup, in case I'm out and I just can't make up my mind!" Emma responded sarcastically.

"Hey, I'm supposed to provide the witty comic relief!"

From the drawer Emma produced six slim leg stakes and pressed them into the clip. When she was finished she slid it back into place and closed the hatch. She then stood the leg up and slammed its heel down onto the counter. Immediately the hatch popped open and a stake went flying back up in the air.

"Now all I have to do is press my tippy toes and it switches to the next shot! Like cocking it," Emma bragged.

"He ha! You said…" Jerome began to laugh at Emma's wording but when he noticed that he was alone in the joke he stopped.

Emma rolled her eyes and went back to her bionic leg. "Anyway, if you thought that was cool wait until you see the rest! Watch this!" She held the leg up and pressed the inside ankle. This caused several tiny spikes to shoot out right into Jerome's arm.

"OW! Dammit! What the hell are these little things going to do in a life or death situation, annoy people to death?"

"No, that's your super power," Layla quipped.

"Just wait." Emma smirked. Two seconds later the smug look on Jerome's face slowly morphed into confusion, then to restraint, to bright red, and then into a mask of pain. He grabbed his arm that was now smoking and sizzling and howled at the top of his lungs. He rolled up his sleeve and watched his skin bubble and burn. He slapped at it violently, trying to make it stop.

"What the hell?! Make it stop!"

"Those were hollowed pellets filled with holy water of course." She put her hand on her hip and winked at him. "Don't be such a baby; I only nailed you with like four or five. It'll stop soon."

Layla couldn't believe all that she was seeing! She knew that Jimmy was a genius but this was unheard of! "Emma, this is like the *Six Million Dollar Man*, or better yet the *Bionic Woman*! How did he know about all of this stuff?"

"Didn't he tell you?" Emma smiled braggingly. "He was a double major in chemical engineering and advanced technologies!" She placed the leg right side up on the counter again and forced it down on the ball of the foot, demonstrating that the wooden dagger feature jutting from the underside of the foot was also available in this model. She gestured for them to step back and she aimed the leg at the cinderblock wall. "And not to be out done, Jimmy added a little something that I think is totally wicked!" She knocked the inside of the foot, forcing it to spin clockwise. In doing so a nozzle was triggered to rise from the shin. Once it had locked into place, Emma touched the inside of the knee and flames shot out and scorched the wall!

"That is BLOODY BRILLIANT!" Layla exclaimed, jumping up and down and clapping.

Jerome stood back in awe. "Damn, I want a fake leg!"

"Yeah and I get all the good parking places, too!" Emma smiled and lowered the flame thrower nozzle back into its compartment. "That's why it's made of CERAMIC Kevlar. With the flame thrower, the steel Kevlar was just cooking the dummy legs like they were in a microwave. Ceramic isn't a good conductor of heat. This way I don't roast when I'm flaming. And I totally get I just said that." She pressed inward on the heel as she had when she began the demonstration and the rubbery synthetic skin returned. "And now for my favorite part." She squeezed the foot and the heel lifted and the arch increased, putting it into the perfect position for high heels. Emma and Layla both sighed in reverence.

"You have a freakin' flame thrower that shoots out from your freakin' shin and this is your favorite part? Our lives are in the hands of no better than a shorter, gimpier Paris Hilton!" Jerome turned and walked away with his hands on his head.

"Hey! This happens to be very important in the business of Slaying I'll have you know!" Emma defended, pointing a firm finger at the vamp.

"Oh yeah? What's that?" he asked arrogantly.

She reached down and pulled up a high-heeled, laced-up leather boot. "A wider variety of fashionable footwear for stylish ass kicking!"

"Yeah, but what kind of damage can you do in heels?" he pointed out.

Emma raised an eyebrow and held up the heel of the boot. "You never saw *Single White Female* did you?"

Jerome acknowledged the reference and caught himself slowly covering his right eye with his hand. He turned to inspect the punching bag hanging from the ceiling across the room.

Emma waited for him to be far enough away and then turned to Layla. She spoke softly. "What's he thinking? Is he lying to us?"

Layla looked up abruptly. "Oh, I don't know. You can't read a vampire's mind."

"What? Why not?"

"When I read a mind it's not like I am in there jumbling. It's kinda like I have sonar I guess. I have an antenna that throws something out at your noggin and your thoughts bounce off. But with vampires, they've been dead, their souls are gone into the ether already, there's nothing to bounce back. My power lies in spirits, not demons."

Emma bit her lip. There had to be some way for her to be sure he wasn't going to double cross them.

"Why don't you use your telepathy that much anyway?" It had come to Emma's attention during this conversation that the most she had ever seen Layla use her ability was when they first met. She thought that if she had something like that it would serve as an advantage and she would use it all of the time.

"Because, there are things that people shouldn't know about other people. There are things in the dark recesses of the mind that should never be brought to light and things that are meant to be left unsaid. That is a door that shouldn't be opened. It's taken a lot of time and practice but I've learned to control it. If I let it go full blast, it would open me up to countless doorways and not just to this dimension but to the spirits who follow me around. And that's something I don't know if even I could close." Layla looked at Emma closely. She was deep in thought. Layla noticed this a lot with her. Emma would stare off into space with the look of torture on her face. She tried to break through the barrier that Emma kept up, but to no avail. Layla looked at her with narrowed eyes and leaned in.

"What are you hiding behind your door?" she asked with genuine care.

Emma awoke from her silent torture. She was lost in the thought of Jimmy being taken by that monster and that she wasn't there to stop it. Nica was looking for her and got Jimmy instead.

"Sorry, I was just thinking about what you said about you having sonar. With me and Jimmy it's more like feelings and instincts we share. Sometimes if we are close enough to each other and have a strong thought, then the other will share that. Almost like we have one mind for a split second." She laughed softly as she explained and hobbled over to a stool to sit down.

"In a way you're not wrong," Layla said, walking over with her.

"What do you mean?"

"Well, there have been several studies in the scientific community regarding the special bond that twins share. And not to mention the mystical beliefs that say twins are also twins of the soul, sharing that as well as their likeness. But as you well know, you two are something unique and very special. There has never ever been a Slayer with a twin. So not only would you already have the connection that normal twins share, you are a Slayer! You share that spirit with your brother!" Layla paced back and forth in front of Emma and it was clear that she was now thinking out loud. "So yes, in a sense, there could be times when you share the same mind and, therefore, it really wouldn't be telepathy would it? Which would explain the proximity issue! The closer you are to each other…"

Emma tried to put on her bionic leg but the wound she had patched up earlier was getting in the way. "Ouch!" She grimaced and seethed.

As an after thought, while Layla was pacing in front of her, she laid her hand on Emma's wound and said, "Here, let me get that for you," and then continued on with her pacing.

Emma removed the bandages to find that her wound was completely healed! "Goddammit, Layla! Why didn't you just do that in the first place?!"

"You didn't ask, and I got tired of listening to you whine!"

Emma rolled her eyes and then rolled the form-fitting silicon liner on over her stub and then pushed on her bionic prosthetic.

"Cool!" she mused.

Jerome marched back over to the two girls, obviously frustrated. "Ok, now that you have your rocket launcher fancy schmancy leg on and we have established that vampires can't have their minds read, shall we start with a plan to get our brothers back!"

"Just waiting on you, fang boy!" Emma taunted.

"You know what I do to little girls like you?" Jerome asked, walking menacingly toward Emma.

"I don't know, threaten a lot?" They stood within inches of each other, staring one another down. Layla jumped and stood between them.

"Ok, guys, look, we are here to stop Naberius and Nica and get our people back!" She turned toward Emma. "You need to focus on getting Jimmy back and killing Nica. And then you can do whatever you want to this wanker here." She then turned to face Jerome. "And you need to bloody realize that you sought out the help of a Slayer! You either need to start showing some bloody respect or we'll just kill you and you'll never get to see your boyfriend again! So start talking!" Jerome fumed for a moment and then walked over to the work counter in the middle of the shop. He reached into his back pocket and pulled out a folded piece of paper.

"Since I left the farm over a week ago, I have been sneaking in to find out everything I can. I paid off a couple of brethren on the inside to give me information as it comes." The folded paper was actually a couple of pages. The first was a crude pencil drawing of the farm's layout. The other two pages looked like notes. He pointed to the largest square central to the simple map. "This is the main house; the cellar is where the ritual was performed to raise the Inanna. It is also where Naberius spends most of his time. He is fond of sulking and plotting and meditating, gathering strength; that's where he does it. If the effigy would be anywhere it would be in there; he would want to keep it close to him."

"Good. Now, how do I kill him?" Emma asked, staring at the paper.

"I think I'm starting to warm up to you. But I don't think you're going to be able to pull it off."

Emma looked offended and then he continued.

"It has nothing to do with your slaying talents. Naberius' power lies in and over the dead. Although the shift of balance has affected him as well, he is still pretty powerful. To kill him you would need to be able to cut off his power source." He looked at Layla and she looked up and pointed to herself in surprise. "That's why he fears you. As strong a medium and witch you are, you have the potential to be an amazing necromancer and that scares the begeezus out of him."

"Right, he's a demon king, so that means he's an old one and would be like Aslyn. He has a foot hold on this world and the next, drawing off the souls of the dead to gain strength! All I would have to do is remove that grip and he would be like any other demon! Great, now how am I supposed to depose a Demon King?" Layla looked over and tapped her teeth with her fingernail.

"Wait a minute, Nica is the Inanna, the Soul Eater, and Naberius is a glorified necromancer. If Nica is able to get the soul of a Slayer she would be unstoppable, and as Layla just said, right now Naberius is vulnerable!" Emma slapped her hand down on the counter in celebration of her clarity. "He doesn't want her to stay here! He isn't looking to control her as a foot soldier! He wants her to get a Slayer soul so he can take hers, making HIM the unstoppable one!"

"Blow me, that makes perfect sense!" Layla said in agreement.

"That's right, and her plan is to lure you there to rescue your brother and then kill you both! That way she would have double the potency. And after she does that, Naberius is going to kill her and drink the remaining blood that's left in the effigy, making him the most powerful being in this world and several others, and if he kills her, he'll kill Leo, too." Jerome looked down at the papers and shuffled them.

"Isn't that what you vampires like, though?! Death and destruction? Total chaos and mayhem?" Emma said sarcastically.

"Yes, but on our terms, and this is NOT on my terms! I thought it would be cool at first. Big time blood sucker coming out to kill off all the Slayers, and then SHE put some kind of whammy on Leo and he just completely changed! Leo never cared about anything else other than going home to Italy. That's all we wanted! We signed up for this Order because they promised to get rid of the Slayers, no offense."

"None taken," Emma said simply.

"But when he said that he was going to stay, I knew something was wrong. So I left, but I came back to see if maybe he had come to senses and decided to leave. When I did, I found out what had really been going on. And that's when I chose to seek you out." Jerome stopped and walked away with his hands in his pockets and sat on the stool Emma had just been on.

"Ok, here's what we need to do now. Layla, find a way to take away Naberius' power source and break the effigy."

"I'm already on it." Layla ran upstairs to start her research.

"Jerome, you need to come up with a distraction to give us time to take down Naberius and the effigy so we can get to Nica and rescue Jimmy."

"I think I can come up with something." He stood from his stool and grabbed up a notepad and pen that was laying on Jimmy's desk. "What are you going to do?"

"I'm going to plan our attack and try a little target practice." She grabbed the bag of stake clips for her leg and headed out.

Upstairs, Layla began tearing through books and notes, looking for anything on The Effigy of the Inanna or deposing powerful demon kings. It wasn't long before that familiar nagging began again. A tenacious spirit broke through the blue and began their plea. Layla tried to ignore it but it was becoming more and more persistent.

"Hey! I know you can hear me! Quit ignoring me! I just want to help you!" was the message the male voice kept repeating. Layla continued to do her best to block him out. He would come around to face her and she would just turn the other direction and continue reading.

"Fine. If you want to do it the hard way go ahead! Far be it for me to ruin your fun and tell you EXACTLY HOW TO KILL NABERIUS BY USING THE ORB OF PURE LIGHT!"

Layla jerked up and looked right at him. "Oh my God! You're Brahma Siddig! You're my ancestor! The one who started our diaries!"

"Yes! And it's about time you noticed. I didn't use my yearly pass to the Earthly Realm to be ignored by my direct descendant!"

"You get a yearly pass?" Layla asked in disbelief.

"Yes. Anyway, you need to get the Orb of Pure Light. It can only be touched by earth bound creatures. If a being touches the orb and they are straddling dimensions, it will burn away the part of them that isn't in this plane. If you take the orb to Naberius and force him to touch it, his god-like powers will be burned away and he will unable to derive strength from the souls of the dead and be stuck in this dimension!"

Layla shook her head in astonishment. "How do I get it? Where can I find it?"

"Well, conveniently enough it's actually right down the street. Emma accidentally sold it in a yard sale five years ago."

"You mean the Hogans had it?"

"Yes, until unbeknownst to her Abgal Da parents, Emma sold it for fifty cents to Mrs. Doane down the street. She believes it's a blue Faberge egg."

Layla blinked and threw her hands up to her face. "Well, that was easy."

"Well, you better hurry; Naberius knows of its existence and has his lackies out looking for it."

"Thank you, Brahma! By the way, where do you go on your other yearly passes?"

"Disneyworld, actually. There's a really nice one over in…"

They chimed in unison… "Shrimp Hell!"

"Yes, if you can get past the smell…Anyway, good luck, try not to screw up, subsequently destroying reality as we know it." Brahma waved and disappeared into the blue.

Layla shook her head from the last comment. "Easy for him to say, he's already dead." And then she ran to tell Emma the news.

CHAPTER SIXTEEN

Power Struggle

Jimmy sat on the cold mud floor of the Kender Farm main house cellar. His arms and back were sore and tired from being chained in this position for so long. And he was getting weaker from loss of blood. He was wet, filthy and cold from being stripped of all his clothing, save his blue plaid boxer shorts. He stopped shaking from the cold over six hours ago. But he could still feel the pain from the hole Nica made with the stake in his left shoulder, broken ribs on his left side, fractured wrist, black eye and fat lip. Nica and her little cronies had made him their personal "dammit" doll. He tried to kick his feet out from under him, but whenever he tried he winced in pain and quickly stopped.

"Sorry, I keep forgetting how easily you things break." The sultry, menacing voice came from the center of the cellar. She was perched seductively on the stone altar that she was raised from. Using his right eye (because his left was swollen to the size of a golf ball and shut) he could see that she had cleaned herself up from their initial meeting. She had exchanged her tattered and burned red silk corset for a black, backless halter with a plunging neck line and her burned black leather pants for a fresh pair. She reached up with her hand and smoothed her onyx bob and twirled her finger around her dangling ruby chandelier earring.

A trickle of water rolled down the mud wall and landed on Jimmy's bare shoulder. The sensation shocked him into shivering again.

"Oh I'm sorry, love, but after that little incident with your annoying exploding watch, I found myself unable to trust you. So, we removed your clothes to make sure you didn't have any other surprises for us. This is why we left you with your underwear, no surprises there." She giggled and looked down, referencing his manhood. He wanted to cover himself to stop her from visually violating him, but his hands were chained against the wall behind him.

"My apologies, did I strike a nerve there?" The sound of a click and then a flash of a flame, signaled that Leo was there as well and was lighting his usual roll-your-own. He stepped forward, exposing his face to the small amount of light streaming down from the stairs. Nica looked up at him and grinned. She grabbed his hand and stuck his finger in her mouth and slowly pulled it out. The smoke from Leo's cigarette puffed and billowed. It drifted along the room until it reached Jimmy's blood-crusted nostrils.

"Do you mind? I happen to like my lungs and don't plan on being a second-hand smoke statistic!" he forced.

Leo walked up to Jimmy, took a deep drag from his smoke and blew it back out in a huge cloud in Jimmy's face. "You're going to die soon anyway. Just a few more hours."

"You live with whatever delusion makes you happiest," Jimmy groaned. "When my sister gets here she is going to be sooo pissed that I don't think they make a rating for the amount of violence she's going to do to you." He smiled the best he could with his puffy lips.

Nica slid from her stony perch and glided over to him. "Your faith in your sister is touching." She crouched down in front of him. "But naïve." She stuck her finger into the half dollar size hole she had inflicted the day before and twisted, forcing more blood to ooze out and run down his chest. He grunted and clenched his teeth in pain. She yanked her finger back and sucked the blood from it. "Face it, book worm, she can't stop me. She isn't strong enough. And from what Leo here tells me, she's too busy with her own issues to worry about me or you!" She stood and walked backward away from him. "So relax! Enjoy your last few remaining hours! Because, when the sun goes down, you are going to die!" She threw her hands up and laughed. "And when I have what I need, I am going to take my best guy to see his hometown!" She held Leo's face in her hand and kissed him. "And we are going to have ourselves one hell of a party getting rid of all those little girls playing commando!" Leo clutched her hips and kissed her forcefully.

"Your malice is perfect, mia caro! You are la mia bella distruzione." He kissed her once more. He had found in her what he couldn't find anywhere else. She was his lover, his confidant, his teacher, his equal and his superior. He had traveled with Jerome for thirty-some odd years and still he felt nothing more for him than teacher to student. With the moment he felt her presence, he knew that a new world of possibilities had opened up to him and he wasn't about to let it pass. His time of disillusion had come to an end with the beginning of Nica.

Jimmy turned away and groaned in disgust. Their display, however excessive and bordering on the pornographic, did turn his thoughts to Layla. He wondered if she was ok, if Emma had gotten to her in time. Who was he kidding? Of course she had! This was Emma he was talking about! She probably saved her first and then bitched at her for an hour for making her exert herself! Yes, he was sure of it. And he knew that she would be here soon to save him and then save the world from Nica and her butt boy.

"What's the matter, junior? Jealous?" Nica teased as Leo nuzzled her neck.

Jimmy scoffed and looked away again. "Yeah, right. God only knows where all you have teeth," he mumbled.

Leo heard this and stormed over. He punched him across his jaw, knocking him unconscious.

"That is what makes you lesser beings so intolerable." Naberius had entered the cellar from his chamber down the tunnel. He walked determinedly over to Nica, Leo and the newly unconscious prisoner. "You have no patience. Or control over your tempers." He nodded to acknowledge Nica. "And you, my queen. Did I not ask that you refrain from cavorting with this filthy one?"

"Yeah, I thought about it, but then I decided that that didn't sound like any fun." She slapped her hips and propped herself against the stone altar. "We both know that you won't do anything to me until you get what you want, Naberius. So quit trying to scare me."

"We've already had this conversation! So if you want to stick around after I do get what I want you better start being a lot nicer!" He stomped over to the sleeping Jimmy and lifted his face with his massive hand. "Hard to believe that this little vermin possesses the spirit of the Ba Musal. What a waste." He stood there, bent over, inspecting Jimmy, poking at his wounds with his large index finger. "He's so fragile, nothing like his warrior sister."

While Naberius was hunched over their captive, one of the lackey vampires snuck down the stairs quietly and gestured for Nica. She motioned for him to be quiet and met him at the banister.

"The Orb was missing from its resting place, My Lady. We were unable to find it in time." Nica rolled her eyes at the news. "We were, however, able to get the other thing you requested." The lanky vamp pulled his hand out of his pocket and slid something small and wrapped in a white cloth into hers. She smiled and waved him off, instructing him to disappear, and she unwrapped the gift. It was a tiny vile filled with illuminated blue liquid. Leo looked back at her and grinned when he realized what she held.

Nica reached into her cleavage and pulled a small syringe from her halter. She stuck the needle into the vile and drew a small amount. After retrieving the correct dosage she placed the vile in the same hiding place that she had had the syringe. Nica looked at Naberius and zeroed in on the back of his neck. She aimed and shot it from her fingertips into her target. Before he could reach up to touch what had stung him, she used her blink ability and was within inches of him in a fraction of a second to shove the plunger in with the palm of her hand so hard that the needle broke off. She blinked back again in time for him to stumble to a stand and touch the back of his neck. His vision blurred and he continued to struggle to stay on his feet.

"Wha... Wha..." He couldn't form words. Nica stood with her arms crossed across her chest, smiling.

"Nectar of the Gods. It's a bitch ain't it? It won't kill you, that's what the Orb is supposed to do, but we couldn't find it. Arturo was kind enough to tell me about it before I plucked his head from his shoulders like an apple. Surprised, Naberius? I find it hard to believe that you didn't see the betrayal of your most trusted High Priest coming. This little magic solution that's made from all kinds of interesting things that I can't pronounce won't kill you. But I do know that it renders you as weak and harmless as a kitten! Night night, Daddy!" She wiggled her fingers as he fell to the ground in front of Jimmy.

Nica snapped her fingers twice and her attendants emerged from the steps in a twinkling. She pointed to Naberius and they bowed and went straight to him dutifully. They lifted the still conscious Demon King off of the mud floor and carried him over to the stone alter where they laid him. The three removed their sheer wraps and began to tie him up. His eyes rolled as the world around him swirled, wobbled. Nica instructed her attending Priestesses to call for Naberius' monks and stood above him running her fingers down his stone chest.

"Now, you might feel a little funny. Like your arms and legs are too heavy, takes every bit of concentration to form coherent thought. But don't worry, that part will pass. You still won't be able to move your limbs, but your thought process will soon come back. And when that happens, you are going to tell me where my effigy is so I can stay and play for a while. Ok? So until then you can just rest right here. And just in case you do end up retaining a little remnant of your strength, we've got ya tied down with my Priestesses' silk wraps, blessed of course. You'd have an easier time ripping apart steel." She kissed her fingertips and pressed them to his.

The Priestesses returned with several monks and genuflected.

"Hello, boys! You have a new boss! ME!" She outstretched her arms and threw her head back. "Well, more like your old boss is back." Leo came next to her and kissed her hand. "Naberius has decided that he is too old and grown weary of being a powerful ruler and has graciously handed the reigns over to myself." She laughed insanely. "If you believe that!" Nica tapped her hand in Naberius' thigh and continued. "You will do as I command from now on, or you will die. Now, I won't have you making any rash decisions and I will understand if your religious beliefs and your loyalty forbid you from staying here under my command. So for those of you that that wish to, you are free to go. All I ask is that you step forward and pay your respects to your former liege before you go on your way." She stepped back away from the altar against the mud wall, away from the vampiric monks. "Go ahead, I won't harm you!" she assured.

A monk stepped forward sheepishly at first, but then gained confidence when he saw that Nica didn't make a move. Once he started to walk up to the altar that Naberius lay on, some others began to move in the crowd. He genuflected before him and then turned to go. He nodded to the others that wanted to leave as well, letting them know that it was ok.

He made it a couple of feet when Leo, who had not moved from his spot, in one clean move, produced a stake from inside his jacket and planted it deep into the monk's back, piercing his heart and reducing him to dust. The group froze.

"Like I said, I won't do anything. But lover here just hates to see me with hurt feelings." She batted her eyes and moved back in front of the group.

The dust from the dismantled vamp made it to Jimmy's nostrils. It swirled around with his breath and tickled the tiny hairs that covered the fleshy walls. He awoke as he sneezed. When he looked up he saw the room full of vampires and Naberius tied to the stone altar.

"Mornin', sleepy head!" Nica greeted cheerily.

"Oh no," he groaned. "This can't be good."

Chapter Seventeen

Hula and Hats

Emma and Jerome came briskly through the front door of the Hogan home with exhausted looks on their faces.

"Did you get it?" Layla asked urgently.

Emma reached into her jacket pocket and pulled out the blue egg-shaped Orb. "Yeah, here." She slapped it into her hand and walked to the refrigerator in the kitchen. "Next time the mission calls for a B n' E you're playing point man." Emma toasted Layla with the orange juice carton and took a long gulp.

"I am not the one who sold a crystal containing powerful, mystical properties at a rummage sale for fifty cents! And at any rate, all you had to do was break into an old woman's house down the street and nick a little bobble. How hard could that be for a superhero and a vampire? What took you so long? You've been gone for over three hours," Layla demanded, tapping her finger on her hip.

Emma and Jerome looked at each other and flashed back to the day's earlier events.

They had been scouting Mrs. Doane's house with Jerome under a black umbrella. Emma had spotted the Orb sitting on a tiered table with several other eggs of many colors and sizes, when Jerome allowed his hand to be caught in the sunlight and caught himself on fire. He dropped the umbrella to put his hand out and began hissing and jumping up onto her covered front porch to protect himself. Emma tried waving her hands and grunting to get his attention to make him stop. She gave up on the charades and leapt up to the porch as well. She was slapping his hands and arms when the front door opened and Mrs. Doane stood there looking very confused.

"Emma? Emma Hogan? What in the world are you doing?" the small lady with large square glasses asked. Emma and Jerome stopped and looked like a couple of deer caught in headlights. Emma blinked rapidly and puckered her lips, scrambling for an answer.

"Well, hi, Mrs. Doane! I'm sorry, this is my cousin…Jerry!" She started patting and smoothing his arms with her hands and smiling awkwardly. "Yeah, uh, he's our um, 'special' cousin. He wandered off and saw…your…lovely decorative eggs in the window and just couldn't help himself!" She then gave an uncomfortable laugh and Jerome looked at her with a sneer. She kicked him with her plastic leg in the shin and he looked at Mrs. Doane with roving eyes and a blank look and said:

"I like…shiny…?"

"Of course you do, dear! And you know I like shinies, too! Would you like to come in and have a closer look, honey?" she asked with charm and grace.

There was a moment of silence and then Emma stomped on Jerome's foot to make him answer.

"YES! Like Shiny!" he grunted. Mrs. Doane ushered them into the house.

"You're so pale, dear," she commented, concerned.

"Yes, Aunt Judy doesn't like to let him out much, you know around people; he tends to bite."

"Oh my," Mrs. Doane said, stepping a couple of inches away from "Jerry."

After perusing her extensive collection, Emma spied the very "egg" she had sold to her five years ago. As soon as Mrs. Doane moved on to the next table, Emma scooped up the Orb and placed it in her pocket. She moved a few of the other nick nacks around to camouflage the missing one.

"Well, thank you, Mrs. Doane, for showing Jerry your lovely collection, but we must be going now. It's time for his snack." Emma looped her arm around Jerome and started to drag him away.

"I like cheese," he said.

"Apish posh! I have cheese here! I'll make both of you kids a nice glass of milk and a plate of cheese for Jerry here! It's been so long since I have seen either of the Hogan twins and I am not letting you go that easily!" She ushered the two over to her plastic-covered love seat and sat them down. Within minutes she returned with the glasses and a plate of cheese slices.

For the next couple of hours she jumped from one subject to the next without allowing any interjection from her visitors. During her story of her and her sister's trip to Hawaii she told them about the hula lessons they took and even, to their dismay, gave a demonstration. Whenever she would turn or look the other way, Emma and Jerome would argue over finding a way to escape. Finally, Emma gave him the international hand signal for "I will stake you" and he blurted out the first thing that came to mind.

"I poopie!"

Mrs. Doane stopped in mid "Kahele" and looked back at the two with wide eyes. Emma sat in surprise as well at his choice in rouse.

"Did you say you had an accident, hon?" She lowered her arms and turned to face them. "Because that's ok, I actually have those quite often myself! That's why I buy the special pants!"

~~~~~

Minutes later Emma and Jerome had made their escape and were entering the Hogan home.

They returned to reality and both said at the same time, "I don't want to talk about it." Emma went back to drinking her orange juice.

Emma emerged from her carton and wiped her mouth with the back of her hand. "How do we know if it's the real deal?"

"Well that's easy." Layla stuck her arm out and opened the hand that held the Orb. "We just turn it on...Ena Nita!" With that the Orb began to glow with a soft blue light that grew brighter and brighter. "Why Tah Heo." And that shut it off.

"Ok. So that's taken care of. What about the effigy?" Emma asked.

Layla picked up the book off the kitchen table that she had been reading. "It translates to shatter the image of the Inanna and to burn away her dark heritage. Whatever that means."

"I think I know what it means," Jerome spoke up. The girls looked at him questioningly. He rolled his eyes and spoke again. "What's another way of referencing your heritage?" The girls looked at each other and thought for a moment.

"Ancestry?" Emma said.

"NO! Bloodlines! Key word, BLOOD! It says to burn away her dark blood!" Jerome said proudly.

"We should set her on fire?" Layla asked.

"No! The Effigy houses a vile that holds HER blood, not the host's blood but the Inanna's, you know that already don't you? Anyway, we have to burn that!"

The girls looked at one another and nodded in agreement.

"Ok so now that we have that all worked out, what's your plan for a distraction?" Emma asked Jerome.

"I'll just go in there and start an argument with Leo, try to make him see what's happening to him. I'm only in this to get my brother back; I don't give a shit what happens to you or anyone else for that matter. So once you and witchy woman bust in and go all good versus evil, Leo and I are gone!"

"Poetic almost," Emma said sarcastically. "Fine, all that matters is we get in, after that whatever you do, so long as it stays out of my way, is your business. Go back to Europe and let The Brotherhood deal with you." Emma put the carton back into the refrigerator and turned back to face them. "Where would they be keeping my brother?"

"I'm not really sure. If Nica wants to keep an eye on him she might keep him in her room. Or she might want him in the ritual chamber so he'll be ready for the ceremony. Or Naberius could want to keep him in his Chamber to make sure that Nica doesn't take off with him. There are all kinds of possibilities." Jerome walked over to the table and sat down.

Layla made a disgusted face and walked over to stand in front of Emma. "Why don't you ask Jimmy yourself?" she asked.

"But I haven't really been able sense him for a while now."

"Meditate!" Layla led her down the hall to her bedroom and sat her down on the floor. Layla disappeared for a moment and then returned with three pillar candles and a lighter. "Here." She lit the candles and sat across from Emma Indian style. "Give me your hands." She held out her hands and grasped Emma's. "Now close your eyes and concentrate on Jimmy. How he looks when he smiles, the color of his eyes, that little wisp of hair he always pushes out of his face..."

"Hey! Are we talking about my brother or your would-be boyfriend?" Emma asked with one eye open.

"Just close your eyes and think of Jimmy! The more you go into detail the deeper you will go into your mind. That's where your connection lies. Now shut your yapper and get to thinking."

Emma closed her eyes and listened to Layla as she described Jimmy in detail. Slowly, her voice became a distant echo. The colorful shapes that one sees when they close their eyes tight began to take form out of the blackness. What she thought was a light was in fact the White Woman again.

"Am I sleeping?" she asked herself out loud, but no one answered. "This is my dream! What is going on here?"

The woman was close to her now and held a finger to her own lips. She was instructing Emma to stop asking questions, she would have her answers soon enough.

"Where's Jimmy?" Emma asked softly. The woman turned and began straightening some objects on a shelf. Emma looked around and realized that she was in some sort of store.

"Please, I need to get to my brother. Are you here to show me where I can find him?"

"Oh, dear, no, that's not my job. My job is to help you find the right hat!" She turned back and faced Emma, holding a large pink tea bonnet.

Emma scowled and looked around herself again. The place was wall to wall hats! Of every different shape, size, color and design. Emma looked down to her right and saw a small end table awkwardly stacked with fez after fez on top of one another. She ran her fingers through one of the golden tassels and tried to concentrate. How did she get here?

"Hats are important you know. You can't just wear any old one! It has to be just the right one!" The lady looked down at the pink hat and then back to Emma. "No, I don't think this one will do at all."

Emma rushed up to her side and leaned over to make eye contact. "I need to get to my brother; I was looking for him when I found you. Can you tell me how to get out of here?"

"Well, you can't go out there without a hat! Just be patient, I'll find the perfect one! I'm sure with a pretty head like that there is bound to be one in here that was made for you!" The woman went back to work in her search. She left the large oak table for the incredibly high wooden shelves that bordered the entire shop. Everything was over stacked, and the tables looked like they would lose their merchandise to gravity at any moment.

"Looks like the book shop in *Harry Potter*," Emma mumbled to herself. She decided to she could wait no longer and would try to find her own way out. But when she tried pushing and pulling on the front door nothing happened. Even though she could see a bright sunny day with droves of people walking up and down the streets through the two large picture windows that flanked the wooden door, she couldn't get to it! Suddenly the door opened and a couple walked in. The man and woman brushed past Emma happily and immediately began trying on hats. Emma quickly grabbed the door, trying to escape while it was still open but to no avail. It passed through her hand as if she were nothing more than air!

"I told you. You can't go out there until we find you the right hat!" the woman said with her back turned to Emma, still searching the stacks.

Emma became frustrated and she began to hyperventilate. Looking around the shop she noticed that there were more people hat shopping than those who had just entered. Across the room, there was a blonde girl and what looked like her mother trying on purple and blue straw beach hats. Next to them was a man trying on a ski mask. When she looked to her left she found another woman trying on three and four hats at a time.

"Where in the hell am I?" Emma asked herself.

"You are in luck, dear! I found two! Either one will suit you perfectly! Which one would you like?" The White Woman held out two hats before Emma.

As Emma looked at the hats presented to her she heard the door open again. The mother and daughter were wearing the purple and blue beach hats and were leaving.

"See how nice they look! They did a good job finding the right hats! It's so important you know!" the woman mused. Right behind the mother and daughter the man who had been looking at the ski mask was leaving, wearing what looked like a Viking helmet.

"Now he really should have asked for help! It's a shame that he won't realize until later that that hat just isn't for him! Now look here, which hat would you like? As I said both are perfect matches!" She stuck her arms out farther, prodding Emma to look.

The one in her left hand was a black fedora with a shiny metal feather sticking out from the silk band. Emma lifted it and was amazed by its weight.

"It's so heavy; it doesn't look like it weighs that much!" she commented.

"That's the matching baggage that comes with it," the lady informed.

Emma replaced the fedora and looked over to the hat in her right hand. It was leather, simple and worn. It had a very slight lip to it. She didn't think it looked like much at all.

"These are the hats that you think were made for me? The first one you picked up was pink and frilly and those women got nice, normal-looking hats, but you bring a hat that looks like it was worn by Al

Capone and weighs a ton and another one that looks like it's at least a hundred years old! This is stupid! I am leaving and you are going to let me!"

Emma stormed over just as the woman with four hats on was leaving.

"Oh my, someone should have told her that she only needs one!" The White Woman shook her head.

Emma tried grabbing the door again but just as before it passed right through her.

"I told you, you have to pick a hat!" the lady reiterated.

Emma plopped her hands to her sides and spun around, puffing out her cheeks. "So you're saying that all I have to do is pick a hat and I can go?"

"Yes."

Emma walked back over to her and looked at the hats again. She thought that the fedora looked nicer, but she didn't want to put that heavy thing on her head. She picked up the leather one and turned it over in her hands. It was much, much lighter than the other and it did have a certain antique charm to it.

"There's a lot of history in that hat," the woman said. Emma smiled as she smelled the leather and smoothed her hands over its surface.

She lifted it up and placed it on her head. "There, I'll take this one. What do you think?" Emma posed right and left while the woman smiled. She put the fedora on the table and brought her fingertips to her lips.

"I think that you made the right choice!" The woman brought a silver hand mirror form her white robes and lifted it to Emma's face to see for herself.

Emma looked and was immediately confused. "Hey where'd it go? I don't see a hat?" When she looked away from the mirror, she saw that everything was gone. The hats, the shop, and more importantly the Sentinel. "Well, that's just great! Now what?!" With that, far off in the distance she heard Layla's voice still chanting away about Jimmy. "Ok, we'll try that again. But this time if you detour me, make it a shoe store!" She closed her eyes and focused. "C'mon, Jimmy, it worked when I was in trouble. You have to tell me where they are keeping you at that farm!"

Through the darkness she found him. He was huddled in a ball, broken, bloody and half naked. Emma ran to him and crouched down, wrapping her arms around his shoulders.

"It's ok, bubby! It's ok!" she cried. "Oh God! Look at what they have done to you!" She held him and rocked. "I'm coming, don't you worry! They won't get away with this! Just tell me where they are keeping you!"

Slowly a room emerged. She found herself in a damp and musty cellar with a mud floor and mostly mud walls. There was a large stone table at the center and an old wooden, rickety staircase against one of the remaining stone walls.

"Ok, ok. I see it. Don't worry! We are on our way!"

Emma emerged from her trance, gasping for air. "Cellar, cellar, cellar!" was all she could manage. In her disorientation, she tried to stand and ended up turning around and around and falling over.

"Emma! Are you with me?" Layla was holding her shoulders, trying to help her focus. "Easy. You came out of it too fast; your brain doesn't have the capability to comprehend all of this at once. It needs time to adjust!" Layla was able to force Emma to sit on the edge of the bed and help her breathe slowly.

Emma closed her eyes and relaxed her mind. Steadily, the world stopped spinning and she was able to reopen her eyes. She saw Layla hovering over her with the look of worry and concern on her face.

"I lost you for a moment. One second you were with me, the next you were somewhere else, but it wasn't with Jimmy. I could tell when you found him." She squared her eyes and looked deep into Emma's. "You did find him, right?"

"Yes! They're keeping him in that cellar where they do the rituals, the one Jerome told us about. He's hurt, really bad. I have to get to him!" Emma tried to sit up and leave the room, but Layla stopped her.

"We will get him, don't worry. We have a few more hours before sunset. They won't do anything more until then. Are you feeling better?"

Emma laid a hand aside her face and thought. "It was the weirdest thing. You said I went somewhere? I did! The Sentinel was there. And she was making me look at hats! She wouldn't let me leave until I picked out a hat! Funny huh? Either I was dreaming, or that Sentinel is getting old and senile."

"That one's all you, hon. Maybe you'll figure that one out in time. How bad is Jimmy?" Layla softened her voice and her expression. Poor Jimmy.

"His face was swollen and bloody. He had a black eye and a split lip. From what I could tell, I think he has some broken ribs and his shoulder had a huge hole in it."

"From the stake," Layla said. She bit her lip and squeezed her eyes shut. She couldn't let herself drown in her sorrows right now. Jimmy and Emma both knew what it could mean to pick up this proverbial sword and Jimmy would want Layla to be focused. She swallowed deep and pushed it away. If she pushed it down and carried it with her, she could unleash it when she needed to, at just the right moment, at just the right person. And Layla wasn't about to allow another person she cared for to be taken from her. Even if these feelings just began, she knew they were precious.

"Where's Jerome? We need to start loading up." Emma slid off of the bed and marched down the hall. "If that bitch wants a fight, I plan on giving her one hell of a scrap!" Emma turned and jaunted down the stairs to the basement.

Layla stopped at the doorway and thought for a moment. "What should I wear?"

Chapter Eighteen

Kender Farm

Sunset. Emma and Layla stood behind a large walnut tree on the outskirts of the Kender Farm. They watched with racing hearts as Jerome walked across the now barren corn fields to the graying main house. Emma's breath was halted, her palms were sweaty. She kept rubbing her hands up and down on the bark of the tree, hoping the dirt would keep them dry. In the vanishing light she could make out two vampires pacing in front of the building.

"I can tell they intend this to be a trap becau—" She was interrupted by the sound of crunching. She looked over and was appalled to see Layla stuffing Cheeto's from a snack bag furiously into her cheese-coated mouth. "Layla! What in the hell are you doing? We are supposed to be incognito right now! Hello! Vampires have, you know, vampiric hearing and NOSES!"

"I can't help it! I get hungry when I'm nervous!"

"You're hungry all the time!" Emma grabbed the bag and threw it behind them. Layla grimaced, dusted the cheese from her hands and face and straightened her ponytail. Earlier that day, it took Emma all that she had to drag Layla from her closet. She had been digging through everything she owned looking for the perfect "ultimate battle" outfit. Apparently, that consisted of black Capri cut, cotton spandex work out pants, a white sleeveless tank top and an indigo blue zip-up hoodie.

Layla bent down to tie the laces to her brand new matching Nike tennis shoes and dust the dirt from them.

"You kill me. We're supposed to concentrating on saving the world from evil, and my brother, and here you are trying to make a fitness fashion statement!"

"Just because you don't care if you look like a homeless person while you are fighting evil doesn't mean I don't have to either!"

Emma looked down at herself. She wore the same thing she always did. Blue jean culottes, boots to accommodate for her supped-up leg, dark t-shirt (so you can't see blood stains) and her black leather jacket for cool nights such as this one. "There's nothing wrong with what I'm wearing! It's comfortable!"

"It's ok, duck, you just don't know any better!" Layla patted her shoulder and looked back over the corn fields.

It took Emma a minute but she caught on to the jab at her personal tastes. She had begun to defend herself with a witty, cutting remark at Layla's expense but Layla spoke first.

"There, look. There's the signal." Layla pointed out to the main house. What looked like the living room light was flickering.

Emma slung her backpack over her shoulder and Layla picked up her small bag containing the Orb of Pure light and they made their way as stealthily as possible across the barren field.

~~~~~

Jerome flipped the light switch several times while no one was in the room. He hoped the slayer would see it in time. He felt his stomach sour. He knew that he may not live through this. If Nica suspected for a moment what he was planning, he would be dead before he would even feel his heart ripped from his chest.

He looked down at himself and inspected his black suit, with silk burgundy shirt and tie. It was important that he not look rushed or disheveled in any way. He stopped as he passed an old tarnished silver Victorian mirror and hesitated. "A reflection would be helpful right about now." He looked at the empty mirror and its ornately-carved frame and dusted his shoulders one last time before heading up the stairs. He assumed that Leo would be in Nica's room, probably licking her toes or whatever she had him do. He kept his pace steady and sure, continually reassuring himself that the Slayer would take care of everything. He reached the top of the steps and inhaled deep through his nostrils. He caught the scent of Leo's self-rolled cigarettes and followed it to the end of the hall.

Finally, he had reached the door that went to Nica's salon. "Here we go!" he whispered to himself. But as he reached for the door knob, it turned on its own and the door swung open. Jerome tried to mask his shock by clearing his throat and smiling slyly.

"Vecchio, amico!" Leo greeted him. "I am so glad that you changed your mind and returned!" He held out his arms and embraced Jerome.

"What a pleasant surprise," cooed Nica from behind Leo. She raised an eyebrow and grinned like a Cheshire cat.

Jerome offered her no such courtesy in return. Leo pulled away from their embrace and straightened his gray pinstriped suit jacket. "I see you have had a change of heart?" Leo asked Jerome.

"Actually, that is what I came here to discuss with you. I will stay here with you, but I need to know how much longer you plan on staying because I don't think I can stand living in this tree-infested back water area for a couple of decades."

Leo put his arm around his friend and escorted him through the door, shutting it behind them.

"Don't worry, lovey, we won't be here much longer! At least not after tonight!" Nica sat in front on her vanity table and snapped her fingers. Her attending Priestess Lunera arrived and began to perfect Nica's makeup. She swirled her small brush in the circular container of black shadow and slowly applied it to Nica's lids.

"Word is you have the Slayer," Jerome said in a praising manner.

"Well, almost, we have her brother, she should be here shortly." Nica grinned again.

"Using the brother as bait. Good idea." Jerome put his hands in his pockets to keep from fidgeting and paced to the window. He could see the girls were almost to the house.

"Yes, well, I plan on eating him, too. As it would turn out, since they are twins, they share the spirit of the Ba Musal." Nica chose the color for her lips, dark crimson, and Lunera began to apply it.

"Two for the price of one," Leo chimed in. Jerome walked over to his friend and placed a hand on his shoulder.

"Brother. When this is over and she has her Ba Musal, will you join me once again?"

Leo put his head down. "We are brethren in the blood of the forsaken, yes. We have been companions in our travels, ci. I have schooled you in the ways of stalking the night, this is also true." He looked up and looked sternly at Jerome. "But I have no obligation to you! I have chosen my path and I am sorry that it does not follow yours!"

Jerome gripped his friend's shoulder tightly and Leo reached up with his hand and gripped Jerome's. "But it WAS your path, Leo! Not a few minutes before she had been raised, you were furious that we had to stay here longer! Don't you get it? She has done something to you! There is something she has done to make you this way! Please! Old friend, come with me now and we can return to your home!"

Leo blinked and hesitated for a moment. "Are you so certain that creatures, such as we, are incapable of love? Why does it have to be a spell or a curse? There is nothing you can say that will change that, Jerome! I taught you well enough to survive on your own. It is time to practice that and allow me to live my own life." Leo removed Jerome's hand from his shoulder in one poignant gesture.

Nica, who had been listening closely, dismissed her attendant and joined the men in the middle of the room. She peeked her head over Leo's shoulder with her Cheshire grin and winked at Jerome.

"Leo! Don't you see? When she's done getting what she wants, she's going to kill you!"

Leo grimaced as he heard these words.

"Don't listen to him, lover. He's just jealous. He could never imagine the connection we have. He's never been in love." Nica purred in Leo's ear and glared at Jerome, smiling all the while.

"I think it's time you left, Jerome." Leo grunted through his teeth as he closed his hand around Jerome's throat and lifted him from the floor.

Jerome could feel things snapping and twisting in his neck. His hands went to pull and claw at Leo's. He fought to free himself, but Leo was much older and that meant he was much more powerful than he. The blood in his veins began to boil with frustration and anger, warming his cold skin. He could feel his neck slowly begin to snap and thought to himself, *Emma better hurry up because she's about to lose her distraction!*

~~~~~

Emma and Layla snuck quietly into the dusty house. They shot a quick glance up the stairs to make sure they were in the clear. The two slowly stalked their way through the living room and headed for the kitchen. Layla couldn't stop herself from opening her mouth.

"Oh my God, Emma. I didn't think it was possible, but this house has accomplished a level of tackiness that actually surpasses yours!"

"Layla, can you not channel HGTV right now? We are trying to save the world and my brother!" Emma slid her bag from her shoulder and crouched down next to the door that led to the cellar. "Here it is. Just where he said it would be."

While Emma prepared to storm the cellar with her back to Layla, one of the grunt vampires snuck up behind Layla and wrapped his arm around her throat. Before she could call out, he covered her mouth with his hard, cold hand. She tried to wrestle free, but his grip was too strong. Emma continued on, oblivious to her partner's plight.

"So when I get Jimmy free, I want you to be ready with that egg thing so we can get him the hell outta here. I want to know he's safe before I go after Nica. Ok? Helloo? Are you not talking to me now after that the HG…?" Emma turned around and fell over when she saw that a vamp had Layla in a head lock. "Whoa! Sorry!" She leapt to her feet and ran for Layla and the vamp. She jumped and somersaulted over his head, landing behind him. While he was still in awe of her gymnastic prowess, she had removed the long-bladed dagger from her boot and sliced through his thick neck. As his head slid from its base, rolling to the floor, his body flashed as embers and then turned to ashes.

Layla immediately started to frantically slap the dust from her shoulders and chest, hopping around like a mad rabbit. "EW, EW, EW! OH my God! That is sooo gross!" She turned around and slapped Emma on the shoulder. "You barmy git! As much as I yammer on, you didn't think anything was wrong when I didn't answer you?!"

Emma shushed her and angrily apologized. "Look, I said I was sorry! Besides, I thought you knew how to take care of yourself, Ms. 'I was raised around the Legacy!'"

Layla threw her arms up and turned away. Emma shook her head and went back to her backpack by the door. She reached in and pulled out a handful of what looked like white ping pong balls. She rose and began to stuff them into Layla's sweater pockets.

"Eh, what are you doing?"

"These ping pong balls are filled with holy water. You see another vampire, chuck one of these babies right at his face. Ok?" Emma stopped and went back to the door. She swallowed deep and prepared for the worst.

Jimmy stirred in his chains. He was still too weak to change his position, and with the night coming, it was getting colder in there. They had left him chained to the wall in the same room that they had Naberius drugged and tied up. He knew from what they were saying earlier that Naberius wasn't able to move, but it still made him uneasy. The only comfort he had had in the last twenty-three hours was the visit he received from his sister in his subconscious. He only hoped that she got the message.

Suddenly, the deafening silence was shattered in Jimmy's ears by the sound of creaking wood. He quickly shifted his line of sight to the stairs at his far right. He knew in his heart that it was Emma! He watched intently, waiting for the moment that he could see even the toe of her shoe. The soft creaking continued until the silhouette of his sister and their roommate emerged in the blackness. He yanked his body forward, wanting to wave but forgetting that he was still in chains. He could see her step off from the stairs and crouch down, searching for him.

"Emma!" he whispered. "I'm over here!" It took all of his strength to mutter these words. She heard this right away and quickly made her way through the dank dark to release him.

When she found her way to him she embraced him and covered him in kisses and warm tears. "I thought I had lost you there for a minute!" she cried. "Ok, let's get these chains." But as she started to pull the chains away, a flashlight hit them out of nowhere!

"Hey, who's there?" a gruff-sounding voice asked. They were blinded by the white light coming from the flashlight and they couldn't see who was carrying it. But Emma decided that whoever it was wasn't there to give her the key to the chains!

Emma slipped back swiftly out of the beam of light and disappeared from the torch bearer's vision. While he searched the room, Emma stalked just behind him. But as he backed up a few inches, forcing her to do the same, she stepped on something that snapped loudly under her foot. He whipped around and pointed the light right in Emma's eyes.

"Oops," she said. The vampire dropped the flashlight and attacked. He went to claw her face, but she was able to catch him in time and throw him back. He stumbled over some crates but came right back toward her at top speed. "See, this is where most of you make mistakes!" She stomped her right foot and it activated the stake-launching mechanism. A fresh stake flew up to her awaiting hands and she buried it deep into his chest as he fell upon her. As he lit to embers and then reduced to ashes, she replaced the stake like a cowboy holstering his six shooter.

"See what I mean, they don't think, they just act!" She dusted herself off and met Layla where Jimmy was chained.

"I can't get them loose! The chains are too dense!" Layla grunted as she tried to pull them from the wall with both hands and a foot planted on the wall for counter weight.

Emma reached up with one hand and pulled both chains from the wall along with some stone and mud. "Freakish strength remember?" Emma shrugged.

The relief Jimmy felt in his arms was immeasurable. When the chains were pulled free, his weary arms dropped to his lap and blood was allowed to circulate once more. Although he could not move them, he couldn't be happier. Layla and Emma began to pull him away from the wall and this allowed for his legs to stretch out from under him. He changed his mind from his earlier feelings and decided that this moment was where he would mark not being any happier! He laid his head in Layla's lap and rested contently. Emma retrieved the flashlight from the floor and set it down next to them. After the initial shock of the sudden exposure of light, his eyes burned then adjusted. Now Jimmy could make out Layla's face in exquisite detail and his heart soared. In his delirium he spoke what he was feeling.

"Thank God for light."

"Yeah, I bet it was miserable being trapped in the dark for so long. I'd be glad to see anything myself!" Layla smiled as she cleared the dirt and debris from his curly brown hair.

"No, thank God for the light that I can see your face." He began to drift and Layla felt her chest swell with affection and flattery. "Such a beautiful face, I love your face." He tilted his head and closed his eyes. Layla's sweet symphony was turning into a bitter requiem. Emma saw him slipping away and her heart stopped.

"NO!" she commanded. "You are not going to leave me now! You hear me! You are going to wake up right now…or…" She began to cry. She couldn't fight these tears. Jimmy was the last soul on this Earth that she had and she wasn't letting him go this way! "Or I'll kill you!" She sobbed and laid her head on his chest.

Jimmy roused, slowly batting and rolling his eyes. He heard his sister and Layla's cries and fought to hold on to his life's breath. "Hey, what's with all the boo hooing? Klingons don't cry!" He winced.

Emma shot her head up and cried for joy. "You dick! Don't ever do that again!" She hugged him and he groaned in pain.

Layla couldn't contain herself anymore and she bent forward and kissed him on his mouth with passion and sincerity.

Emma sat up instantly and felt like she was in the way.

Jimmy was pleasantly surprised at her display and kissed back as best he could despite his split and swollen lip. "Wow, so all I had to do to win you over was get my ass beat to a bloody pulp. Nice to know you have standards."

"If I may be so bold to interrupt this touching moment."

The voice came from behind them. It was deep and forced. Emma grabbed the flashlight and shone it on the large stone table. There they saw Naberius tied down.

"I just thought I would let you know that we are all about to die," he said forcibly again. Layla and Emma jumped and quickly moved Jimmy farther away from the altar. Emma tossed her backpack, which contained fresh clothes for Jimmy, to Layla who began dressing Jimmy. Emma retrieved the long bowie knife from her boot and, holding the flashlight still, walked carefully to the subdued Naberius. She stood over him with the black-handled bowie stuck to his chest.

"No need for that, incarnate one. I have been poisoned with the Nectar of the Gods. It is difficult for me to even form sentences let alone tear your limbs from your body. This, by the way, is what I would do if I wasn't poisoned," he grunted. Emma looked back at Layla who was busy dressing her injured brother.

"It was Nica, right?" she asked him, still not trusting his condition enough to remove the bowie.

"Of course it was the Inanna! She's been plotting her revenge for millennia! I just wasn't able to control her movements this time! I just didn't expect it this way! I must be getting old!"

Emma slid the monster knife up to his blood-red eyes and pushed down his lower lid with the tip of the blade and added pressure. "Tell me, Naberius, where is the Effigy? Tell me, or I will pop out your eyeball like a pimento!"

Naberius forced a smile and blinked the eye that had the knife held to it. "Do your worst! I would rather my Dark Queen ravage the earth than your kind continue to infest it!" Emma pulled the knife from his eye socket, realizing that it was doing no good. "And you, you filthy little Abgal Da!" he grunted, addressing Layla, "I thought we had rid ourselves of you along with your parents when they attacked the London Motherhouse!"

Layla stood from caring for Jimmy and ran to Naberius. She pulled the Orb of Pure Light from her pocket. She slammed it down toward his chest, stopping millimeters from his skin. Emma grabbed her shoulders just in case she went too far.

"ENA NITA!" Layla yelled. Naberius' eyes grew wide in fear. "Yeah you recognize this don't you, asshole! It was you! You killed my parents! YOU! And now I am going to return the favor!"

"Layla!" Emma protested. "Don't! We need to know about the Effigy!"

"Don't worry, he's going to tell us! Aren't you?" The Orb glowed bright blue in Layla's fist and illuminated Naberius' stone face.

~~~~~

They heard distant voices shouting. Leo immediately dropped Jerome to the floor and he and Nica looked toward the door.

"She's here." Nica smiled. She snapped her fingers for her Priestesses and they appeared. "Watch him. Don't let him leave." The three stood over Jerome as he rubbed his bruised neck.

Leo stood at the door and held it for Nica. "After you, Mia Caro!" he gestured.

"Let's go burn the world!" she cooed as they marched down the stairs.

~~~~~

Layla held the Orb over his chest, gripping it tighter and tighter. This was the bastard that killed her parents! Even if he was just the one that placed the order and not the one who actually wielded the sword, he was just as guilty! But then at that thought it became blaringly clear.

He tried to kill her not once but twice! Jerome said that Naberius was afraid of her because of her powers as a medium. And that Naberius was a necromancer himself! It was obvious what she had to do.

She pulled the Orb away from him and handed it to Emma. "Hold this for me!"

"Why? What are you going to do?" Emma asked

"See dead people!" Layla slapped her hands together and closed her eyes. She began to mumble, and when she opened her eyes again, they were glowing blue. Emma instinctively moved backward to where her brother, now dressed in gray sweats, was leaning against the wall.

Layla held her hands to her side with the palms facing out. The energy began to build around her, causing a blue aura to grow and fill the room. She stretched her arms out to her sides and commanded:

"FROM BEYOND THE VEIL, REVEAL!" Suddenly the room filled with spirits! Emma stood in awe and respect of what she was seeing. Hundreds of spirits from the other side overflowed the cellar. There were so many that each face seemed to blend into the next. They shown ethereal blue and stared at Layla blankly, waiting for her next command. "SHOW ME WHERE THIS ONE HIDES HIS SECRET!" The multitude looked up and opened their mouths. From inside them, blue mist flowed and collected in the center of the room above Naberius. It hovered for a moment and then shot down into Naberius' torso.

He grunted, trying to fight against it. "Get out of me!" he futilely commanded. His body spasmed violently and uncontrollably. Finally, after several seconds the spasms slowed and then stopped altogether. But then Naberius' abdomen began to glow with the same blue aura that spirits were.

"That's where it is!" Emma spoke out loud. "To get it safe, he put it in his stomach!"

"WE ARE THANKFUL! RETURN!" Layla clasped her hands back together in front of her and in a twinkling the masses of other worldly spirits vanished. Emma rushed up to an astounded Naberius and, without hesitation, stuck the knife into his gullet and sliced upward. He howled in pain as the knife tore through his leather-like flesh. Emma reached in with both hands and fished around until her fingers found their way to something that wasn't spongy and slimy. She gripped it tight and pulled it from his body. She held it up with her black, blood-covered hands for her and Layla to be seen. As soon as it was clear from his body, Layla grabbed the Orb from Emma's pocket and held it up to Naberius' eyes.

"Now you get to feel what my parents did, you bastard child of hell!" She stuffed it into his mouth and shouted the incantation again. "ENA NITA! FUCKER!" The Orb glowed again and Naberius began to scream. He howled and shook his head. His body began to glow from the Pure Light and then ignite into blue flames. He screamed louder and louder until his body burned away to nothingness. All that was left was the Orb and the silken wraps that held him to what was now his funeral pyre. Layla picked up the Orb and studied it in her hand. "Why Tah Heo," she stated and the light faded. Emma put her arm around Layla's shoulder and embraced her.

"You just saved me a lot of time and effort! I guess I should thank you for that!" It was Nica's voice. The girls turned around and found that she was standing merely feet away with Leo by her side, smoking away as usual, and several more of her followers on the stairs behind them. But what was really alarming was that she held Jimmy by the throat! "But it's really not in my nature to show gratitude!"

CHAPTER NINETEEN

Rock the House

Nica held Jimmy up in the air by his throat with one hand and the other on her hip. He groaned weakly, still unable to help himself. For a moment Nica and Emma stared at each other fiercely until Nica spoke.

"You see, we both have something the other wants. You give me my toy, and I'll give you the boy. OK?"

Emma twitched. She looked at Layla but Layla was focused solely on Jimmy. Emma looked down and could see her fingers wiggling, signaling that she was about to do something. Emma looked back up at her poor brother whose life was now in the hands of a psychotic, exiled vampire Goddess. She looked down at the blood-soaked trophy she held in her right hand and felt the pressure build inside her chest. Her heart beat rapidly and her stomach cramped.

What do I do? she asked herself in her mind. If she refused to give up the statue, then her brother would die. But if she gives Nica the statue, reality could crumble! But would her life be worth living knowing that her brother had to sacrifice his life for it?

She looked up at Jimmy and gave him a pleading look.

He tried his best to shake his head. "No, Emma, don't give it to her!" he croaked. Nica squeezed his neck tighter and raised a well-manicured eyebrow.

"I'll do it, bitch. Hand it over." Nica stuck out her hand that was on her hip.

Layla began an incantation, but Emma gently laid a black-stained hand in her arm. "No," she said softly. Layla looked at her, confused and shocked. "I couldn't bare it if he was gone."

Emma stepped forward and held out the statue.

~~~~~

Jerome stood caressing his sore neck, staring back at the three white marble beauties who kept vigil over him.

"So what does one have to do to become an attending Priestess?" he asked. There was no answer.

"Doesn't sound like a very fun job to me. You are at the beckon call whenever someone snaps their fingers, always trying to please the boss, no sick days, and I hear you get crap for dental." Still no response.

"I don't know about you but I am running out of small talk and it really doesn't work anyway unless the other people involved participate. So, why don't we just skip the attempt at chit chat and get right to the fighting." With that, he grabbed the one on the far right by her throat with his right hadn and kicked out with his left leg and sent the one on the opposite end flying into the wall. That left Lunera in the middle who produced a dagger in each hand.

He pulled the Priestess he held in his grip toward him and spun her around to where she faced the dagger, wielding Lunera. As she jabbed at him with her silver daggers, he dodged side-to-side, taking steps backward until he stumbled into an end table. He looked down to see what he had hit and saw a pair of elegantly-carved wooden hair sticks.

As the Priestess in his arms bit and clawed to break free, he reached down with his left hand, retrieved one of the sticks and jabbed it into her heart. For a fleeting moment she burst into flames and then reduced to ash.

Lunera looked up and began her attack again. She jabbed right and left and then swiped both at him criss-crossed but he deflected her advances. She was becoming frustrated and swung with her right, only to be caught by his hand. She then tried her left, but was received with the same results.

They struggled against each other for a moment. Ultimately, Jerome was able to bend her arms back against her shoulders with each hand, holding a dagger resting on the opposing side. He pushed them closer together as she fought back with all of her strength. But when the blades began to cut into her neck on both sides she realized she had been beaten. Jerome winked and then pulled her arms out straight, forcing the blades to cut through her and sever her head. Another pile of dust collected on the floor.

As he dusted his hand to remove the remains of the two Priestesses, the third that he had knocked into the wall came to and ran screeching for him.

He ducked just in time to flip her over his back and send her crashing through the window. Conveniently, she landed on the picket fence that surrounded the house and she, too, was now ashes.

"Women!" Jerome said as he looked out of the shattered window. "I guess I'll go tell Leo it's time to leave." He turned away to exit the room, first adjusting his jacket, and shut the door behind him.

~~~~~

Emma stepped closer to Nica, holding the Effigy out in front of her. Nica flashed her familiar Cheshire smile as the statue loomed closer and closer.

With each tiny step, Emma's heart sank. She knew the actions here would have ramifications that even she couldn't imagine. *Sever the arm.* Emma tried to brush out the tiny voice that whispered in her mind. *Sever the Arm.* It demanded to be acknowledged. *You must choose a hat!* She continued to walk forward, blinking to try and erase the voice from her head. *Sever the arm! Choose a Hat!* Emma had reached the point where the statue was just a fraction of an inch from

Nica's fingertips. Suddenly she repeated what had been playing in her head out loud and then it made sense! As she reached up with the statue, she slyly reached behind her and pulled that bowie knife from her back. Instead of putting the statue in Nica's hand she dropped it, making Nica reach for it, and when she did, Emma let fly the bowie knife and it sliced through Nica's right shoulder, severing her arm and dropping Jimmy to the floor!

Nica screamed in pain and astonishment. Layla rushed to Jimmy's side, removed the wriggling arm and drug him to safety. Emma quickly retrieved the statue and slid it behind her.

A very pissed Nica picked her arm up from the floor and stuck it back to her shoulder. It quickly reattached itself.

"That's it! I have been more than fair with you! Your ass is mine now!" Nica started for Emma and she was ready.

Layla had pulled Jimmy around the corner and kissed his cheek. "I'll be back, love, try not to run off, ok?" She smiled and squeezed his cheek.

"I'll do what I can," Jimmy muttered.

Just as Layla came running back around the corner, she saw Jerome running down the stairs, slicing the head off of one of the vampires there with a sword. "Where the hell did he get that?"

~~~~~

Emma locked arms with Nica. They spun around, knocking each other into walls, trying to break free from the other. Leo had left Nica's side to see who was chopping heads on the stairs.

Emma finally pushed back from Nica and kicked her in the chest with the bottom of her spike-studded right foot. Nica brushed it off and the tiny holes in her chest healed quickly as she landed a right hook across Emma's face. Emma returned the attack and added a roundhouse that released the tiny holy water pellets into Nica's face. They simply evaporated on the surface of her skin.

Thinking quickly, Emma used the stone altar as a launch pad for a spinning kick but was foiled as Nica grabbed her leg. With one swift move, Nica threw Emma to the ground and removed her prosthetic leg.

As Layla entered the epicenter, a vampire caught her by surprise and grabbed her by the face. Without thinking, she reached into her pocket, pulled one of the ping pong balls out and smashed it into the vamp's face. He immediately started screaming, shaking his hands in front of his melting face. Layla wasted not a moment and retrieved a stake from her bag and plunged it into his heart. When he fell as ashes to the floor Layla started jumping and shaking her rear in celebration.

"HAHA! I dusted my first vamp! WOO HOO!" But her celebration was cut short by another tackling her into the mud floor.

Jerome continued to burst down the stairs, swinging his blade at Nica's followers as they came at him. Suddenly a familiar voice called out to him.

"Jerome! What are you doing?" It was Leo. He was jaunting up the stairs as the few other followers were making their way past him.

"I'm saving you!" Jerome yelled back with conviction. He grabbed for Leo's arm to lead him out but he just swatted Jerome's hand away.

"I told you, Jerome! I don't need saving! I don't want to be your big brother, Jerome! Stop trying! Don't make me kill you!"

Jerome gripped his simple broad sword he found by the stairs and lowered his eyes in contemplation. Betrayed! By one he respected and loved as his own brother! The burning in his chest became an inferno of rage and hurt. He quickly opened his eyes and his face twisted into a psychotic fury.

"Then try if you must, brother!" And then they clashed.

Luckily for Layla the vamp that tackled her landed on the stake she was holding and was virtually compost before they hit the ground.

"Bloody brilliant!" Layla complained. "It's going to be murder getting this mud out!" she said as she batted the sleeves of her hoodie. She looked up when she heard the snarls of the three remaining vampires coming directly at her! Her fear was quickly changed to confidence when she remembered that she was in fact a WITCH. "Heya, fellas! I have a bright idea! LUMINESCA! GRANT ME YOUR GIFT!" She held up her hands and the bright ball of light that she had used at the book shop to take notes by appeared above them. Then, biting her lip, she hurled the light, emolliating all three in one fail swoop. "HAHA! Take that, forces of darkness!" And she ran to check on Emma.

Jerome swung the sword at his mentor and brother Forsaken. But Leo easily dodged it. He tried this time hitting him with the hilt and then kicking at Leo, but all for nothing. Leo was far older, wiser and stronger than Jerome, and inside he knew that this was a fight he was not going to win. But he would rather die than spend an eternity feeling the sting of betrayal.

Jerome took a symbolic deep breath and made his last swing with the blade. Leo caught the blade with his hand, not caring that it was cutting deep into him. As Jerome resisted, Leo pulled back hard and flipped the sword over, catching the hilt in his right hand. Jerome stopped and looked straight into Leo's eyes.

"Goodbye, vecchio amico." And then Leo swung the blade, sliced through the flesh and bone of Jerome's neck and lopped off his head.

Nica had Emma's leg in her hand. The commotion around them was dying down and from the sound of it Layla had notched a few victories on her belt. Emma pushed against the floor with her hands and her left leg and stood back up without her prosthetic.

"Wow," Nica said sarcastically. "That was just inspirational and stuff. You must be like, proud!" She walked a little closer to Emma, spinning her bionic leg around in her hands. "But if you really want to be impressive, let's see ya tap dance!" She erupted into maniacal laughter at Emma's expense.

Emma felt the sickness of bitter anger well up inside of her. She posed with her hands out and did a little squatty dance that resembled an incompetent chicken. Nica stopped laughing long enough to look utterly confused at Emma. Seizing the opportunity, Emma burst into forward handsprings and knocked Nica to the ground. "Back at ya! You loony bi…AHHH!" Nica had used the prosthetic leg to knock Emma's remaining good leg out from under her, knocking HER to the ground and hitting her head.

"Now that was funny! I've heard of tripping over your own feet, but DAMN!" Nica tormented as she rose to her feet. Confidently, she sashayed over to the toppled Emma who was now trying to scoot away.

"You've lost, gimpy! I've taken your job, your brother and now," she held up the leg and tilted it back and forth, teasing Emma, "your leg…"

As Emma continued to back away her hands happened upon a hard, heavy object on the floor. It was the EFFIGY! She felt carefully so not to be discovered and gripped it tightly as she scooted closer to the stone altar.

"And now I am going to take your life! So why bother? Why do you keep fighting?"

"For Shea!" Emma spat back. She used her free hand to help herself up from the floor while hiding the statue behind her. "For my sister who will never get to fight for anything!"

Nica threw her head back and laughed. "You are so predictable! Do you know why? Can't you feel it in you? The Darkness inside? We're a lot alike, that's why! Deep down inside, Emma, you are just as twisted as I am, you just don't want anyone to know!"

Emma clutched the statue behind her back so tightly that her hand began to bleed. She squared her eyes and looked fiercely into Nica's. "I am NOTHING like you!"

"Sure you are, lover! You use your power for vengeance just as I do! I just admit it! At least I live in harmony with my darkness! If you would just embrace it, the torment you suffer would become a distant memory! Accept what you are, Emma. A cold-blooded killer!"

Emma's anger was further fueled by Nica's accusations and assumption. But then that voice rose again inside her mind. "Choose a hat." The image of the two hats flashed before her and she knew what it meant!

"That's what she was trying to tell me!" she said out loud, searching with her eyes.

"What?" Nica asked flatly.

"I just realized something! That it's not my past or the things I have or don't have that define who I am. It's what I do with it! It's the decision that matters! I wasn't created for anything other than what I choose to be!"

Nica placed her hand on her hip and smiled cocky at the slayer having an epiphany.

"And do tell, what's that?"

Emma smiled and produced the statue for Nica to see. "The Hero!!!!" Nica's jaw dropped as she heard these words. Emma held the statue over her head and brought it crashing down onto the altar, smashing it into tiny pieces! The force of the powerful magics released, knocked everyone around off of their feet and shook the foundations of the already rickety house. Nica cried out as her Inanna spirit drained from her being in flashes of white light. Emma scurried across the mud floor to her discarded limb and slid it back onto her leg.

The force of the energy expelling from Nica's body was shaking the house apart. Bits and pieces of wood, stone, and dust were falling onto everyone in the cellar. If Emma, Layla and Jimmy didn't leave soon, they would be buried alive!

"LAYLA! GET JIMMY! WE NEED TO GET OUT OF HERE BEFORE THIS PLACE FALLS APART!" Emma yelled as loud as she could, but even to her own ears, it sounded as if she were yelling in a wind tunnel. Emma rushed behind her and picked up her backpack. She took the vile of the Inanna's oily blood and stuffed it into one of the pockets.

After the last of her Godly powers slipped away, Nica fell to the mud floor of the cellar, the Inanna no more. Leo, who had been standing in the background watching, confident that she would prevail, rushed to her side and cradled her in his arms.

"Don't worry, Mia Caro. We will find a way!" He rose to his feet and, carrying her, ran up the stairs and out of the house.

~~~~~

Layla came from around the corner, doing her best to carefully drag Jimmy along with her. The house shook more violently and more chunks of the house fell onto the group as each tremor passed. Layla looked toward the stairs and saw Leo flee with Nica in his arms.

"EMMA! THEY'RE ESCAPING!" she yelled as she pointed to the stairs.

Emma looked up just in time to see Leo's feet disappear above the ceiling of the cellar. As she flung her backpack on with both straps, she whipped around and grabbed Jimmy from Layla, slinging him over her shoulders. "COME ON! THIS PLACE IS GONNA FALL ANY SECOND!"

They ran from the house, across the barren field, not stopping until they reached the truck. With Layla's help, she slid Jimmy gently into the cab of the old blue Ford. And as the main house at the Kender Farm fell in on itself, the trio tore out into the night, speeding off to Walnut Grove General Hospital.

The Picnic

Two Weeks Later

The sun shone brightly over Webster Park. Children ran in the large, open, lush green field, kicking bouncy balls and playing tag. Families barbequed and lovers snuggled on benches in the shade of a large oak tree. Everything was perfect, everything was serene, and most of all, it was all still there.

Emma, Layla, and Jimmy, who was in a wheelchair, all sat in the middle of the park with a large picnic spread out before them. Emma lounged in the sun for the first time in a pair of shorts and a pink sleeveless tank top. The fact that her prosthetic leg was visible was the last thing on her mind.

Layla sat next to Jimmy and fed him forkfuls of apple pie while they exchanged googly eyes. Poor Jimmy was pretty banged up when they reached the hospital that night. In fact, today's outing wasn't only to celebrate saving the world from the Inanna; it was to celebrate Jimmy's first day out of the hospital. Though he had received fifteen stitches above his right eye, five over his top lip, fifty stitches to close up the wound to his shoulder, a cast on his wrist and around his ribs, he looked blissfully happy to be out and about and in the care of his new love, Layla.

Layla gave Jimmy another bite and leaned forward, giving him an Eskimo kiss.

"Oh will you two stop that for two minutes!" Emma teased. "I have been waiting two weeks to do this!"

"Ok fine!" Layla produced a black cast iron bowl and broke some small sticks and twigs into it.

"I knew it!" Jimmy proclaimed. "I knew you had a cauldron! Do you have a broom, too?"

"You're lucky you're cute!" Layla said, slapping his knee.

"Hey, I'm crippled here!" He laughed. "Now I get all the good parking places!" He winked jokingly at his sister who just shook her head.

"Ok, pour it in," Layla gave permission to Emma who pulled the vile containing the black grease-like substance that was the Inanna's blood from her pocket. She held it up to the sunlight and tipped it back and forth to watch the sun glint off the glass vile.

"Goodbye!" she said as she opened the cork and poured the contents into the cauldron. She looked at the vile and saw that some had stuck to the sides and could not be poured out. She shrugged and tossed the vile in as well.

"Here we go," Layla said as she lit a match and dropped it into the pot. Initially there was a bright flash and then the contents burned uniform and bright.

"And good riddance!" Jimmy cheered. "I will NOT miss that crazy bitch!"

"Yes, thank God that's over and I can get back to my normal life of not having any friends and killing the evil undead every night," Emma added.

"Oh you two, she was just misunderstood!" Layla said.

The Hogan twins stopped and stared at her in shock.

"God, I was just kidding! Lord!" Layla leaned over and kissed Jimmy on the cheek and smoothed his hair.

Emma looked out across the park and breathed in the relaxation. True, they still had to renovate the shop, but that was stress she could save for another day. For now she was happy to lay in the late spring sun, listening to birds chirp and watching people as they went about the happier parts of their lives.

"What happened to your leg?"

Emma looked up to see a sweet little girl no more than six standing next to her. With one hand she fidgeted with the hem of her pink denim jumper and with the other she twirled one of her white blonde pigtails around and around.

Jimmy and Layla froze, afraid of Emma's reaction to the girl's innocent question of childhood curiosity.

The girl's mother had heard her daughter's inquiry and ran to apologize. "Carrie, no, honey! You shouldn't ask questions like that, it's very rude! I'm so sorry she bothered you!"

But to her companions' surprise, Emma simply smiled. "Oh no, it's fine!" she said to the mother. She then looked back over to the little girl and smiled bigger. "Well, my old one didn't work very well, so the doctors had to take it away and give me a new one. Does that make sense?"

The little girl puckered her lips and looked up at the sky, thinking before she answered. She tapped her chin with her finger and then smiled, looking back down at Emma. "Yeah! I understand! That's neat!" She turned abruptly up to her mother and pulled on her skirt. "Mommy! I want a new leg, too! Can I get one?"

Emma laughed at the little girl's reaction as her mother led her away. Jimmy smiled proudly at his sister. She was at peace in a way and that made him happy. She had learned what the White Lady had been trying to teach her all along. That choosing who you want to be is a simple as picking out a hat; it just has to fit. Happiness with one's self doesn't just happen, you have to choose it.

~~~~~

He tapped his pen nervously on the brown leather folder. He looked around the long, lacquered conference table at the five others who sat with him. Two were women, three were men all dressed in fine suits.

"How could we not have seen this coming?" he asked aloud, looking to the others for an answer.

"There's no use in questioning that now. What we need to be asking is what can be done about it now? As it stands, there is still an unbalance and we don't know how to fix it without cutting away what we and our ancestors have worked so hard for." It was the blonde woman farthest from the right. She looked about the dark room and sighed.

A Middle Eastern man scooted forward, closer to the table. His large belly squished against it. "If we don't find the answer, Martin, not only will there no longer be an army, there will be no single incarnate of the Ba Musal again!"

Martin pinched the bridge of his nose and closed his eyes. "Assemble the Congress of Elders. Addar is right. If we don't find the answer, soon there will be no more Vampire Slayers."

Printed in the United States
61016LVS00006BA/25-36